CONGO VARIANT

ROBIN CRUMBY

NOVATUM PRESS

❀ Created with Vellum

"The Dark Ages may return...on the gleaming wings of science, and what might now shower immeasurable material blessings upon mankind, may even bring about its total destruction. Beware, I say; time may be short."

Winston Churchill, 5 March 1946

PROLOGUE

UK Government Research Facility
Near Salisbury, United Kingdom
2 March 1998, 0400 hours

The darkest hours before dawn held few surprises for an expert in infectious disease. Safety was a mantra so routine as to be instinctive. Antisocial hours, icy roads, the impenetrable darkness of tree-lined roads in winter were all part and parcel of the night shift.

Doctor Ben Littlejohn turned right at the bottom of a steep hill, full-beam headlights illuminating the low stone wall that still bore the scars of the last person who failed to negotiate the tight corner on a country road notoriously slippery in early spring.

He yawned and rubbed the sleep from his eyes, turning again onto an anonymous approach road, lined with a high chain-link fence topped with barbed wire. A sign at the entrance gave little indication of the clandestine activities undertaken at this industrial facility located next to a nondescript business park.

He fumbled for his ID in a black leather day bag on the passenger seat, a birthday gift from his wife. He rolled to a halt at the checkpoint. The security guard shone a penlight at the security pass before waving him through with a polite nod. Littlejohn parked up next to an austere warehouse building.

Wisps of smoke or steam from the chimney towering over the complex caught the light from below before disappearing into a moon-lit sky. Pinpricks of light from a sleepy village less than two miles south-west of the installation twinkled in the darkness, its stalwart residents oblivious to their proximity to danger. A serious accident here could extinguish human life in a heartbeat. Littlejohn had dedicated his career to ensuring a leak like that could never happen on his watch.

When friends and family asked about his work, he trotted out well-rehearsed lines about tracking outbreaks of various tropical diseases, annual visits to monitor cases wherever they occurred in the world and the development of vaccines. Depending on who he was talking to, he might throw in a mention of biocontainment, gene therapy or drug development, by which time most people's eyes became sufficiently glazed to deter any follow-up questions.

He hung up his raincoat and scarf in a locker in the staffroom, changed into a starched white lab coat, clipped a security badge to his top pocket that displayed his name, military designation, identification number and the unflattering photo he had always hated. There was something about the overhead strip light that made his forehead appear shiny, thinning grey hair too greasy. Frozen across his unsmiling lips was the dark mood from that particular morning. The argument with his wife. Words she could never take back. Personal criticism he would never entirely forgive.

Littlejohn nodded at the disinterested security guard on reception, whose sidearm lay next to the keyboard in its holster, alongside a half-eaten packet of biscuits. The heavily reinforced security door buzzed open, giving access to the bio-secure containment zones beyond. The electrical hum from a generator filled the air, running day and night in case of temporary interruption to mains power.

Even at this early hour, the inner sanctum was busy. Littlejohn recognised the same handful of scientists and military personnel, night shift workers like him, scuttling along narrow corridors, heads down, immersed in their thoughts. He passed successive laboratories where lone technicians peered down microscopes, running tests, absorbed by their work. Those already finished for the night would be heading home to their beds.

The far end of the complex was even quieter. He keyed in an access code and the pressure seals around the door hissed open. The specialists who worked here knew this secure area of level three and four biocontainment zones as "Hades". The name had always struck Littlejohn as fitting in so many ways. In Greek mythology, Hades had been the god of the underworld, a place of the dead and dying.

The day-to-day reality of working here was a little less dramatic. A suite of negative-pressure ultra-secure biocontainment laboratories allowed the study of the planet's most deadly pathogens. Marburg, Ebola, even the bubonic plague. Mistakes here incurred heavy consequences: quarantine, hospitalisation, even death. Hades was reserved for the most experienced scientists, requiring additional precautions, multiple vaccinations and two-person safety protocols at all times.

Through the reinforced Plexiglas, almost an inch thick, was the so-called "red room", a cramped office used by Littlejohn's team. Beside his desk was an airtight medical crate that resembled a cool box, or hot box, depending on your point of view. Such deliveries were a regular feature of their work here. A plastic wallet attached to the crate would provide need-to-know information as to the sample's contents and provenance. Sometimes, they tested blind. Littlejohn's security clearance meant that he knew more than most, but occasionally, samples crossed his desk that he was required to identify with minimal context. That was the job. No questions asked.

On the whiteboard, Littlejohn's day-shift counterpart had scribbled the other items of note, including priorities for this morning.

The diminutive scientist pulled with all his might against the negative-pressure door, which resisted his slight frame until the rubber seal gave way and the air pressure began to equalise. Inside was a staging area where Littlejohn's fellow technician, Major Andrea Pollard, was already half-dressed in a surgical scrub suit, tapping her watch, waiting to help him get ready.

"What's so urgent this couldn't wait till morning?" Littlejohn asked, unbuttoning his shirt and closing the cubicle door. The two of them had worked together for so long, the awkwardness had gone. He barely thought of her as a member of the opposite sex. To him she was a colleague and partner. Their lives depended on each other's vigilance and professionalism.

"Your guess is as good as mine. I got the same pager message you did, Ben. Anyway, it wouldn't be any fun if they gave us clues."

"Certainly keeps things interesting," observed Littlejohn with a wry smile.

Above the white noise of the air handlers, he could just make out the muffled screech from what they called "the zoo".

Housed in separate cages in a sealed environment next to the laboratory were two dozen marmoset monkeys. To a virus, the primates looked almost identical to human beings, making them ideal subjects for the tests they were undertaking.

Littlejohn showered, wrinkling his nose at the stink of powerful disinfectant gel. He dried himself with a fresh towel, donned clean socks and underwear and a green surgical gown to match his colleague's. He wrapped tape tight around his ankles and sleeves to make a seal. Next came latex gloves, completing his first protective layer.

He turned his attention to assist Pollard as she wriggled into a biohazard suit that resembled a pressurised spacesuit, holding her arms out for him to secure the chest zip, before checking the seals at the wrists and ankles, closely inspecting the heavy-duty rubber gloves until he was satisfied there were no tears in the material. The puncture-resistant rubber made handling laboratory equipment somewhat cumbersome but protected the most vulnerable areas of the body, the hands, from accidents or contamination with a hot agent. Then came his turn. She repeated the process, meticulously checking his seals and equipment before giving him the thumbs up.

Last came their helmets. The instant he squeezed his head through the narrow gap, the Perspex screen began to fog until all he could hear was his own laboured breathing. He remembered the first time he had put on one of these suits, how claustrophobic it had felt. The rising panic that could make even an experienced lab worker claw at their face and try to tear the suit clean off. Doing that inside a level four laboratory would be a death sentence, like a deep-sea diver removing their helmet at the bottom of the ocean.

He reached over and calmly connected the coiled yellow hose to the socket on his suit. After the stifling suffocation, the roar of air flowing around his body was intoxicating. He watched the arms and legs of the yellow suit inflate with the positive pressure. There was a slight metallic taste to the recycled air that reminded him of diving holidays abroad with rented scuba gear before he signed up for this demanding role. He admonished himself for wandering thoughts. In this environment, concentration and discipline were critical.

Staring at the steel door to the airlock that separated them from the biocontainment area beyond he marshalled his breathing, falling into a steady rhythm like his instructor and mentor had taught him years ago, waiting for Doctor Pollard to carry the samples into the airlock and finish her preparation.

The door sealed behind them with a hiss, and nozzles began to spray them from top to toe with chemicals, draining away through a grill on the floor. The red light above the exit turned green and the door unlocked, allowing access to Hades, the secure biocontainment area beyond.

In the red room, Littlejohn logged into the computer terminal and read through the notes left by his day-shift counterpart. The previous "cool box" emblazoned with a biohazard warning symbol had arrived almost four days earlier with instructions to test for all known pathogens. A full screen and battery of tests took time.

The monkeys in the zoo greeted the scientists' arrival with a cacophony of screeching, fiercely territorial in their individual cages. Littlejohn reconnected his air hose to a central supply hanging from the ceiling in the middle of the room, and got to work.

He retrieved the clipboard listing the observations for each monkey, flipping through for anything of note. Twenty-four test subjects. They had injected twelve with what they were calling

XC-4328. A digital clock counted down every second since exposure. Just under ninety-six hours so far. The other twelve monkeys were the control group, administered with a harmless placebo. It was hard to hear anything over the roar of the air in the suit but the first test subject "Alpha", one of the controls, bared its teeth, screeching a warning as Littlejohn approached with clipboard in hand. The monkey repeatedly charged the front of the cage in a show of aggression that suggested the adult male was in rude health. Littlejohn's eyes flicked to the padlock to make sure it was secure and the key removed. Despite their diminutive size, these were dangerous creatures. Escape was unthinkable.

The next two monkeys rattled their cages in protest, but were more muted in response. The condition of the fourth was of immediate concern. Subject "Delta" lay on its back, staring at the ceiling, eyelids flickering as if in a dream-state. Littlejohn tapped the cage door with a pen, but there was no reaction. He leaned closer to get a better look, feet planted behind the yellow safety line painted on the linoleum floor. A half-eaten biscuit lay by the monkey's side. The subject's lethargy and shallow breathing concerned him. There was no question the mystery pathogen had attacked the immune system as predicted. Littlejohn noted his observations on the sheet before moving on to the next cage.

"Ben," shouted Pollard, tapping him on the shoulder and pointing to the penultimate cage. His colleague's concern was understandable. The marmoset's torso appeared twisted, legs contorted as if in some frozen spasm. Eyes half-open, almost glassy in appearance, he noted later. Blood trickled from one nostril before pooling beside its tiny body. There was no sign of pain, its cheeks and forehead seemed drawn downwards by an invisible force. Subconsciously, Littlejohn distanced himself, determined to remain calm, working through the probabilities. The cage was a vision of hell, worthy of Hades himself.

He exchanged a concerned glance with Pollard. There was little that surprised the team down here. They had worked with almost every pathogen known to man and yet the sight of this tiny monkey's body, ravaged by disease in under four days, terrified him. He checked the sheet again, barely believing the transformation. Yesterday's lethargy and loss of appetite had mutated into full-blown haemorrhage and fever.

The monkey's motionless ankle and foot lay tantalisingly close to the cage door. Littlejohn deliberated whether he could take a sample safely without exposing himself to danger should the infected monkey stir. Safety protocols dictated the use of a tranquilliser. A bite or scratch from a monkey could easily puncture a glove or suit. Caution prevailed, and he resolved to return with the tranquilliser once he had completed the inspection.

Two further marmosets were at a similar stage of infection. However, what concerned Littlejohn most was the sight of one of the control subjects slumped against the back of the cage, staring blankly into the distance, totally unresponsive. He checked the notes again, assuming a colleague had made a mistake, or they had moved the animals for some unknown reason. Scientists jumping to unsubstantiated conclusions had undone hard-won reputations for rigour. He would not make that rookie mistake. Before raising the alarm, the experienced scientists would need to be certain.

One by one, they injected the affected monkeys with a tranquilliser until each cage fell silent, their heaving chests settling into a relaxed rhythm and he could safely draw blood and tissue samples for further analysis.

Back in the laboratory, he carefully prepared the samples before peering down the high-powered electron microscope. His normally steady hand trembled with excitement, impatient for the image to come into focus.

Littlejohn zoomed in further into an alien world of valleys and mountains hunting down the microscopic virus invisible to the naked eye. A force of nature so destructive it could detonate inside individual cells like a nuclear bomb. It didn't take him long to pick up its trail. Millions, perhaps billions, of tiny snake-like strands. Threads of virus tangled together as if in the throes of ecstasy. There was no question. It was a filo virus. From his extensive research, he was aware of only two pathogens that could wreak this level of damage, but had never come face to face with either. Marburg or Ebola.

He checked the textbook next to the keyboard, cross-checking what he was seeing with the black-and-white photo. Something about the sample looked different. Only further tests would determine for sure. He zoomed in further, zeroing in on a single strand of virus silhouetted against a cell wall from which it had emerged. His index finger fumbled for the red button, capturing the image and sending it to the printer on the far side of the room, a mug shot of the offender that might just seal the deal on a long-overlooked promotion. Littlejohn tilted his head, studying the print-out, allowing himself a moment of self-satisfaction with his handiwork.

Back in the red room, he hesitated before reaching for the telephone mounted on the wall, checking the time. It was only a quarter past five in the morning. Perhaps he should fax the photo to his boss's home number and wait until after six before calling? No, Major General Phillips would want to know immediately. He rifled through the staff Rolodex until he located the number.

"Sir, it's Doctor Littlejohn from CT6." He swallowed his nerves, listening to the rustle of bedclothes, his boss clearing his throat, slowly levering himself upright, perhaps taking a sip of water from a bedside table.

"Do you have any idea what time it is, Littlejohn?"

He sounded groggy, irritable, like always. Perhaps it had been a mistake not to wait until six.

"Yes, Sir."

"What on earth couldn't wait until the morning?"

"The samples we received last Tuesday?"

"Yes, what about them?"

"We believe we're looking at a novel strain of haemorrhagic fever."

There was a stunned silence. "Who else is there with you?"

"Major Pollard."

"And she's corroborated this?"

"Yes, Sir."

"Well, let's not get ahead of ourselves."

If there was an explanation, Littlejohn didn't know what it was.

"Run the tests again, can you? And when you've done that, run them again."

"Sir, we've double-checked the results. It's haemorrhagic fever all right. I can fax you a photo."

He could hear Phillips sitting up straighter now, fully awake. "Back up, will you? Tell me exactly what tests you've run."

Littlejohn walked the major general through the detailed notes he had scribbled down in preparation for the call. One of the subjects had died, two others had advanced symptoms. He hesitated before mentioning the control subject, knowing only too well the gravity of what he was about to say.

"Sir, one of the controls has developed early-stage symptoms."

There was a pause as Phillips considered what Littlejohn was saying. "Could it be cross-contamination, somehow?"

"We're waiting for confirmation from the day shift, but it looks like they followed all the protocols. We believe XC-4328 could be airborne." Littlejohn swallowed hard.

"Now listen carefully. Here's what I want you to do. Call Farrier and Cooper. I want the whole CT-6 team in my office by 10am. Until then, you're to mention this to no one. I want everything typed up and faxed to my office within the hour."

"Yes, Sir. I'll need to tell the others something."

"Tell them you have a suspected case of haemorrhagic fever, nothing more. I'll be there within the hour. This stays between us, Ben."

"Yes, Sir." Littlejohn's boss had never called him by his first name. It took him by surprise.

The line went dead as he stared at the receiver, imagining the chain of events their discovery had just initiated. He thumbed through the index cards, looking for Major Farrier and Doctor Cooper's numbers.

Major General Phillips replaced the receiver on a cluttered bedside table and ran a hand through thinning grey hair, marshalling his thoughts. He grabbed the handset and punched the numbers he knew by heart. After half a dozen rings, the line connected.

"George, it's Tom. Those lab results came in. You were right. It's not monkey pox. Littlejohn thinks it could be haemorrhagic fever. It might even be Marburg or Ebola."

There was a light static on the line, but no audible response.

Finally, Curran cleared his throat. “We should wait for the autopsies to be certain.” There was no emotion in his voice, as if he half-expected to be having this conversation.

“It looks like our friends are up to their old tricks again.”

Curran hung up without answering.

PART I

IRAQ 1998

CHAPTER 1

United Nations Special Commission
Inspections team
Iraq: 50km southwest of Baghdad, Iraq
12 April, 1998

~

The lead vehicle in the United Nations convoy rolled to a halt at a deserted intersection on a dirt road to nowhere. The radio crackled into life. One of the Iraqi minders spoke in rapid Arabic, asking for instructions.

Blake Harris shook his head and sighed deeply. They were already half an hour behind schedule, left waiting outside the hotel for their Iraqi escorts. The driver, Sadi, lit two cigarettes with a disposable lighter from his top pocket and offered one to Harris, the imprint of an oily finger on the filter. Harris thanked him with a nod, cracking open the window an inch to expel the plume of smoke. The tobacco was American, no doubt bartered from one of the inspectors. Harris reached into the back and grabbed two cans of tepid Coke from the cool box between the seats and handed one to Sadi.

Beyond the bulletproof glass of their lightly armoured Mitsubishi Land Cruiser a gust of wind toyed with a cardboard coffee cup left discarded by the side of the road. Harris lost sight of it as it skated across the tarmac and disappeared beneath their vehicle. Normally alert to danger, Harris slumped back in his seat, unpolished boots resting on the dashboard. There was nothing they could do now but wait. Harris knew better than anyone that it didn't pay to linger too long at intersections. The UN presence was, at best, tolerated by the locals.

A burst of static returned him to the here and now. A rapid exchange in Arabic followed on the CB radio mounted between the seats. Harris rotated the crumpled map across his lap to match their direction of travel. They were still almost twenty kilometres from their destination for today's inspection. It would not pay to be late. Saddam Hussein's own presidential camera crew would be waiting to record the UN team's every movement. Another box-ticking exercise to prove to the world that the Iraqi government was complying with the latest resolutions issued by the United Nations Security Council.

Despite his professionalism, Harris doubted today's visit would be anything other than another wasted journey. To their Iraqi hosts, the inspections had become an elaborate charade to avoid further sanctions, to silence the threat of war. Any hard evidence of non-compliance had so far proved impossible. Depending on who you believed, the bulk of Iraqi stockpiles of weapons and munitions had already been declared and destroyed years before. Harris had seen first-hand the intelligence reports that suggested otherwise. What remained of Saddam's weapons programme was believed to be hidden in bunkers and underground facilities whose locations remained unknown. There was no question. In recent months, the Iraqis had gained the upper hand, but the game was far from over.

Harris shifted in his sticky seat, adjusting the hip holster digging into his thigh. The Land Cruiser's engine spluttered momentarily before settling back into a rhythm. It would be a miracle if they actually made it to a single destination and back without at least one of the vehicles in their convoy breaking down. Most of the cars in Baghdad had body panels salvaged from the scrapyard, parts cannibalised, engines stripped for spares. Despite the presence of today's VIPs, the vehicles they had provided were no different. Beneath a thin veneer of white paint and the supposedly reassuring livery of the United Nations, the trucks and people carriers in the convoy were as old and tired as the lies they heard from those they interviewed. Like most things in the desert, the truth lay half hidden under a thick layer of sand and dirt.

The one exception was the vehicle immediately behind which carried their military chaperone, a Saddam clone in uniform with an obligatory moustache, like some jumped-up warlord in his executive saloon. Sadi noticed Harris admiring the pristine BMW in the wing mirror. "My cousin can get you one if you like," he joked in Arabic, grinning a crooked smile, two of his front teeth were missing. "A *gift* from our friends in Kuwait. Very good price." Harris remembered the triumphant footage of Saddam parading an entire fleet of luxury sedans seized in the chaotic aftermath of the invasion of Kuwait that precipitated the war that had first brought Harris to Iraq in January of '91.

In the rear-view mirror, Harris could make out the Iraqi colonel speaking on a handheld radio, no doubt reporting the convoy's progress to a national monitoring centre in Baghdad. At the first sign of trouble, they would despatch a government minister to "manage" the UN inspectors. The colonel would do nothing without first getting approval. Under Saddam, it did not pay to stick your neck out.

Harris wound down the window and flicked his cigarette into the wind, shielding his eyes from the sun. The featureless, narrow desert road stretched into the distance. Late spring was Harris's favourite time of year. Blue, cloudless skies. Not too hot. In a couple of months, the heat of early summer would become suffocating once more.

In the air-conditioned minibus behind them were the weapons inspectors. The international team hailed from almost a dozen countries, including the United States, France, the United Kingdom, Canada, Germany and Sweden. Beards and wild hair, pens in shirt pockets, briefcases and bundles of paperwork. Scientists through and through. Eccentric in the extreme. Harris was the lead for today's security detail, responsible for their safety. He likened his task to "herding cats". A couple of the Americans seemed friendly enough. He couldn't say for sure, but to his trained eye, at least one of the American minders was CIA. There was something about the way he carried himself. Ex-military. It took one to know one.

There were others in the security detail. Private contractors like Harris. Men he had worked with before. People he could trust to do their job. Of course, some, like the Americans, he suspected of having an agenda beyond the pay cheque. It didn't pay to ask too many questions.

Everyone assumed Harris belonged here. He had been living in the Middle East long enough that it never occurred to those visiting from the West that he wasn't born here. Dark hair, deep tan, heavy beard and piercing blue eyes that rarely provoked a second glance.

He had his mother to thank for his olive skin. Born in Egypt, she had been something of a beauty. Even in her fifties, she retained the same striking features that had courted the attentions of at least one Sheik. His father had called her his "Cleopatra". Harris's parents had met in Riyadh, while his father was stationed there as an oil engineer working at drilling sites throughout Saudi Arabia. Young Blake Harris had moved from school to school wherever the work took the family. Kuwait, Saudi, Iraq. He had inherited his mother's good looks and his father's grit. His school maths report memorably recorded "something unquantifiable" about the young Harris. Brooding, moody, dangerous. An intensity that made others uncomfortable, apparently.

The convoy finally received permission to proceed. Forty minutes later an Iraqi soldier waved them to a halt at a checkpoint on the approach road to an anonymous industrial facility miles out of town. A chain-link fence stretched as far as the eye could see. Signs in Arabic informed visitors of their arrival at the Iraqi State Facility for Pesticide Production and Animal Feed, warning of dog patrols. Trespassers would be arrested or shot on sight. This was a military facility in all but name. The guards went through the motions of checking the United Nations paperwork until the Saddam lookalike colonel grew impatient. Harris was too far away to hear what they were arguing about but he got the gist from their body language.

Finally, the guard raised the barrier and they drove the remaining half a mile to the first building in a complex that Harris recognised from the aerial photos, laid out over fifty acres.

In the distance, Harris noticed clouds of dust kicked up by a column of trucks and tankers leaving by an entrance at the far end of the facility to the West. It didn't take a genius to grasp that the Iraqis were well practised at staying one step ahead of the inspectors. According to the satellite imagery, anything illegal simply moved to a new location. Everyone knew the game. They just couldn't stop it.

In the pocket notebook Harris carried everywhere, he kept a coded record of everything he saw. Vehicle movements, the location of CCTV cameras, any significant military hardware, air defence, even surface-to-air missile arrays that might suggest a high-value military target. He noted the number of security personnel assigned to guard each facility. His ultimate paymasters had tasked him with grading the Iraqis' level of professionalism, from rookie recruits to Saddam's own Republican Guard. If further air strikes were authorised, Harris's first-hand intelligence would prove invaluable.

A welcoming committee stood waiting outside the building's glass and steel reception to receive the UN delegation. When the cloud of dust had dispersed, their hosts approached the minibus and shook hands with each of the inspectors, under the watchful eye of the security team and a camera crew recording every interaction. The Saddam clone introduced a handful of suits, including the Head of Production, Chief Scientist and Head of Research and Development tasked with answering the inspectors' questions and conducting a walking tour of the pesticide research facility and production line.

Harris kept a respectful distance but remained close enough to listen out for any discrepancies between the Iraqi scientists' answers in Arabic and the translation given to the inspectors by their military guide. The group began their tour of the first building, stopping at the first production line, said to be for animal feed. Harris noted vast hoppers and conveyor belts, fifty-feet-tall storage containers that soared towards the roof where raised walkways were lit by fluorescent lights dangling from high beams. The modern machinery was silent but well maintained. He noticed much of the assembly was on wheels, so it could be moved to another location if production lines were altered.

Flashing lights on a control panel suggested the line was

merely paused and in regular use. Harris noted the make and model of the plant equipment. The air handlers drew his attention. High-capacity air filtration system. He had seen units like this before, but not normally used in the production of animal feed.

The Iraqis had mastered the art of hiding evidence in plain sight. A lick of paint proved extremely effective in masking the true purpose of certain specialist equipment. Their programme of deception and concealment had proven very convincing. The burden of proof remained firmly on the inspection team. The Iraqis would admit nothing without incontrovertible evidence and the United Nations had set a very high bar. Non-compliance was proving very hard to substantiate. Data had become politicised and the word of scientists was universally distrusted.

Marchand, one of the French scientists, took photos, checking the United Nations tags on each piece of equipment, noting those missing from the previous inspection the year before. The Frenchman asked factual questions about daily production targets, the manufacturing process they followed and the output achieved. At first the responses came easily, fluent explanations that suggested years of experience in agrichemicals, but as the inspectors dug deeper, the answers became vaguer. Occasionally, the Head of Production appeared guarded, glancing at the Iraqi colonel for guidance.

"These are busy people," the colonel explained, beads of sweat forming on his brow, "we should not keep them too long from their work. I will make sure the team provides written responses to your questions. We should move on," he insisted, impatient to proceed with the tour.

Before continuing, members of the UN team collected swab samples from each piece of equipment using what looked like six-inch-long Q-Tips with absorbent pads on one end, thrust into the corners of empty containers. They put the samples into test tubes and filled them with liquid. It would be several days before they knew for sure what the tests revealed. Harris listened carefully to the explanation of why the silos were empty. The Head of Production explained that delivery lorries had left this morning.

"How convenient," thought Harris, remembering the convoy of trucks he had seen leaving prior to their arrival.

The next building housed the research and development division, tasked primarily with testing and quality control. Harris recognised the layout from the blueprints he had studied. Beyond the security door were half a dozen laboratories they were all keen to get a closer look at. Five women staffed the front office, sat at desks, tapping away at their keyboards with long varnished fingernails. They paused in their work, their movements strangely synchronised, smiling at the visitors. Their lipstick and make-up made Harris think of airline stewardesses rather than workers in an industrial facility. Their host introduced one of them as a doctor. She bowed awkwardly, nodding at each of the inspectors in turn. Something about the moisturised, delicate hands and their gold jewellery suggested to Harris that these were actors. It seemed unlikely those hands had ever handled industrial chemicals, laboratory equipment or heavy machinery. It would not be the first time the Iraqis had used stand-ins in place of scientists.

"We've prepared the samples your team requested," explained the colonel via the translator, opening a briefcase with foam cut-outs, each space filled with a test tube.

"We were told we could see the labs," challenged Raus, the Swedish inspector.

"I'm afraid that's not possible today. We'll have to rearrange."

"May I ask why?"

"There was an accident." He seemed embarrassed by the admission. "A chemical spill."

"Why weren't we told?"

"Bad news is not always shared in Iraq," he admitted. "We only found out on our way here."

"Was that the reason for the delay?"

"I'm afraid so. An unforeseen change to today's schedule."

"We could have saved ourselves the long drive. I hope no one was injured."

The translated question prompted a rapid exchange followed by a look of bewilderment. No one seemed to know what they were allowed to admit. After a brief delay, conferring in whispers, the colonel explained, with some embarrassment.

"Two of the lab team were hospitalised. He says they had to evacuate this entire building, shut down the line until the clean-up crew got here. All because someone fitted a filter incorrectly. I can only apologise," explained the colonel via the Iraqi translator. "He would be happy to arrange a return visit. Perhaps later this week? In the meantime, he hopes the samples of their research will suffice."

"Thank you. Can he tell us what they were working on?" asked Doug Mathews, the Australian inspector, his pen poised to record the response.

"A modified version of malathion."

"Ah. We call it maldison where I come from," confirmed the Australian with a smile. "Can I see the production records?"

"Of course. We have made the copies you requested," said the translator as someone presented Mathews with a ring-binder file, stuffed with documents.

Before they continued on to the next building, more through habit than necessity, Harris made a mental note of the make and model of the key code security entry system, together with the location of cameras, blind spots and potential entry points. It might come in useful for a return visit. Next time, he would come alone.

CHAPTER 2

Baghdad, Iraq
17 April, 1998

Harris made sure he was at his assigned rendezvous early the following morning. Keeping a close eye on the main road for any sign of a tail, he reassured himself that he had taken every precaution.

Most of the Iraqi intelligence operatives were easy to spot in their Brooks Brothers chinos, dark glasses and checked shirts but those from other countries less so. In the last few weeks Baghdad had become a hotbed of intrigue and espionage once more. The longer the inspectors went without finding evidence of non-compliance, the more vocal America and its allies had become in demanding tighter sanctions to punish Saddam.

Harris had left the hotel at daybreak for his morning jog before the heat of the day. He wore the same dusty running shoes and carried just enough dinar in notes to buy breakfast. He doubled back several times, exploring the roads around the plush hotel the UN team were using as their base, until he was satisfied he was not being followed.

Compared to his humble rented apartment on the top floor of a purpose-built concrete and glass block in the Al Shorja district with views over the Bab Al Sharqi market, the Western-style hotel was positively decadent. Hot showers, buffet breakfasts, cappuccinos and cocktails. He pushed himself harder and longer every morning just to keep the pounds off.

Harris circled back and made his way to one of his favourite haunts. Not far from the hotel, Café Kerrala still served their coffee in antique silver jugs called Dallahs with curved handles and tapered spouts, ornately decorated with birds and flowers. He ordered a selection of pastries made on-site by the bespectacled owner whose nephews helped him get ready for the day before hurrying off to school. It was still early, before the main commuter rush for those working in nearby factories or offices downtown.

A sixth sense made Harris glance across the street. David Brokenshire, his MI6 contact, was leaning against a lamp post, scanning the café and its surroundings. Harris ran the fingers of his right hand through close-cropped hair to give his British military intelligence handler the all-clear. If he had used his left hand, Brokenshire would have continued on to an alternate rendezvous point where they would try again, this time hopefully unobserved. As Harris's counter-espionage instructor had once so eloquently explained, meeting your handler is a lot like porcupines mating: it should be done very carefully, if at all.

Harris caught the attention of the café owner and gestured for another place setting for his guest.

"How was yesterday?" asked Brokenshire, taking his seat with no fanfare or greeting.

"Waste of time. We were too late. There was nothing there. It's all gone."

"Shame. The intel looked so promising."

"Maybe a week ago, but not now. They'd cleaned house."

"We should still pick up chemical traces."

"If they were ever there. The whole place stank of disinfectant. They'd scrubbed that place clean."

Brokenshire shrugged his shoulders. "Let's see what the experts say. We may still get lucky."

"I'm telling you, Saddam would never have allowed the inspections to go ahead if he thought they would find anything."

"Unless he didn't have a choice."

"Until the UN grow a pair and start enforcing no-notice inspections, we're never going to catch them red-handed."

"Patience. Let the inspectors do their jobs. We might get lucky."

"There's too much at stake. We had the bloody camera crew yesterday following us around. They're unlikely to slip up now."

"Of course. It plays well for an international audience. Saddam still has many allies. It's going to take hard evidence to persuade the council."

Harris looked unconvinced. "We need better intelligence. There's a limit to what I can accomplish on my own."

"I'm working on it."

"What happened to your source?"

"He got sloppy." Brokenshire ran his fingers inside the starched collar of his checked shirt, scratching at a sunburned neck. "They reassigned him to Basra."

"Any chance of blowback?"

"No, you're in the clear. But we're back to doing things the old-fashioned way until my new contact comes good."

"Nothing's going to change until we stop playing by their rules."

"My hands are tied. We don't have a choice."

"What more do they want? Your own satellite data confirms they're moving UN-tagged restricted industrial equipment from site to site. We have tyre tracks disappearing into the desert.

Convoys leaving by the back door, just as we arrive. The deception is blatant."

"It's a misdemeanour at best..." Brokenshire's voice tailed off, unconvinced.

"You can't expect me to get results with both hands tied behind my back. Cut me loose."

"Believe me, I'm trying. There's still no consensus for stronger enforcement tactics."

"Why?"

"This is coming from the top. You know better than anyone, the UN operates under an international mandate—"

"So, what? We carry on going through the motions and nothing changes?" interrupted Harris with heavy sarcasm.

"I wouldn't say nothing. The council just voted to increase our budgets for aerial reconnaissance and remote monitoring," confirmed Brokenshire with a wry smile.

"Big deal."

"They want to give the inspectors more time."

Harris shrugged his shoulders. "Most of that lot wouldn't know a weapon of mass destruction if they tripped over one."

"They're the best available."

"On paper, maybe." Harris could barely hide his derision. "I'm telling you. Half of them are still wet behind the ears. They look without seeing."

"So you keep saying."

"Why is there never a proper handover? Every new inspection team asks the same old questions and gets the same answers."

"Sorry, I thought your job was to advise them?"

"On security, sure. Not on how to run inspections."

"We see to it the UN teams are well briefed. They have all the relevant intelligence."

"Does anyone actually bother to read my reports?"

"Look," interrupted Brokenshire, growing tired of Harris's whining. "Do you have any idea how hard it is getting scientists to come out here in the first place? The layers of UN bureaucracy we're dealing with are unreal. Trust me when I say they are the best team in the circumstances."

"If this is the best the West can muster," Harris sneered, "the Iraqis must be laughing at us."

"Perhaps if you actually co-operated and worked with the inspectors..."

"And blow my cover?"

"Look, all I'm saying is that if you see something that's not right, call it out."

"I'm not the expert."

"No, but your instincts serve you well. You know how to ask the right questions."

Harris shrugged his shoulders in response.

"Anyway, isn't that what I pay you for? Very handsomely, I might add."

Harris let out a long sigh. He knew Brokenshire was right. He could sit on the sidelines and sneer at the inspectors or lean in and make a difference.

"You said yourself," continued Brokenshire, "it's amazing how much you can learn over a shared cigarette. A bit of empathy goes a long way in this game."

"And respect. Respect matters. When you bother to get to know people, take the time to cultivate friendships, they talk."

"They talk to no one but you, Harris. That's the point. As we both know. All those little details matter. How busy the bus is on the way to the factory, the number of deliveries, how many visitors. They help us build up a picture of activity levels. Gives the analysts back in Whitehall a baseline to work from." Brokenshire paused. "Of course, they take everything we tell them with a pinch of salt."

"Because?"

"We can never discount the fact that the Iraqis are telling us what they think we want to hear."

"Why would they lie? They think I'm one of them."

"Because everyone in Iraq lies. I've never known a country so wedded to deceit."

"Outside Russia and China, you mean?"

"What do Iraqis have to gain by telling us the truth?"

"Not all Iraqis are the same, Brokenshire. When you get to know them, they're good people."

"Look, all I'm saying is that, since Saddam came to power, there's no cultural taboo about lying any more. It's seen as a means to an end."

"Only because people are too scared to tell the truth. People learn to keep their heads down. Mind their own business. Keep their families safe. It's much too dangerous."

"MI6 has drafted in an entire team of psychologists and cultural experts to help us figure out how Saddam and his henchmen think. Their mentality. This obsession with obfuscation, disinformation."

"You should have asked me."

Brokenshire rolled his eyes. "In time, those psychologists should help."

"Sure, but there's no substitute for boots on the ground. We both know people here live by a strict code. No one in Baghdad wants to be a whistle-blower. And someone should tell those Americans, people don't respond well to threats."

"What is it with these damned desert cultures?" Brokenshire smiled, remembering something. He drained his coffee before refilling from the jug. "Do you remember Tehran?"

Harris shook his head. "You never let me forget."

"What was it you wrote in your report? That the desert breeds 'a determinism based on insecurity and uncertainty'," regurgitated Brokenshire from memory, as if reading from an intelligence report. "Where 'tribal and sectarian politics inter-pollinate'."

Harris winced at his amateur attempts at social commentary. He knew better now to leave the analysis to the experts. Stick to the job of gathering intelligence, not interpreting it.

"Iraqis will never tell Westerners what they really think. They pay lip service. Go through the motions of compliance. The UN shouldn't expect anything more."

"Unpicking a multifaceted lie takes time. Trust in the process."

"Sure, but until the inspectors start using a bit of imagination and a critical eye, they're never going to get beyond first base."

"Then I say again. It's up to you, Harris, to show them the way. Help them see what you see. Remember: they just got here. You've been in country for years. Help them get up to speed."

Harris shook his head, snorting in mock disgust. "Those American inspectors can go to hell for all I care."

"Fine words from the man paid to protect them," Brokenshire said, changing tack, perhaps remembering how stubborn Harris could be.

"Remember what our Russian friends used to say: 'Doveryai, no proveryai'. *Trust but verify*. Keep sending us those samples and they'll give us the evidence Whitehall needs."

"What if they don't?"

"Then we'll do it your way."

Harris leaned forward across the table, fixing Brokenshire with a purposeful stare. "It would be a damned sight quicker."

Brokenshire nodded, reflecting on their conversation. Under the table he kicked a rucksack to rest beneath Harris's seat.

"What's this?"

"What do you know about Al Daura?" asked Brokenshire.

Harris threw his head back, rubbing his eyes, trying to recall. "Former military research facility. Suspected of manufacturing biological weapons. Declared to the inspectors in '95. Converted over to the production of vaccines later that year. Why?"

"Because we think the switch to vaccine production was temporary." He gestured towards the intelligence folder in the rucksack under the table. "I got you the architect's drawings for a level three biocontainment laboratory."

"Now we're talking."

"We think they completed it within the last twelve months. Our new source claims they've restarted their research."

"Into what?"

"You name it. Camel pox, rotavirus, haemorrhagic conjunctivitis, enterovirus."

"Not exactly Doomsday weapons, then."

"No, but the experts think those may be stepping stones towards Saddam's ultimate goal."

"Which is?"

"We don't know yet. Whitehall thinks Saddam never gave up his obsession with developing biological weapons he could use against the West."

"And you believe them?"

"We don't think they're acting alone."

Harris mulled over this information. "Why would anyone help Saddam develop biological weapons?"

"We don't know."

Harris patted the satchel containing the photos and intelligence briefing under his chair. "Al Daura, eh? You really think Saddam has an active programme?"

"Don't you?"

"If he does, Al Daura is not a bad shout. State-of-the-art, modern research facilities. It's capable of huge production volume."

"We're pushing the security council for a no-notice visit."

"The Iraqis won't like that."

"They won't have a choice."

"It's about time we changed tactics."

"Oh, and there's one other thing."

Harris noticed a hesitation. That never bode well.

"How good is the UN's security detail?"

"Why?"

"I hear things."

Harris picked something out of his teeth with a toothpick, one eye half closed. "You know me. I leave nothing to chance. What did you hear?"

"Word on the grapevine is that Tehran is smuggling weapons and explosives across the border again."

"What's their play?"

"The Americans tracked bank transfers totalling several millions. We think an Iranian-backed militia group is preparing an attack."

"Against the UN? Why would they do that? The repercussions would be severe."

"A false flag attack could prompt further sanctions."

"Not if we could prove the attack came from Iran."

"Look, brief your team. Double security. Do whatever you have to do. On the quiet, of course. Where would they hit you?"

"Let me talk to the Americans. The hotel is secure. Guarded by Iraqi soldiers day and night."

"Then an IED attack or ambush?"

"We only release the convoy routes at the last moment. An ambush takes planning."

"Look, I'm not telling you how to do your job, but take the tip-off seriously, will you?"

Harris nodded. "Anything else I should know?"

Brokenshire thought about saying something, but changed

his mind. "Look, I know you find this process frustrating. But we've got to give the inspections more time. Sooner or later, Saddam will mess up. I guarantee it."

"You make your own luck."

"I'm sure you're right, Harris," said Brokenshire, with heavy sarcasm. "We're all counting on you."

"I hate it when you say that."

CHAPTER 3

What happened on the morning of the fourth day of inspections caught Harris completely by surprise. For a man with his fabled monk-like routine of meticulous preparation, that was unprecedented.

McIntrye, a tall American inspector in a Stetson, it amused Harris to discover, did actually hail from Fort Worth, Texas, summoned the Iraqi colonel chaperoning their visits to the hotel lobby prior to departure. In no uncertain terms, he demanded that the convoy be redirected to the Al Daura Foot and Mouth Disease Vaccine facility, located some five miles south-west of Baghdad. Overnight, the powers-that-be sitting some six thousand miles away in Washington had finally grown tired of all this obfuscation.

The tone and directness of the American's request seemed to surprise the Iraqi colonel. At first, he point-blank refused, insisting they stick to the agreed itinerary, already approved by Saddam and his Iraqi high command. A tense stand-off ensued between the two groups. Both men stood toe-to-toe, voices raised. The American warned the colonel what might happen if he refused. The Iraqi officer stood his ground, referring to the American as a "cowboy" in broken English.

Only when the Iraqi minders threatened to draw their weapons did Harris intervene. His calming words in Arabic seemed to give the colonel pause. Much to everyone's relief, both sides backed down, de-escalating their macho posturing. Harris would later admit to Brokenshire how much he enjoyed the morning's drama.

Harris took the colonel to one side and recommended he talk to his superior. At first, the military man appeared implacable, incensed at having his authority challenged in this way. Harris suspected it was as much about loss of face in front of his men as fear of repercussions from his superiors. After a protracted radio conversation between the colonel and his commanding officer at the national monitoring centre, they finally approved permission for the convoy to proceed to Al Daura.

Time was of the essence. The faster they got there, the more likely they were to catch the Iraqis napping and discover the truth. Harris herded the UN team on to the waiting transportation, except this time he heeded Brokenshire's advice, choosing to ride with the scientists in their luxury minibus. In the peace and air-conditioned calm, he sank back into the plush seat, allowing himself an ironic smile, reflecting on the Iraqi colonel's momentary loss of composure. Perhaps Brokenshire was right. The Iraqis really did respond better to threats.

Harris tuned into the inspectors' sporadic conversation, biding his time until they were on the main road and he could move around the vehicle's interior without fear of injury from the violent bumps in the uneven roadway.

"Give them a chance," Brokenshire had encouraged. "Get the inspectors on side early."

Harris was considering how to initiate a conversation when

Marchand, the French scientist, sat immediately behind him, tapped him on the shoulder.

"Do you speak English?"

"Only when called upon to do so," answered Harris, affecting his adopted Arab accent. He had used it so often, it was like putting on a comfortable pair of slippers. He could have replied in passable French, but he didn't want to encourage too many questions.

"My apologies. I assumed you were..."

"That's okay, I grew up here. But my father was Scottish," he added, which was only half a lie. "The name's Harris," he added, extending his hand. "And you are?"

"Christophe Marchand, OIAC."

All the inspectors seemed to belong to some non-governmental organisation or other. Each had its own acronym. Perhaps if Harris had paid more attention to Brokenshire's briefing notes, he would already know that.

"Chemical weapons specialist," Marchand added as if registering Harris's confusion. "And I assume you're ex-military like the rest of the security team?"

"Something like that." Harris grimaced in response, turning to look out the window, checking the rooftops overlooking their route. More out of habit than necessity, mindful of Brokenshire's warning about Iranian militia operating this side of the border.

"I just hope today's visit is more productive than yesterday's," continued Marchand with a sigh.

"When you've done as many of these as I have, you learn to manage expectations."

"But driving all that way for nothing?"

"Accidents happen rather a lot round here. You get used to them."

Marchand nodded, tilting his head in acknowledgement of Harris's world-weary experience.

"First time in Iraq?" asked Harris.

"Is it that obvious?" replied Marchand, with some embarrassment. Harris didn't answer. "You must tire of people like me, scientists asking the same questions?"

"Not really. We all have a job to do."

"The sooner we return home to our wives and girlfriends..." Marchand paused and leaned in conspiratorially. "May they never meet."

A scientist with a sense of humour, thought Harris, wonders will never cease. Harris wanted so desperately to tell the Frenchman what he really thought of the inspections, but he decided to let it slide, for now.

"May today's visit be more productive than yesterday. Santé," said the Frenchman, taking a nip from a hip flask before offering it to Harris who declined. "Been to Al Daura before?"

"Twice." If truth be told, when Harris closed his eyes, he could visualise the facility's entire layout from the architect's blueprints. Harris had waited a long time for this one. A return visit to Al Daura, the state-of-the-art facility built to conduct research into infectious diseases. The latest intelligence suggested the Iraqis had configured the production line to manufacture a vaccine for foot and mouth, but this had not always been the case.

Working with live virus would require enhanced security protocols, high-level biocontainment units that could easily be repurposed for the study of other pathogens. The last time Harris was here, the job of the inspectors had been to determine whether Al Daura's production lines had been altered and to understand what else they might be producing. Seven years earlier, in 1991, military intelligence had classified Al Daura as a priority target for allied bombing in the *Desert Storm* campaign. Since then, much of the site had been rebuilt and repurposed. Harris had seen intelligence reports that suggested there was an entire suite of secure laboratories they had never inspected until now. This time Harris hoped their visit would be different.

Before they left the hotel, there was some commotion as the Americans unveiled their new mobile detection system. The inspectors were eager to try out their new toy. The handheld units were said to accurately detect the presence of a whole range of foreign particles. If the claims were true, it might be a game-changer for the work of the inspectors.

The convoy rolled to a halt at the front gate to Al Daura. It soon became clear that the message had not reached the guards charged with manning the facility.

"On whose authority?" demanded the Iraqi commander in Arabic, summoned by his guards to talk to the visitors.

"By order of resolution 687 of the United Nations Security Council," replied the American, towering over the Iraqi as he waited for the translator to catch up. "This document authorises me to inspect this facility under suspicion of illegal production of chemical and biological agents." Unsurprisingly, the commander had never heard of such an order, but the Iraqi colonel joined them and quickly explained what had been agreed.

Once inside the compound, the Iraqi base commander became more concerned with appearing in official photos documenting his team's cooperation, no doubt aware that they would use the footage in Saddam's propaganda machine. Local news stations and CNN had taken to running rolling repeats of the inspectors shaking hands with smiling Iraqi soldiers and government officials, eager to convince their many allies around the world, notably Russia and France, that they were doing everything expected of them.

The Americans unloaded the mobile detection equipment and removed one of the two handheld devices, referred to as HANAAs. It was the first time Harris had seen one in the field but had read the one-page specification sheet Brokenshire had supplied in his intelligence briefing. Harris was already sceptical. The devices looked like prototypes, totally unproven in desert conditions swirling with dust and sand. The Iraqis seemed spectacularly unaware of the capabilities of this new equipment, crowding round the device to see what it did.

They began their tour, drifting from room to room, cataloguing each piece of equipment. Even to the untrained eye Al Daura was state of the art. They had spared no expense.

Harris had become well versed in Iraqi concealment tactics. After endless briefings from experts, poring over transcripts from previous inspections, he had developed a sixth sense for high-end industrial equipment that just seemed out of place. Telltale signs of deception suggested all was not as it appeared. Harris's role as a front-line observer was never more important than now. To see without being seen. While the Iraqis scrutinised every movement and request by the UN team, Harris was free to apply his particular skill set few others possessed.

Harris wandered outside and offered the guard an American cigarette. He had a knack of breaking through by playing along, engaging with the Iraqis without judgement. As one man to another. He always made a point of removing his sidearm on-site, remaining professional and civil at all times. He had witnessed first-hand American attempts to intimidate the Iraqis. Classic good cop, bad cop routines that rarely worked here. Sure, some, like the Iraqi colonel responded better to authority but, to the working man, different tactics were needed.

Harris relied on putting workers at ease, getting them to lower their guard and talk to him. A free pack of cigarettes or a Zippo lighter was normally all it took to loosen tongues. Harris had developed a healthy respect for the locals. They had a habit of playing their hand well. In poker terms, a game of which Harris was particularly fond, one never knew for sure whether the man opposite was bluffing with a pair of threes or whether they really did have the winning flush.

As Harris had explained to Brokenshire countless times, unless you're actually there in the room, listening carefully to the Iraqi scientists' answers to the inspectors' endless questions, it is almost impossible to say whether the purpose of an industrial facility is what they said it was or not. The colonel overseeing the inspections had become a past-master at stage-managing the entire process. They showed the inspectors exactly what they expected to see, told them what they wanted to hear. Had Harris not known better, it would be easy to go along with the consensus of the French and Russian inspectors that, superficially at least, the Iraqis were in full compliance. To all intents and purposes, the inspectors had found nothing illegal. Any normal person would be satisfied with what they found. But not Harris.

Harris had come to understand that the Iraqis would admit only what the United Nations could prove. Unlike many of the inspectors who saw extracts only of the intelligence gathered, Brokenshire fed Harris a rich diet of aerial photography, import paperwork for specialist equipment, high specification air handlers, bioreactors, growth medium consistent with an advanced bioweapon programme. The challenge was to find it. Harris knew better than most that several of the civilian factories and facilities they visited concealed a darker purpose. Earlier inspections had revealed weapons programmes on an altogether different scale and while they had destroyed stockpiles of chemical weapons, the research into viruses and bacterial agents had been driven underground.

Harris finished his cigarette, nodded at the guard and wandered back inside. He paused at what looked like a water tank, absent-mindedly scratching at the flaking paint with his fingernail. Underneath was the unmistakable sheen of stainless steel. Why would someone paint what, to all intents and purposes, was a brand-new piece of equipment? Awfully high spec for a water tank, thought Harris.

He nudged Marchand's elbow to get his attention. The Frenchman looked up from his task, checking a piece of tagged equipment against the inventory on his clipboard, his steel-framed glasses perched on the end of his nose, ever the scientist. Without overtly drawing attention to what he had discovered, Harris surreptitiously nodded towards the flaking paint. Marchand nodded in gratitude and took a closer look at the water tank.

"Why is this equipment not tagged?" he asked the nearest Iraqi scientist. The Frenchman retrieved a new tag from his bag, wrote an identifying code sequence and secured it to the storage tank. "What happened to the one that was here before?"

"They replaced it. Or moved it to another facility," the Iraqi admitted with a shrug.

"Either way, I'll need to find it."

More paperwork. That didn't seem to please their Iraqi host. The bureaucracy was excruciating, but was the only way for the inspectors to unpick the truth and build a complete picture of Iraqi production. Slowly but surely, first-hand intelligence was making a difference, at least according to Brokenshire.

Once inside the laboratory suite, they suited up in protective equipment before entering what Marchand explained was a secure, level three biocontainment zone.

The inspectors paid particular attention to a stainless-steel cylinder connected by more than a dozen tubes and pipes to other laboratory equipment. They took several photos and catalogued everything. From the briefing document, Harris recognised the centre piece as a second-generation GTC bioreactor used for the production of bacteria or viruses.

Inside the cylinder, through a narrow viewing panel, a soft

yellow light bathed the contents in a warm fug. Alongside the reactor was a computer monitor whose green screen displayed the rotating Al Daura logo.

Via the translator, the Iraqi technician explained what they were making and detailed the production methods in terms Harris struggled to follow, though the responses seemed consistent with the inspectors' expectations.

In another half-empty storeroom Harris noted grooves in the floor where heavy equipment had once stood. Row upon row of twelve-inch-high storage racks were fixed to the wall. Hundreds of what looked like empty egg cups, which the technician explained, were used to grow foot and mouth virus for testing purposes. An industrial fridge and freezer, now empty, had storage space for a significant quantity of vaccine.

While the inspectors documented everything, re-tagging each piece of equipment, Harris was running complex calculations in his head. For the last few minutes, his sixth sense had been screaming at him. It was an old habit of counting steps wherever he went. He had memorised the approximate dimensions of the building from the architect's blueprints. Unless he had miscounted, which would be most unlike him, there was a another set of rooms beyond the concrete wall, but there appeared to be no obvious way of accessing them. Harris nudged Marchand again, pointing at the dead end, and after a moment of confusion the Frenchman understood.

"What's on the far side of this wall?"

"Nothing," explained the guide.

"The floor plans show a research wing."

The Iraqi appeared flustered. "That entire section was closed years ago. After the war."

"We'll still need to see inside. Is there another way to access it?"

"There's an entrance on the far side of the building, but..."

"Thank you. I insist."

Once they were back outside, they walked around the side of the building. The technician tried the door but found it locked. He summoned the janitor on a portable radio who tried each of the keys on his fob, but none of them seemed to work. After a brief delay, the building supervisor arrived red-faced with another set of keys. The door swung inwards to reveal a darkened suite of shuttered rooms. Mothballed equipment, grey sheets covering work stations, chairs turned upside down. Several years of dust covered every surface, and much to Harris's disappointment, there were no footprints, no obvious signs of recent activity, exactly as the Iraqi technician had suggested. It was rare for his instinct to let him down.

"We'll need to take samples in here too," confirmed the American inspector.

"Looks like another wasted journey," whispered Marchand to Harris in muted resignation.

Harris nodded, but something still seemed off. He just couldn't put his finger on what exactly. He watched the Americans use their handheld detection equipment again. A continuous alarm sounded from one unit until the operator silenced it, blaming a false reading. Too much dust in the air, disturbed by their movements, catching in the light that penetrated between the blinds. Perhaps it wasn't working properly.

The supervisor waited patiently by the door until the inspectors had completed their checks, relocking the door behind the team. Harris couldn't be certain, but he noticed a silent exchange between the colonel and his aide. A look of relief, perhaps.

"Satisfied?" asked Marchand of his American counterpart. "There is nothing here. No evidence of non-compliance. Oui?"

"Let's wait until the results are back, shall we?" replied the American in the Stetson.

CHAPTER 4

As the sun set on another hot Baghdad day, Harris was relaxing in a busy café, absent-mindedly watching the world go by, enjoying an intense game of dominoes with his good friend Sadi. The southern district of Dora had become one of Harris's favourite places to hang out, home to bustling markets and restaurants, where office workers gathered in the evening. Families filled the streets, perusing market stalls, buying fresh produce before heading home for dinner.

Earlier, Harris had taken Marchand, the French scientist, to his favourite fish restaurant on Abu Nawas Street before heading across town to meet Sadi and his brother for their usual dominoes round robin. The contest was evenly matched, as always. Uncharacteristically, Harris had taken his eye off the ball, his thoughts clouded by another long day of inspections, allowing his opponent the upper hand. All was not lost. Not yet at least.

Harris leaned forward and took a long hit on the floor-standing shisha pipe they were sharing. He took a sip of sweet tea, studying his old friend deliberate over his next move, little finger resting on upper lip. His Iraqi friend wore faded denim jeans, checked shirt and sockless leather loafers, the informal uniform of a small army of fellow United Nations staff working as interpreters, drivers, guides and local liaison.

Each table had its own floor-standing polished brass and liquid-filled glass hubble-bubble pipe, or Argilah, as Sadi called it. Harris blew out another sweet cloud of honey-scented tobacco smoke. He allowed his eyes to glaze over, fighting to concentrate on the game and his opponent's next move. Sadi stiffened in his chair, eyes fixed on someone standing behind Harris, who was pretending to read the menu but paying particular attention to their table. Sadi kicked Harris under the table.

Without looking round, Harris whispered, "Don't tell me. Six feet tall. Pale skin. Foppish, light brown hair, blue eyes. About forty?"

"How do you do that?"

"Years of practice."

"Wait. He's coming over."

Harris reached over and pulled up another chair, patting the cushion. "How did you find me?"

Brokenshire's eyes narrowed. "It's my job." He took the seat offered without ceremony.

"I think you know my friend Sadi," said Harris.

"Salaam alaikum," said Brokenshire, faltering over the pronunciation.

"Alaikum salaam. Peace be with you," replied Sadi, taking a long draw from the shisha pipe, never taking his eyes off Brokenshire. He offered the military intelligence officer a turn on the pipe. Brokenshire hesitated before accepting. He inhaled from the brass nozzle, perhaps too deeply. The smoke caught in his throat and, much to the amusement of those around him, the Westerner's face turned puce. He coughed for a full twenty seconds, gulping down successive glasses of water.

"You get used to it. Eventually," conceded Harris with a mischievous grin. "Sadi, this is the man I was telling you about."

"The Englishman who closed my son's school for three days?" accused Sadi with an air of mischief.

Brokenshire's face flushed crimson. "I'm not sure why anyone would tell you that." He challenged Harris with a forced smile.

"There are no secrets in Baghdad," added Harris.

"Well, in that case, I apologise. Let's just say that it wasn't our finest hour," he acknowledged with a shrug.

Sadi raised his glass. "American dollars make people do crazy things."

"Sorry?"

"In Baghdad it doesn't pay for locals to tell Westerners the truth."

Harris remembered the scenes with some embarrassment. Under his watchful protection as Head of Security that day, the UN inspectors had wasted precious time on what seemed, from the start, a fool's errand. A supposedly reliable local source had claimed there were missile components buried beneath a school playground. No doubt the sizeable reward for information had something to do with it. After all, this wasn't the first or the last time false leads had surfaced.

"You should have seen the look on the Americans' faces when their expensive ground-penetrating radar found nothing," sneered Sadi.

"I wouldn't say nothing." Harris laughed. "We found several water pipes."

"It's hardly a laughing matter," cautioned Brokenshire. "Next time, the Yanks will think twice about trusting my sources." He shook his head. "And to think I allowed myself to be convinced there was a cache of SCUD missiles components buried there. What did we find? Diddly squat."

Harris noted Sadi's puzzled expression. "He means nothing," he translated.

Sadi sniggered into his sleeve, enjoying the Englishman's self-deprecation.

"If that angry mob hadn't showed up when they did, we would have excavated the whole site."

"People were angry. Our children couldn't go to school. We had to take the day off work, look after them ourselves," explained Sadi.

"Let's just say we were all deceived," said Brokenshire with a shrug. He took another sip of tea, allowing a pause in the conversation, leaning in so his voice could not be heard above the hubbub of the café and passing traffic. "Is there somewhere more private we can talk?" Brokenshire glanced at Sadi and back to Harris, seemingly reluctant to continue in the Iraqi's presence.

"I would trust Sadi with my life," reassured Harris.

"As would I, but this is for your ears only."

"Fine. Sadi, give us a minute, would you?"

He rose without objection. "Gentlemen."

Brokenshire waited until Sadi was out of earshot, watching as he shook hands with friends and family members at a nearby table.

"I didn't realise you two were so close."

"Sadi? Oh, we go way back. If ever you need a driver or a local guide, he's first rate. Totally trustworthy. Nerves of steel, that one. Unflappable."

Brokenshire nodded, unzipping a rucksack and sliding a folded newspaper across the table. Harris snatched it away and hid it from view on his lap. Inside was a brown envelope.

"We've identified another site I need you to look at."

Under the table, Harris half-removed the briefing documents and flicked through the dossier, pausing on the black-and-white aerial photos.

"I'll need blueprints, floor plans."

"I'm working on it. Right now, this is as good as it gets."

"What's the job?"

"Reconnaissance."

Harris groaned with disappointment. "Can't you find someone else? I've got my hands full baby-sitting inspectors, in case you'd forgotten."

"No one knows the lay of the land like you do. Anyway, this is a night job. The inspectors will be safely tucked up in bed."

"As should I." Harris looked up and noticed the intelligence officer's air of desperation. "Okay, okay. Where to this time?"

"Al Hakam."

"You're kidding. That place is a fortress."

"Exactly. Way too much security for an agrichemical production facility."

"You've changed your tune. Last time I was there, you said we were wasting our time."

"Circumstances have changed. It's all in the briefing document."

Harris crossed his arms, frustrated that Brokenshire didn't feel the need to level with him, as if the money alone was enough to get Harris to do his bidding. The intelligence officer picked up on the lack of engagement and reconsidered. "Remember last time? We only got access to about sixty per cent of the site."

"So?"

"New information has come to light. Our analysts think they've identified the location of an underground bunker complex in the north-east corner of the compound."

"This entire country is full of bunkers. What's so special about this one?"

"Judging by the amount of night-time traffic going in and out, it has to be something important."

"You think, or you know?"

"High probability."

"Or they may just be storing animal feed for the winter."

"Just read the dossier."

"If this is another wild goose chase..."

"The intel is solid," reassured Brokenshire. "It seems the threat of no-notice inspections has forced their hand. They've centralised more of their weapons programme to Hakam."

"And your guys figured all this out from some infrared satellite data?"

"You're going to have to trust me on this one. Look, I wish I could tell you more."

"If I'm going to put my life on the line, I need more than sketchy intelligence from some geeky photo analyst sat in a basement in Whitehall."

"Fine," said Brokenshire, leaning closer. "Remember your trip last week to the Iraqi State Facility for Pesticide Production? Well, one of our analysts noticed something off in the Australian inspector's report."

"You mean Mathews?"

"That's the fella. He wrote that they had relocated equipment from Al Hakam."

"So?"

"They changed the production line at short notice. At first we didn't fully understand why."

"Go on."

"The samples tested positive for minute traces of thiophosphonate."

Harris was unfamiliar with the compound.

"Nerve gas," explained Brokenshire.

Harris remained sceptical. "We've had false positives before with organophosphates."

"True, but there's more. Much more. In the background of one photo, our analysts identified what appears to be an air handling system used for creating negative air pressure."

"Pretty fancy for an agrichemicals facility."

"Exactly. Of course, they heavily disguised it. Painted to look old. By sheer luck, they installed the same system at Porton Down a few weeks back. Someone recognised the intake pipe."

"I'm sure our Iraqi friends have a good explanation."

"If they do, I'd like to hear it."

Harris sat back, taking it all in. Could this finally be the break they had been waiting for?

"Didn't I tell you, sooner or later we knew they'd mess up," added Brokenshire.

"They've been getting away with this for so long. I suppose it was inevitable." An unspoken question had been troubling Harris for the last few days. "Wait, how the hell are they still getting their hands on this kind of specialist equipment? I thought there was an embargo."

"So did we. Our friends in Stuttgart were good enough to furnish us with copies of export records, detailing historical black-market shipments from Germany to Iraq long before they introduced control orders."

"What are we talking?"

"High-end air handlers, fermentation equipment, growth media. One order last year was for two brand-new GTC bioreactors. Like the one you saw at Al Daura last week. They took delivery less than three months ago."

"How is that possible?"

"Assembled and shipped through Turkey. Somehow slipped through the net. Manufacturing issues meant they delayed the Iraqi order by fourteen months."

"And what about the other reactor?"

"We think it's at Al Hakam."

"Okay. So, what do you need me to do?"

"Phase one: monitor and document everything that happens there. Figure out what they're up to."

"Satellite data?"

"In the folder. Everything gets moved in and out at night."

"Smart."

"Too smart. Somehow, they figured out when our satellite passes over."

"Why not re-task it?"

"This isn't our only surveillance operation, you know. Do you have any idea the strings I'd need to pull? They'll only authorise the request with hard evidence."

"Which is where I come in."

"Correct. I need eyes on the ground. Vehicle movements, deliveries, activity levels. The lot."

Harris shrugged. "You know I hate stakeouts. What's next?"

"Depends what you get me."

"Their security is good. It won't be easy."

"From what we know, they're more worried about threats from above. A man with your skills could get in and out."

"This is a two-man job. Minimum."

"I only have authorisation for..."

"Sadi knows that area like the back of his hand. Every gully, every hiding place."

"Fine. But it comes out of your share."

"Then I want double."

"You're kidding."

"Double or you find someone else."

Brokenshire put a hand through his foppish hair in a rare display of frustration. Harris already knew the answer. There was no one else.

Brokenshire nodded. "Get me what I need and I'll make it worth your while..." His voice trailed off. "Who knows? This could be your way back."

"There is no way back," Harris replied flatly.

Brokenshire shrugged. "Times change. What you're doing here hasn't gone unnoticed."

"Don't try to play me," dismissed Harris. "I'm not one of your wetboys."

That seemed to give the intelligence officer pause. Harris hadn't always been on the outside. There was a reason he still enjoyed access to the highest levels of intelligence.

"I've read your file, Harris. I'm well aware of what you once were." His eyes narrowed, letting his message sink in. "But that was a long time ago. You're on the outside now. A hired gun."

"A *ronin* without lord or master," said Harris, through gritted teeth. "Expendable."

"You chose this path, not me. The sooner you trust me, the better."

"I've been burned by your people too many times."

"That was then, this is now. There's a war coming. Times are changing."

"Right. Which means you need me more than I need you."

Brokenshire sat back and let out a long sigh. "What do you want, Harris?"

"Half now, half on delivery."

"Bloody cheek."

"You know I'm worth it."

"You better be. If we don't give Whitehall something soon, we'll both be out of a job."

"How long have I got?"

"You'll go in tomorrow."

"That soon?"

"The Americans are pushing for air strikes as early as next week."

"What about the inspectors?"

"I'll tell them you're on compassionate leave. A medical

emergency. Car accident. Family member in hospital. You got a sister back in the UK, right?"

Something about the mention of his sister unnerved Harris. To someone in his line of work, family ties were a weakness. A point of leverage. A pressure point to be exploited. And Brokenshire knew that better than anyone.

CHAPTER 5

Sadi picked up Harris at midnight, just around the corner from the hotel he shared with the UN inspectors. Harris transferred his equipment from the boot of his city runabout into the back of Sadi's flatbed truck next to a rusting bicycle and climbed up into the cramped cabin that stank of stale cigarettes and sweat. Sadi turned down the tinny music and shook hands with Harris.

"Sadi, my smooth operator." Harris greeted his old friend with a familiar grin, much to Sadi's puzzlement.

"If this is another one of your sad eighties jokes..."

"Don't make me explain it again, please." He paused, waiting for the penny to drop. "Remember? Sade? Pronounced *Sha-day*? 'Smooth Operator' was her big hit."

"Time to get some new jokes, old man."

As the truck moved off, Harris noticed Sadi's expensive gold necklace and identity bracelet in the dim street lighting. He was wearing his usual loafers and jeans. Working for the Americans paid well.

"Jeez, Sadi. I said dress for a night operation, not a nightclub."

"I thought maybe we were going out on the town."

Harris shook his head and laughed out loud, patting his friend on the shoulder. "Don't worry. I've got some spare clothes, enough for both of us."

"Where to, boss?" asked Sadi.

"We're going camping."

"At this time of year? It's going to be freezing."

As they pulled off the service road that ran parallel to the boundary fence to the Al Hakam compound, Sadi extinguished the headlights. Harris had already scouted the area earlier in the day and chosen somewhere to leave the truck. They parked up behind a derelict structure that Sadi said was a storehouse he and his friends would play in sometimes when they were kids. Its windows were shattered and part of the roof was missing, but it would serve their purpose. It was also far enough from the main entrance and the approach road that they were in little danger of being discovered.

From the storehouse it was a two-kilometre hike with all their equipment up the backside of a slope that overlooked the western end of the facility. As they approached the crest of the hill, they lay on their fronts and edged forward to get their first look at Al Hakam in the darkness through the night vision scope Harris produced from his top pocket.

A two-metre-high perimeter fence ran left and right as far as the eye could see, enclosing a compound of some twelve square kilometres. The fences were standard chain link, topped with barbed wire. Two fortified entrances bathed in orange neon from the floodlights towering above. They had equipped the entrance to the north and the other to the west with tyre-slashing barriers and a chicane made from heavy concrete blocks to slow the approach of vehicles.

What surprised Harris was the space between the buildings, which he knew to be connected underground, by dozens of tunnels. The layout was a carbon copy of similar research installations in Russia and America. The briefing documents suggested up to thirty soldiers guarded the Al Hakam facility, day and night.

"Pretty good security for a fertiliser factory," thought Harris as he swept his scope over the main buildings, scattered with pinpricks of twinkling lights, barely visible from this distance. A compound this large was almost impossible to patrol effectively, even with the size of the security force assigned to protect it.

Once Harris satisfied himself there were no patrols operating on their side of the fence, he turned his attention to the slope below them, seeking a site for them to set up camp.

Sadi nudged Harris awake. It took him a moment to remember where he was, his mouth dry and gritty. He rolled over onto his belly, limbs aching, wrapping the sleeping bag tighter around his shoulders to peer out of their observation post on the hillside overlooking the Al Hakam compound. Dust had found its way into every crevice.

Sadi passed Harris the night scope, pointing towards a column of vehicles approaching in the distance. Five trucks and two support vehicles, front and back, bouncing along the dusty road towards the western entrance, closest to the suspected storage bunkers to their left. Harris made a note of the activity in his pocketbook, documenting everything they had observed in the last forty-two hours since they arrived.

This was their second night on-site, positioned beneath a

camouflaged tarp strung between four posts driven into the ground. Its construction shielded them from direct sunlight during the day, while allowing air to flow in all directions when there was any breeze. During the heat of the midday sun Harris claimed the tarp reduced ambient temperature by as much as ten or twenty degrees, but by night, temperatures in the desert plunged. Much to Sadi's consternation, Harris had brought bundles of newspaper to stuff inside their sleeping bags, insulating themselves against the long hours lying motionless in the hide. They took it in turns to sleep or read in the shafts of moonlight that penetrated the narrow entrance.

Both men's senses had become finely tuned to even the slightest of changes in the sounds and smells around them. Every foraging animal, every bird flying low overhead, proved a welcome distraction from the monotony of endlessly waiting. Harris knew only too well that there was no substitute for gathering on-the-ground intelligence, but it was not without risk.

Twice, two-man patrols outside the perimeter fence came within one hundred metres of their position, walking along the bottom of the incline. The soldier appeared to look directly at them, but saw nothing out of the ordinary. They had done their job well. From a distance, the rocks that formed the entrance to their hide concealed them entirely. All they had to do now was lie and wait for the appointed hour.

Harris had reported in at 1900 via an encrypted burst transmission from the satellite phone he had brought with them. After an hour's delay, Brokenshire came back with the go-ahead, granting Harris permission to enter the site and gain access to the bunkers.

Harris changed into his tactical gear. The equipment was a little tighter than he remembered. Just in a few places, but enough to notice. It had been a few months since he'd done one of these.

Sadi watched him change. "I didn't know you had a tattoo," he said.

"This?" he replied, tracing his fingers around the length of a snake's body, curled around a dagger, tattooed on his chest. "My wife designed it. What can I say? She was very into Guns N' Roses."

"Oh. I thought it was a special forces thing?"

"Not everyone in the military has tattoos."

"All the Americans do."

"Says who?"

"I work with a lot of Americans. They all have tattoos."

"Well, that's Americans for you. In my line of work, it doesn't pay to draw attention." He sniggered despite himself. "Special forces tattoos? You make me laugh. To go with my special forces watch and hoodie?"

"I don't know." Sadi feigned embarrassment. "They do in the movies." Sadi knew better than to ask a man like Harris direct questions about his military service. Either Harris refused to answer or he quickly changed the subject, like now.

"When did you start working for the Americans?"

"As an interpreter and worked my way up. No big secret."

"Where did you learn your English?"

"My father always said I had a good ear for languages. I'm a good listener, I suppose."

"Marchand said you speak French too."

"And German. In Iraq, we say you learn a language by listening, not through books."

"You? You never stop talking."

Harris switched on the two walkie talkies, checking they were both working and tuned to the same channel. He gave one to Sadi and tucked the other in a secure pouch on his chest webbing, a concealed wire stretching to his left ear. He repacked the fifty-litre rucksack he carried that contained a full-face respirator equipped with HEPA filters, plus rubber gloves and an airtight case for any samples he might recover. He took one last look at the site map and floor plans of the target building to the west, almost two kilometres from the tower at the centre of the facility. He ran his eyes along the perimeter fence.

"Time check. It's 0001 and thirty seconds, thirty-one, thirty-two," announced Harris as Sadi adjusted his watch to match. "I'll check in with you at 0200. With any luck, I'll be done by 0400. That should give us plenty of time to break camp and get back to the truck before dawn."

"Breakfast at Sami's then?"

"Keep your radio on, just in case. And do me a favour? Try not to fall asleep this time."

CHAPTER 6

Harris checked his pockets one last time for keys or coins, anything that might make a sound and give him away. He secured a pair of bolt croppers to the outside of his rucksack, tightening the straps on the black webbing, pouches packed with emergency supplies and three spare magazines for the 9mm pistol in a holster on his right hip.

With a final nod to Sadi, he checked left and right through his night vision scope and set off on the one-kilometre downhill hike to a section of the chain-link fence he had selected as his entry point for tonight's incursion into the Al Hakam agrichemical production facility. Two tonnes of dirt piled high hid the entry point, presumably debris from the construction of the service road several years before.

At the bottom of the slope Harris stayed low, crawling towards the two-metre-high metal fence topped with razor wire. Crouching down on one knee, he set to work clipping the wire to fashion a man-size rectangle. Once he was through, he wrenched the cut-out shape back into position. From a distance, a passing guard would never notice.

He checked his watch. The next patrol was more than fifteen

minutes away. Plenty of time to cover the kilometre to the nearest building. His meticulous reconnaissance had confirmed there were no dog patrols here nor infrared monitoring to worry about. The guards at Al Hakam were local militia, not in the same league as the highly trained Republican Guard he had encountered sneaking into Saddam's palaces in Baghdad.

The moon slid behind scattered clouds, just enough light to see clearly. The ground was flat and rocky, but allowed him to jog at a reasonable pace without making too much noise. He covered the ground in a little over eight minutes and took up position with his back against the wall of the building. Eight minutes. Not bad for an old man, thought Harris, making a mental note of the time it took for his return journey. He took out his night vision scope and scanned for any movement. The whole place seemed deserted.

There was a low-level electrical hum emanating from the target building. Pre-fabricated, windowless, with walls some forty to fifty feet high. A grill high above his head vented hot air from the inside. He wondered whether he should wear his protective equipment, but reasoned the waste air was almost certainly filtered and non-toxic. At least he hoped the Iraqis wouldn't be that reckless. That said, the nearest dwellings were over ten kilometres from here, presumably in case of accidents. No, he was sure, with the UN inspectors threatening no-notice inspections, the Iraqis would not take undue risks.

He spotted the access door to the maintenance area just ahead, staying hidden in the shadows. He picked the lock within thirty seconds and slipped inside a darkened plant room where clanking, wheezing machinery drowned out all other noise. Back pressed against the wall, he waited for his eyes to adjust to the gloom.

He recognised the air handling unit from the official photos taken by an Iraqi photographer contained in the intelligence folder. Someone had carefully curated the photos to give the appearance of a production line at the end of its life cycle, desperately in need of investment to bring the plant up to modern Western standards. The truth was somewhat different. At the far end, overhead lights framed a doorway to the primary production facility beyond. He listened at the door, satisfying himself that there were no footsteps or voices from within, before nudging the door open an inch.

The more modern laboratories were on the far side of row upon row of enormous rusting steel machinery, which had fallen silent at the stroke of five o'clock. He kept low, skirting the edge of the factory floor, deserted at this time of night. Most of the equipment stood idle.

He paused to listen. A janitor was sweeping the floor with a tinny radio for company, playing a popular tune Harris recognised from the cafés of Baghdad. The door to an adjacent laboratory was exactly where the blueprints had suggested. From his rucksack, he removed the hood and respirator and donned thick rubber gloves before entering the research and development complex.

Once inside the darkened room, he gently pulled the door closed and clicked on a penlight. This was a staging room lined with white coats and protective equipment hanging from hooks. The next room sported row upon row of biohazard suits and respirators. Further down was a scrub room complete with decontamination showers that still smelled of pungent disinfectant. Beyond the glass, Harris could make out the work stations and individual laboratories where the scientists worked. Microscopes, racks of test tubes, tall refrigerators, shelves packed with ring-binder files detailing their experiments. On one side of the room were what looked like the type of stainless-steel fermentation tank you might find in a brewery. Harris remembered the smell from a previous inspection visit. The yeasty odour that reminded him of hops. He moved on, scanning the next room, looking for the specific equipment set-up he would recognise from the briefing documents.

They had listed the make and model of the bioreactor used here in the exportation shipping document. Imported from Germany, high-end specification, used for amplifying a virus, containing a body of liquid heated to body temperature containing living cells infected with virus. They reliably informed him that the storage unit beside the bioreactor would house rows of vials, each labelled with bar codes and number sequences he would need to document. Harris had been told to be extremely careful when handling the samples. Without knowing what the Iraqis were working on, he had to assume each one contained highly infectious and potentially lethal material. The scientists who worked here took every precaution and so should he. Mistakes might prove fatal.

From his rucksack he produced a bright orange, rigid, airtight container. Inside were a dozen empty slots evenly spaced in the protective foam. He reached into the fridge and carefully removed one of the dozen vials containing a clear liquid. He shook the contents. It looked like water to his untrained eye, as he secured it carefully in the space provided. He repeated the process several times, taking one from each shelf. Harris wondered how long it would take for the Iraqi scientists to notice. Securing the first plastic container, he placed it carefully back inside the rucksack, closing the door behind him as he released his breath. Sweat had formed on his brow but the mask prevented him from wiping his forehead.

Harris moved from laboratory to laboratory until he had filled the twenty-four storage slots. He still had almost forty minutes until he needed to be gone.

The jangle of keys in the next room startled him. He flicked off his penlight and sank to his knees, in between two workstations, waiting and listening. He unholstered his weapon, trying to locate the source of the disturbance. A door slammed open. The squeak of wheels across the linoleum floor. Had he miscalculated? He was not alone in the laboratory after all.

Through the glass partition, the overhead strip lights flickered on, bathing his hiding position in bright light. He could see the janitor moving from desk to desk, pushing his cart, collecting the trash, oblivious to Harris's presence. The janitor paused at a workstation, picking up a family photo on a desk, angling it towards the light with a smile. A sixth sense made the man look up, peering into the darkness towards Harris's hiding place. Harris sank lower, confident he was invisible beyond the glare from the glass. The janitor returned to his task, drifting between the desks, emptying wastepaper bins.

Harris checked his watch. He needed to start back towards safety in time to make good his return to Baghdad before dawn. He sized up the janitor. Mid-forties, overweight, wheezing from the exertion. In his protective equipment, the chances of Harris approaching by stealth and overpowering the guard before he could react were slim. Harris considered his options, remembering his orders. Leave no trail. Zero fatalities. His best chance was to wait it out.

Harris ducked down again as the janitor rolled his cart towards the door to the laboratory, but something made him pause, as if remembering something. He left his cart where it was and disappeared from view. Perhaps protocol dictated he wore gloves and a mask or he needed to return to the maintenance area to retrieve additional supplies. Either way, the janitor was gone.

Harris didn't hesitate. He exited the lab, removed his hood and gloves and scrubbed down his hands with disinfectant from a dispenser in his webbing. He cracked open the door to the factory floor and listened for the sound of footsteps. The clanking of metal drums on the far side of the facility confirmed Harris's hunch that the janitor was simply replenishing his supplies.

He slipped out the way he came, covering the ground back to the boundary fence without further incident. With any luck, Sadi would have packed up the hide and be waiting to speed-march back to the truck before dawn broke and the promised slap-up breakfast at Sami's in Baghdad. Harris just hoped that the samples would give Brokenshire the evidence he needed.

PART II

THE CONGO

CHAPTER 7

Yarmouth
Isle of Wight, England
April, 1998

Doctor Alice Bishop had always loved the last leg of her journey home to the Isle of Wight. Savouring that first glimpse of the island as the ferry to Yarmouth left the shelter of the Lymington River.

Whatever the weather, she insisted on climbing the stairway to the top deck, leaning over the railing, drinking in the view of the narrow entrance to the Solent, watched over by Hurst Castle on the mainland and Needles Lighthouse on the island's western tip. There was something purifying about the light drizzle or spray that moistened her cheeks during the crossing, cleansing the months of Oxford city grime. Each nautical mile brought her another step closer to the childhood home she considered sanctuary from the chaos of the modern world.

Returning to Yarmouth, the place where she grew up, was like rediscovering a time capsule, so little seemed to change.

Those same cobbled streets, low-ceilinged pubs, waterfront cottages, windswept beaches and clifftop paths she remembered like yesterday. That first stolen kiss under the pier, taking turns to swig from a two-litre plastic bottle of cider, her first and last puff of a cigarette.

If changes had occurred in the nearly ten years since she first left home to study medicine at Bristol University, then they barely registered their passing. New buildings certainly, others renovated, but the spirit of this tiny seafaring town laid out in an orderly grid since Norman times had endured like the salt stains on the seawall or the seaweed that covered the mooring timbers driven deep into the harbour mud where yachts and power boats jostled for position. Beyond the high defensive walls that surrounded this settlement of less than a thousand people lay the Yar River estuary and tidal marshes before the ground rose sharply towards the western tip of the island. Rolling hills, views that stretched east towards Ventnor, seagulls soaring on the breeze above towering cliffs, maritime landscapes that had inspired poets and writers for generations from Keats to Tennyson.

She had fallen out of the habit of her once regular trips home to see her mum. The unexpected invite to meet up with old school friends for a birthday dinner was just the excuse she needed to break the prolonged silence, to bridge the yawning gap that had developed between mother and daughter since her father's passing.

As a coping mechanism, Alice had buried herself in post-graduate research. Long evenings, working weekends. Her personal time eclipsed by her studies. She and Richard, her fiancé of eight months, had become ships that passed in the night, sharing a bed for a few hours, too exhausted for intimacy, waking at dawn, returning home after dark. Leftovers for dinner.

Her mother would be sure to tell Alice how much weight her daughter had lost since her last visit. How ghostly pale she looked after too many hours in the lab. One of several familiar themes to which her mother returned.

Alice strained her eyes to pick out her family home in the gathering darkness. The Bishop residence for over thirty years was a period cottage of natural stone and brick on a narrow lane that ran along the waterfront, heading out of town. As a child, she had taken for granted the stunning views from her bedroom window of Yarmouth Pier and the many sailing boats and merchant ships that passed on the westward-flowing tide.

The ferry adjusted course one last time to take account of the strong current sweeping around the harbour entrance. The helm delayed its approach, waiting for a local fishing boat to make its turn and clear the dock. A ruddy-faced youth in stained yellow oilskins stared directly at Alice as they passed. Lobster pots and fishing nets cluttered the flood-lit deck. She struggled to make out the boat's name on its weathered stern. *Flipper* or *Nipper*. On the far side of the harbour she noted the reassuring presence of the RNLI lifeboat, its orange and royal blue wheel-house, decks scrubbed daily by an ever-vigilant crew.

A recorded announcement over the ship's tannoy instructed drivers to return to their vehicles. Final call. On the busy car deck she retraced her steps to find the ageing Renault 5 she lovingly referred to as "Cinq" or "Supercinq" on the rare occasions it started first time. The other passengers, island-bound holidaymakers and truck drivers, were already in their vehicles waiting patiently for the familiar bump against the harbour wall that signalled their arrival.

Alice turned the key more in hope than expectation and was rewarded with the familiar cough and splutter before the engine settled into a rhythm. She patted the dashboard like the faithful workhorse the Cinq had become. There was something about that idealised father-daughter relationship from the Renault "Papa – Nicole" TV adverts she had grown up watching that lent some added glamour and allure to her on-off relationship with the car, at least in her mind's eye. Their relationship was fickle, but the Cinq, and the freedom the little French car embodied, was loved beyond words. Most of all, the car reminded Alice of her father.

The ramp began to lower, revealing queues of cars, day-trippers waiting to return to their homes on the mainland. When it was her turn, the deckhand waved her forward down the slope. The Supercinq's low-slung exhaust grounded, momentarily prompting a cheer and a chorus of encouragement from the crew wearing obligatory fluorescent oilskin jackets, much to Alice's embarrassment.

She checked her watch. She would keep the promise made to her mother, at least on this occasion. Home in time for late tea.

Alice found a parking space further down the road and lugged her battered green suitcase along the pavement. She knocked on the door, out of courtesy more than necessity. There was still a key somewhere in her handbag. The scrape of a chair greeted her knock on the stone kitchen floor, a cough and the approach of footsteps.

"I thought you were catching the earlier ferry?" Her mother's reception was somewhat cool, as expected, as if the two had barely been apart.

"Nice to see you too, Mum," she said, leaning in to plant a kiss on a reluctant cheek. "The traffic outside Southampton was terrible."

Her mother's movements were imprecise. She had been drinking again.

"Gloria's made up the bed in your brother's old room. Silly woman. I must have told her three times you were coming."

"That's fine, Mum. Don't worry." Alice would give anything to avoid the inevitable drama of changing sheets and moving all the boxes of her old belongings still stacked against the cupboard in her room.

She dumped her unopened suitcase next to the bed, smiling at her brother's boyhood posters of superheroes and that Nirvana album cover. She ran her fingers along the dusty spines of childhood books, including a full set of Lewis Carroll novels. She removed the illustrated Folio edition of *Alice in Wonderland*, turning to the first page with the handwritten note from her father on her fifth birthday explaining how Alice had come by her name.

Being home evoked so many memories, good and bad. The hours spent in her bedroom, buried in her books, trying to silence the all-consuming grief. Losing her father to prostate cancer before he was even fifty had devastated the entire Bishop family. While they each dealt with his premature passing in their own private way, Alice's mother had coped perhaps the least well. The erratic behaviour, the endless drinking, the angry outbursts. Alice and her elder brother, Tom, left to fend for themselves. When Tom moved to London to embark on a career in the City as an underwriter at a large insurance company, Alice's mother had briefly taken in a lodger, perhaps to fill the deafening silences between them, but it hadn't worked. Her mother preferred the solitude and peace of an empty house. When Alice left home, her mother's ever loyal friends encouraged her to keep busy, playing bridge at the club, church on Sundays.

On the kitchen counter sat a near-empty bottle of Chablis, her mother's favourite tipple. Without asking, she poured a glass for Alice and tossed the empty bottle into the recycling. "Open this for me, could you, darling?" she asked, handing her daughter another from the wine rack.

"Why don't we wait for dinner, Mum? It's not even five thirty."

"Dinner? I thought you were seeing Daisy."

"I meant your dinner."

"I've already eaten," she lied unconvincingly.

"There's some leftover Bolognese you could heat up if you're hungry?" replied her mother.

Alice would admit she was a little peckish, and her birthday host for tonight, Gemma, was notorious in the kitchen. Alice opened the fridge and inspected its contents. A tired lettuce, shrivelled lemon, items past their sell-by date, but the bowl of Bolognese looked recent.

"Is Mark coming tonight?"

"No, Mum. I told you on the phone. He's coming down tomorrow on the train. He had to work."

"On a Saturday? Is he still working for that awful Oxford rag?"

"Yes, Mum." Why was she always attacking his choice of career? "He's got a second interview for that journalist job at the magazine."

"What about that book he was writing?"

"It's almost finished. He's got a friend at HarperCollins who sounds interested."

Her mother snorted and took another sip from her glass. "What on earth are you going to live off when you stop working?"

"Why would I stop working?"

"My dear, you are planning to get married and start a family at some stage?" It was more a statement than a question.

Here we go again, thought Alice. "Maybe next year, Mum. We're both just so focused on our careers right now."

"You're never going to get pregnant if you don't spend more time at home. Always gallivanting round the world. Where next?"

"I told you, Mum. The Democratic Republic of the Congo."

"Where on earth is that?"

"Former Zaire, Central Africa."

"Why ever would anyone want to go there?"

"There's a World Health Organization expedition heading there. Remember? Professor O'Leary invited me."

"All my friends at the club have grandchildren, you know. They're always asking when you're going to get married."

Alice didn't take the bait and remained silent. With a huff, she put the Bolognese in the microwave and stabbed at the buttons to heat it up.

"Your biological clock won't wait, you know."

"Yes, Mum, I know."

"You young people have your priorities back to front. In my day..."

"Mum, please."

"Well, if I didn't say something..."

"Why do we have to have this argument every time I'm here?"

"Well, have you set a date yet? For the wedding?"

"No, not yet. After I get back from Africa, I've got time off booked to do some wedding planning. I promise I'll do it then."

Alice often wondered whether her father would have approved of her career choices. As a civil engineer, he had always wanted his children to take up what he called "proper careers", encouraging Alice's interest in medicine from an early age. Having a scientist for a daughter and a son in the City was not a bad return from all those sacrifices they had made as parents. Putting them through the best private schools, affording them every advantage their middle-class circumstances could provide.

The telephone jolted Alice from her thoughts. Her mother's excited tone suggested it was someone unexpected, though their conversation was short.

"Daisy says she'll meet you by the pier in half an hour. You better get changed, darling. You can't wear that to the party."

CHAPTER 8

The birthday dinner was not until eight. Daisy proposed a quiet drink or three at The George Hotel before heading to Freshwater together. They met by Yarmouth's wooden pier. The two old friends hugged each other, not wanting to let go.

"How was Hong Kong?" asked Daisy.

"Awful. I need a drink first."

"I was so worried about you, Bish."

Only Daisy still called her Bish. A nickname since kindergarten. Daisy grabbed hold of her, linking arms. Alice had confided in an email that she found being away from home for nearly a month much harder than she expected, but had hinted at worse. It took an old friend to read between the lines.

They had been together at college all the way through to medical school in Bristol. While Daisy had chosen to return to the island to become a GP in Freshwater, Alice had continued her studies. An Honours in medicine followed by a Master's in public health, another in natural sciences from Cambridge. Her research into infectious tropical diseases had taken her all over the world. There had barely been a chance to pause for breath. A clinical fellowship in the epidemiology unit followed by post-doctorate research. Alice had more letters after her name than she knew what to do with.

"Your mum sounded well." Daisy meant it more as a question than a statement of fact.

"Yes, she's good at keeping up appearances."

"Is she drinking again?"

"I'm not sure she ever stopped."

"Well, last time I saw her, she was on great form. I wondered whether there wasn't someone new in her life."

"Really?"

"I could have been mistaken but there's a nice man at church I saw her talking to. A widower no less. They were getting on like a house on fire."

"She's a dark horse, that one. Never tells me anything."

"Are you surprised? She's worried you'll judge her."

"Me? Hardly."

"Bish, you're always judging people."

"Me?" Alice said again, wounded by the suggestion, but Daisy was normally right about such matters.

The two old friends made a beeline for their favourite watering hole, safe in the knowledge that they could talk without fear of seeing anyone they knew. The George Hotel was one of her father's old haunts, steeped in history, portraits of local noblemen adorning the walls, symbols of its political and cultural importance as the former home to the island's Governor, next door to Yarmouth Castle. King Charles II was said to have visited on more than one occasion.

Daisy returned from the bar with two enormous gin and tonics in what looked like goldfish bowls. They would take a taxi home later and make the most of their time together.

"So, Hong Kong? Tell me everything."

With a long sigh, Alice explained how her supposed big break had come just before Christmas. Her mentor, Professor

O'Leary, had put Alice forward to join a World Health Organization task force investigating an outbreak of suspected avian flu.

"Professor O'Leary?" swooned Daisy. "Isn't he the one you fancy?"

"Hardly. He's ancient. Anyway, as I was saying, by the time we got there, five had died. One was just a kid. And there were another seventeen confirmed cases," she explained with obvious regret.

"I know. I read about it in *The Lancet*."

"But that wasn't the whole story. Half the people who caught that strain died. The mortality rate was terrifying."

"From bird flu? My God."

"It turned out none of them worked directly with poultry. It was spreading from person to person," explained Alice.

"So what did you do?"

"What we're trained to do. We traced the outbreak to a chicken farm near Yuen Long. And from there to other farms in the area. Within seventy-two hours, the WHO had declared a new strain of bird flu and suddenly it was headline news."

"We were so proud. Local hero Alice Bishop, quoted in *The Times*."

"Hardly."

"What do you mean?"

"The hate mail from animal rights campaigners was hideous."

"How so?"

"O'Leary had to order the slaughter of one and a half million chickens. The local farmers hated us too."

"Jeez. I'm not surprised."

"There was no alternative. We found a link with a previous bird flu strain. The one that caused the outbreak in Guangdong province, in China, two years before. If the outbreak had coincided with seasonal flu, things could have got worse. We couldn't take that risk."

"A tiny chance, no?"

"If you had seen what this thing did to its victims, Daisy, you'd understand. This was a real street-fighter. Tough as they come. One of the worst I've seen. We couldn't take that chance."

"And you won some award?"

"Oh that. A letter of commendation," she replied modestly. "It was nothing."

After the WHO team was ordered to return home, just after Christmas, Alice had received an unexpected letter from Hiroshi Nakajima himself, the Director General of the World Health Organization commending Alice's role in preventing a public health crisis. The letter was now framed and hanging on the wall above her workstation back in the cramped office she shared in Oxford.

"So, case closed?"

"Until next time," said Alice, toasting a job well done with a sip of gin and tonic.

Like so many other variants she had studied in her meteoric career tracking infectious diseases, if they were lucky, they would never see it again in their lifetimes, but somehow Alice doubted that.

"So where to next?"

"No rest for the wicked. Kisangani, in the Congo."

"So your mum said. The Congo sounds dangerous."

"Not really. I leave at the end of next week."

"So soon?"

"I know."

"You and your jet-set lifestyle, you're so lucky. Trampoline injuries are the most excitement I get at my GP surgery in Freshwater."

"Trust me, there'll be nothing glamorous about this one. Kisangani will be a hellhole."

"I'm sure you'll be fine. You normally are." Daisy pulled her old friend closer and gave her another hug. "I'm really going to miss you, Bish."

"I'll be back before you know it. In time for your birthday."

"You can bring me back one of those hideous fertility statues. Like the one awful Angela brought back from Nigeria. You know, the one you insisted I put under the stairs when Richard and your highbrow university friends came round." Alice blushed at the memory, remembering the statuette she insisted her friend hide. "You always were such a prude."

They laughed together, like old times, before careers and travel got in the way.

"Right," said Daisy, noticing the time, "finish that drink and I'll go check on the taxi."

~

The seating assignments at the birthday dinner in her old friend's honour had placed Alice opposite the newly-weds, some smug couple she detested. As if getting married and having children was the pinnacle of success.

Most of the invited guests were old school friends. Several had never left the island, settling down in the towns and villages they had grown up in. Alice struggled to think of anything more unimaginative.

"When's Mark going to make an honest woman of you?" joked Daisy's boyfriend, Paul, helping himself to another glass of Rioja. Alice could always rely upon Paul to stir the pot, knowing how she hated such questions. Alice would settle down when she was good and ready. Not before.

"Just as soon as Alice finishes her research. Whenever that

is," added Daisy, needling her friend.

"Doesn't Mark get jealous of you gallivanting round the world with that silver fox Irish professor?"

"Strictly professional. Anyway, he's too old." Alice flashed her friend a disapproving glance.

"The lady doth protest too much," Paul said with a wink.

"Didn't you hear? Alice is a hero these days. Saving the world, keeping us safe from catching a nasty cold," mocked Daisy playfully.

"Will all of you just stop." The angrier she became the more she encouraged her friends.

"You want to be careful, Alice," continued Paul, sensing weakness. "One of those weather girls at Mark's local paper might just steal him away."

"He always did have an eye for the younger woman," added Daisy.

"He's six months older than me," replied Alice testily, rising to the bait.

"Same old Alice. Head in the clouds." The smug married woman opposite laughed. "If you're not careful, you'll get left on the shelf. End up like your mother."

"Take that back, Jen," growled Alice, subconsciously reaching for her glass of wine. Just like her mother would, she thought to herself.

"Don't be so prickly. You know we all love your mum. How is she?" Jen backtracked, heeding her husband's reproach.

"She's okay. It's hard being on your own. I think she's lonely."

"No doubt. She can't wait to start planning your wedding. Knitting baby clothes."

"Oh, God."

"Why don't you put us all out of our misery and name the date, Alice? I bet you haven't even looked at that list of venues I sent you."

"As soon as I'm back I'll do it."

"Where to this time?"

"The Congo."

"I thought, after what happened in Hong Kong, they'd agreed to let you work more from home."

"Wait, what happened in Hong Kong?" whispered Beth's tipsy friend at the far end of the table.

"I'll tell you later," said her husband.

"I'm not much use in an office," replied Alice. "My place is in the field. Talking to patients, visiting hospitals, gathering data."

"You two were always such nerds."

"That's right, Beth. Remind me what you've done with your life?"

"Now, now, ladies," cautioned Paul.

"I have a beautiful family," Beth replied defensively, staring lovingly at her husband, eager for his support. "What more could any woman want?"

Alice snorted. Pathetic, she thought. "I'll drink to that."

"You always were an attention-seeker, Bishop," added Beth.

"What, because I dared to be different? You really think that's why I went into public health. It's not as glamorous as you think."

"I always hated academia. It all sounds incredibly dull."

"Probably why you make such a great homemaker, Beth," sniped Alice with uncharacteristic bile. There were some people that just brought out the worst in her, and Beth was one of them.

"You always were a spoiled rich kid, Bishop. You've never had to work for anything in your whole life."

"Just ignore her, Alice. She's jealous." Paul's hand lingered on Alice's for a second longer than necessary. There was a flicker of what they once had back in college and then it was gone again. Alice blushed, hoping Daisy had not noticed.

"So tell me about your trip?" continued Paul. "What are you actually doing in the Congo?"

"I'll be away for three months. Part of a World Health Organization expedition to study the spread of infectious disease. There have been three outbreaks in the last year alone."

"Is it safe? I thought there was a war going on there?"

"The WHO wouldn't let us go if it wasn't. Anyway, it's not like I'm going alone. There's a big group of us."

"That's right. You've got your professor to hold your hand," he joked.

"Hilarious. Actually, Stephen's been there before."

Paul mouthed the word Stephen to Daisy, but she ignored him.

"Don't worry. There's an entire army of peacekeepers watching over us, day and night, wherever we go."

"Still. You know there's a civil war going on?"

Alice felt suddenly foolish that she knew so little about the security situation in the country she was travelling to. In Hong Kong, minders had chaperoned them wherever they went, but the Congo would be different.

"I'm not joking. Last thing I heard thousands of troops were pouring over the border from Rwanda and Uganda."

"It's calmed down now. That was last year. Anyway, how do you know so much about what happens in Central Africa?"

"I read the paper."

"Well, they wouldn't let us go if it wasn't safe. Would they?"

"I'd check if I was you. You don't want to get stuck in a war zone."

No, thought Alice. She would be sure to ask the professor next time she spoke to him. Her fiancé would go crazy if he found out she would be working in a crisis zone. She resolved never to mention it.

CHAPTER 9

Cowley Institute for Infectious Diseases
Oxford, England
9 September, 1998

Alice leaned over the electron microscope and flicked the switch at the back, waiting for the machine to power up before squinting through the eyepiece. She pressed herself against the faceplate, adjusting her position until two circles of light merged into a digital image.

The novelty never wore off for Alice. To her it was like being transported to another world, her own private wonderland, where all extraneous noise and interruptions ceased. Her mentor, Professor Stephen O'Leary, referred to this as "a state of flow" where a scientist becomes totally absorbed in the task at hand, demanding every ounce of concentration. For Alice, the extractor fan became a distant hum, blanketing everything else in white noise.

She had spent so much time studying viruses since

returning from Hong Kong that when she closed her eyes to sleep at night, she could comfortably recall the cell scapes, structures and shapes they inhabited like some alien world she had visited in a dream. Through the lens of her microscope she could easily feel godlike, omniscient yet strangely detached, as if orbiting a distant planet, witness to the surface-level carnage wrought by tiny organisms, indifferent to their host's suffering.

She magnified the image of a single lung cell, zooming in hundreds of times. When she had first started as a junior researcher, it might have taken her minutes to locate what she was looking for but experience taught her just where to look. After all, even viruses had a certain pattern of behaviour.

Sometimes she admired the persistence of such tiny organisms. All her years of postgraduate study had taught her a begrudging respect. Survival of the fittest was baked into their every waking thought. Dedication to a single task: replication.

Her mentor's advice all those years ago to "never underestimate a virus" had become almost a mantra for Alice. As a lifelong fan of horror movies, it called to mind all those unforgettable cinematic moments in *Alien*, *Friday the 13th*, *Psycho* or *Scream*, when our plucky hero fools themselves into believing the killer is dead. So it proved with viruses. Just when you think they're beaten, they crawl back into the jungle or some animal reservoir from which they emerged, biding their time.

Theirs was a war that would never be won. It was what made Alice's research endlessly fascinating. Her Master's thesis had laid the groundwork for an early warning system, a live database to track emerging viruses anywhere on the planet. Alice had devoted her career to what she called her "big hairy audacious goal" of bringing an end to deadly pandemics. To nip them in the bud through active monitoring and immediate intervention. In time, she dreamed of a world where we vaccinated future generations, including the world's poorest, against all common infections.

That dedication together with a burning curiosity had been a winning combination for why the professor chose her over several equally qualified postgraduate students. Alice suspected it had something to do with being a woman. Time and again, the faculty handed out promotions to her male counterparts. Decisions made behind closed doors. After several years of disappointment, the committee of middle-aged white men had finally seen fit to award Alice the opportunity to prove herself in a male-dominated environment where misogyny remained rife, even today in the late nineties. The right connections still appeared to accelerate professional development. That and being born a man.

To break through, Alice told herself, a woman scientist had to be exceptional. She shrugged her shoulders at the injustice, committed to redoubling her efforts. The professor assured her things were changing. Centuries-old institutions took time to adjust. She could fight the system or navigate its injustices. Reluctantly she followed his advice.

The professor had served as her advocate for most of her career. She considered him one of the enlightened few who embraced equality and the opportunities it presented. Professor O'Leary seemed to understand that diversity and gender-balanced teams sparked genuine innovation, capable of challenging the status quo. He had seen it repeatedly. International research teams made up of men and women made rapid scientific breakthroughs thought impossible only a few years before.

The challenge before them remained immense, requiring bold new thinking. They would never win the war against infectious diseases. Despite the breathtaking progress they were making as a global research community, their own models suggested the incidence of fresh outbreaks was actually speeding up. Viruses crossing species barriers with terrifying frequency. Mother Nature always seemed to be one step ahead.

Any personal considerations had become secondary to Alice. She rarely indulged thoughts of family. Work-life balance was a regular source of disagreement with Mark, her long-suffering partner. He could never understand her commitment. To her, the potential to make a difference, to stop a novel virus in its tracks, to save thousands of lives through early detection, was worthy of a little personal sacrifice.

The phone next to her workstation rang. An internal call. She recognised the professor's extension number immediately.

"Can I borrow you for a few minutes?"

"Sure."

"Unless you're in the middle of something?"

"I was just looking at those lung tissue samples from Guangzhou."

"Guangzhou can wait. I need a second opinion."

The professor was asking her for a second opinion. Wonders would never cease. He was normally so guarded about his research. He preferred to work alone.

"I'll be right down," she replied with genuine excitement.

She washed up and was outside his door within five minutes, slightly out of breath, still straightening her lab coat as the door opened. He ushered her in and offered her a seat, a steaming pot of tea and two mugs on a coffee table littered with stacks of medical journals, sticky notes protruding from the glossy pages.

As he poured the tea and set out some Rich Tea biscuits, Alice stared absent-mindedly at the cluttered bookshelves stacked with musty brown textbooks, gold lettering on the spines, piles of papers bound with string. An assortment of

African knick-knacks, miniature mahogany carvings of elephants, zebra and monkeys lined the windowsill. His lab coat hung on the back of the door.

"What do you know about Porton Down?"

"I've driven past it," said Alice without thinking, feeling instantly foolish. It wasn't like the professor was asking for directions to the military research facility near Salisbury.

"I've got some VIPs coming to visit tomorrow morning. They've asked to meet you."

"Me? May I ask why?" she replied, trying to control the butterflies in her stomach.

"They've been following your career for some time. Your research paper on disease monitoring and prevention was widely shared in government circles."

"Really?"

"Like I said, you impressed a lot of people when you were in Hong Kong. They think, and I tend to agree, that you're ready for the big time. BSL-4."

BSL-4, or biosafety level four, represented the highest level of safety required for the study of deadly pathogens. Very few scientists were invited to join their elite ranks. Of course, Alice had dreamed of such a progression, but had not expected the invitation so soon in her career. Porton Down was one of only a handful of research facilities in the UK equipped with BSL-4 facilities.

"Don't worry," he countered, noticing her apprehension. "I'll walk you through everything. That way when we get to Kisangani you'll be able to assist me in the full range of laboratory work we may need on the front line."

"In three weeks?"

"I've seen how you work. You're ready for this. And it's not as big of a step as you think."

It went without saying that Alice already followed protocol

to the letter. She never took unnecessary risks. All her vaccinations were up to date. Despite her unquestionable ambition, in a work environment governed by rigidly constructed rules, she never cut corners, never compromised on personal safety. Many of the viruses she would be working with had no vaccine. There was no doubt about it: three weeks was an accelerated timeline, to say the least.

"I want you to start immediately."

"What about the Guangzhou samples?"

"I'll find someone else to take over. You can project manage from a distance if you insist."

CHAPTER 10

The following morning at ten o'clock sharp, the departmental receptionist showed the visitors from Porton Down into a draughty conference room where Alice and the professor were already deep in conversation about the delivery that had arrived overnight.

O'Leary rose to shake hands with the new arrivals, greeting Major General Phillips like an old friend. The other two received a more muted welcome, introduced as Doctor Littlejohn and Major Farrier. Alice knew both by reputation from various published articles and research papers.

"So this must be our rising star? It's a pleasure to meet you finally," said Major General Phillips with a broad smile as he shook Alice's hand.

"Likewise," said Alice, embarrassed by all the attention. She had somehow expected such a senior army officer to be more formal, more medals and gold braid, less dress-down camouflaged fatigues. "How do you and the professor know each other?" she asked, trying to calm her nerves.

"Oh, Stephen and I spent a long hot summer criss-crossing

west and Central Africa, trekking through the rainforest on the trail of a mystery virus."

"We were just kids back then," conceded the professor.

"Looking to make a name for ourselves."

"Little did we know," said the professor, at which they both laughed.

"We never did find the monster's lair," added Phillips with a theatrical flourish, like some dungeons and dragons wizard.

"Lair?" asked Alice, amused by the metaphor. She was somewhat of a fan of *The Hobbit* and other works of fantasy.

"Back then, we were foolish enough to believe that finding ground zero might teach us how to develop a cure."

"As if it was that simple."

Alice was feeling like a child listening to their grandparents recount tales from their youth.

"Yes, everyone else at the institute thought we were raving lunatics."

"And they were probably right," admitted O'Leary with a shrug.

"But that didn't stop you going back for a second and third time, did it, Stephen?" There was an edge to the question, as if rediscovering the source of long-held disagreement.

"Someone had to try."

"And look at us now," said Phillips, changing the subject, shaking his head with a weary sigh. "We were so idealistic back then." He glanced at Alice, as if jealous of her passion, the same ambition that had once burned inside of him. "Science has come a long way. Young guns, like Doctor Bishop here, breaking the mould, challenging the status quo."

"I hear Littlejohn and Farrier are making great strides," countered O'Leary.

"Some modest breakthroughs, perhaps," replied Phillips before the two scientists could respond. "Don't believe everything you hear. We're still a long way from the breakthrough we were promised."

"You always were the king of understatement, Tom. What about all these rumours I hear about genetic revolution?"

"Baby steps. One day I hope to tell you about it." The general glanced at Alice and back again.

"I'll hold you to that. Well, then, assuming this isn't a social call, Tom, how can we be of service to you gentlemen today?"

"Did my package arrive?"

"It did."

"What did you make of it?"

"Yes, fascinating, but all rather cryptic."

"One can never be too careful, Stephen. Someone is always watching," he joked, tapping his Roman nose, mostly for Alice's benefit. Alice found his playful demeanour incongruous for a man in his position.

"Well, I must say Alice and I are intrigued."

"Good. That's the spirit. Now, before we get to the package, we have a little initiation test for Alice. Let's call it a condition of entry to the BSL-4 'club'."

"Tom, I told you. Alice is ready."

"Humour me, Stephen," he insisted. "Reputations can so often disappoint, don't you think?"

From his briefcase, Major General Phillips produced two high-definition photos. Mugshots of pathogens Alice instantly recognised from her studies. She rotated them to get a better look before standing back, hands on hips. "West Nile Virus. This other one is Ebola."

"Very good, but take a closer look," said Phillips, handing Alice a magnifying glass. The professor's pained expression spoke volumes. He had reprimanded Alice before about jumping to conclusions. She studied the photos more carefully this time, scrunching up her eyes, puzzled by something.

"What is it, Alice?" asked Phillips.

"Well, for a start, the protein shell on this West Nile sample is...most unusual and then this," she said, pointing to something else that seemed odd. "Wait, where did you say you got these?"

"I'll come to that. Tell us what else you notice," encouraged Phillips.

"Well, as you know, West Nile is an enveloped virus. Its protein shell is covered by a membrane containing cholesterol. This anomaly," she said, pointing to the photo, "in the envelope's thickness is very unusual."

"Have you seen this before?"

"Never."

"And, in your opinion, what difference could this make?"

"Increased levels of cholesterol would, in theory at least, make it easier for the virus to pass into the target host cell."

"So, in layperson's terms, the anomaly might make the virus more transmissible?" said Phillips, conferring with Farrier and Littlejohn, who nodded in agreement.

"Yes. Although it's hard to be certain from a black-and-white photo. I'd need to conduct detailed tests with live virus to be sure."

"Out of the question," confirmed Littlejohn, amused at the request.

"Then perhaps you can tell me where in Central Africa you got these samples?" Alice was jumping ahead, but she suspected there was a link between these photos and their upcoming visit to the Congo.

"Who said they're from Africa?" countered Littlejohn.

"Why show them to us if they're not?" asked Alice, struggling to hide her frustration with this strange game.

"Alice has a point," agreed the professor. "If you're not going to tell us anything about them..."

"Very well. What we're about to tell you is strictly off the record."

Alice and the professor nodded.

"Both of these samples were recovered from a laboratory in Iraq."

"Iraq? But there are no recorded cases of these viruses in the Middle East," challenged Alice.

"Correct. We believe the Iraqis are attempting to alter their genetic make-up."

"To what end?" asked Alice, incredulous.

"Saddam has made no secret of his intention to develop chemical and biological weapons to target Israel, perhaps even the West."

"With West Nile Virus and Ebola?" Alice couldn't help but laugh at the suggestion. All eyes turned to her, waiting for her to explain. "Sorry. It just seems a little unlikely, don't you think?" rebutted Alice. "Look, if anyone was serious about deliberately starting an outbreak of infectious disease then WNV and Ebola make pretty poor choices."

"Opinions differ."

"Really? I'd like to meet the expert who seriously considers West Nile Virus a candidate for a bioweapon."

The major general seemed encouraged by her forthrightness, exchanging a glance with O'Leary. The professor glowed with pride at the confident display from his prodigy. She was certainly living up to her reputation.

"In its current form, perhaps. What makes you so sure, Alice?"

"Because, in ninety-nine per cent of WNV cases, if there are any symptoms at all, they're normally milder than the flu. Fever, headache, a rash, sometimes vomiting. It's hardly a killer."

"Alice has a point," added the professor. "Both viruses make poor candidates for bioweapons. Ebola or Marburg are deadly all right, but, as Doctor Littlejohn and Farrier know, neither is very transmissible. Unless there's something you're not telling us?"

The three men from Porton Down shared an awkward silence.

CHAPTER 11

There was a pregnant pause in the conversation as Doctor Littlejohn waited for his Porton Down superior to elaborate.

"Let's just say we're dealing with incomplete data right now. The Americans are taking this threat seriously. They've sent live virus samples to Fort Detrick for analysis. We hope they'll be able to tell us more in the coming days."

"The problem, as I see it," continued Alice, with growing confidence, "is less the virus and more the vector. As you know, mosquitoes spread West Nile Virus."

"So?"

"All you'd need is some decent insect repellent and sleeping nets and you'd virtually eliminate infections."

"You mean cut transmission by avoiding getting bitten in the first place?"

"Exactly."

"But for those infected, I'm told there's still no vaccine for WNV," challenged the major general.

"We've never needed one. Deaths from WNV are all but negligible."

"Yes, but we have no way of knowing mortality rates for a genetically modified strain."

"True." A thought occurred to Alice. One that had been bothering her since they produced the photos. The part of her brain that loved puzzles, making links between seemingly unrelated pieces of information, was trying to tell her something.

"Has anyone considered that there might be a common link between these samples?"

"A hybrid virus?" dismissed Farrier with incredulity, shaking his head. "Trust me, it's been tried before. It's actually much harder than it sounds."

"But Jonathan, it's worth Alice knowing, it was an avenue of investigation we considered and chose not to explore," conceded Littlejohn, by way of an olive branch.

"Gentlemen, if we're considering all the options, then Doctor Bishop is right. A hybrid virus should stay on the list," said Major General Phillips. The professor patted the photos on the table in front of him, caressing the glossy paper on which they were printed. His hand froze as if struck by a thought.

"Any number of experts on your payroll could ID these viruses. Why bring them to us?"

"I would have thought that was obvious to you, of all people, Stephen. After all, you're one of only a handful of scientists to have studied these viruses in the wild."

"Only because the others died?" challenged O'Leary.

"I'm sorry. Poor choice of words. I didn't mean to open old wounds."

"Then why are you really here, Tom?"

Phillips took a moment to consider his response. "To put an end to all those sleepless nights. To give you a second chance, Stephen." O'Leary stared back at him, cautioning him against going too far. "I've read your latest evaluation. Blame and recrimination still burn bright, don't they? Losing members of an expeditionary team all those years ago? Wounds that can never heal. Trust me, I know, I've been there."

The professor had never spoken to Alice of past expeditions to West Africa. Now and again, she caught glimpses of his inner turmoil, as if trying to right the wrongs of yesteryear, some debt to former colleagues.

"You have no idea," said the professor, with a flash of anger. "You left. It was me who had to deal with the fallout."

Alice noticed O'Leary's hand shaking, horror frozen across his lips.

"I know you're still angry, Stephen. I reread the report. Saw the photos."

"Photos could never do justice. Watching Graham die in agony like that. Seeing his skin peel away like radiation sickness, blood pouring from his eyes, his organs liquified by that monster."

"What was it?" said Alice.

"Ebola Zaire. Killed seven out of ten of my team."

"Good God."

"If I live another thirty years, I never want to see that thing again."

"You're one of only a handful of people in the UK who have first-hand experience working with Ebola. That makes you indispensable to our mission," said Phillips.

"Your file says you also treated Marburg victims back in the eighties, but it doesn't say where," said Littlejohn, flicking through the folder in front of him, trying to find the answer, oblivious to the obvious pain these questions caused.

"Uganda," said O'Leary.

"It says here it was one of the worst outbreaks ever recorded. Worse than Ebola. Were the symptoms very different?"

"Marburg targets the brain and the nervous system. Victims appear psychotic, prone to extreme violence." The professor stared into space, unwilling to continue. He closed his eyes as if still haunted by the memory. "Entire villages wiped out at a stroke. Marburg has no remorse, no conscience. You can't reason with this monster. It has no heart, just rage."

Littlejohn was scribbling furiously in his notebook. "And the Ebola outbreak you witnessed, where exactly was that?"

"A tiny village called Yambuku. Mongala province, northern Zaire. Very remote. The only way to get there was by motorbike. By the time we arrived, most of the villagers were dead or dying. We were too late."

"What did you do?"

"There was nothing we could do. The missionaries took the survivors into care. Orphans, mostly. Some of them were so young, just babies, really. We found them naked, sitting in the dirt, waiting for someone, anyone, to comfort them, to feed them. Everyone was totally shell-shocked. In the end, most of the locals just abandoned their homes. Villages were left uninhabited for years afterwards. Some swore never to return. They said the land was cursed."

"And yet, despite all that horror, you're going back to Zaire in a few weeks."

"Now the Democratic Republic of the Congo," corrected the professor.

"Right, but why?"

"For closure. To face my fears one last time."

"For an end to all those sleepless nights," added Phillips.

Alice was visibly shocked hearing O'Leary talk this way. Her role model. The scientist who wasn't afraid of anything.

"And then what?"

"Retirement. I'm too old to be trekking in the jungle."

"There comes a time for all of us, Stephen."

"I can't tell you how many times I've woken up in a cold sweat thinking about what might happen if Ebola or Marburg ever escape the jungle and, God forbid, reached our shores," admitted O'Leary.

"It doesn't bear thinking about," replied Littlejohn. "A more contagious variant would make SARS look like a picnic."

"This time, I plan to stop it. Dead in its tracks."

"No, no one can stop Ebola, Professor O'Leary," warned Littlejohn.

"Funny, they used to say the same about climbing Everest or going to the moon," he replied with a faraway look in his eyes.

"Where there's a will, there's a way," added Phillips, feeling that youthful ambition rekindling between the two men.

"If we can study these viruses in their natural environments, learn more about how they jump species, then maybe, just maybe, we have a chance."

"I don't believe we have a choice," challenged Littlejohn. "If the Iraqis truly are as far along as we fear in their research, then we may not have long to bolster our defences."

"Whatever Littlejohn believes Iraq is up to or not," said O'Leary, waving dismissively, "the sooner we flush Marburg and Ebola out of their hiding places the better."

"Except that's not quite the complete story, is it, Professor?" challenged Littlejohn, clearly irritated by O'Leary's dismissive views on the Iraqi threat. "The real reason you're tying your wagon to the WHO horse is that you couldn't get funding for your own expedition. Isn't that right?"

"Who told you that?" O'Leary said, his eyes flashed with anger.

"Come, come, Professor, no one wants to pay for another fool's errand. All the funding is going East. To Asia. To China. SARS is the new threat everyone's talking about. Marburg and Ebola are outliers."

"Direct as ever, Littlejohn," conceded Phillips.

"Did you ever ask yourself why the WHO mission chose Kisangani for its base of operations?" continued Littlejohn.

"I'm a scientist, not a politician. Why don't you tell me?"

"The Congo has seen more novel strains of viruses in the last few years than virtually anywhere else on the planet. It's the new front line against disease and yet no one cares because it's in Africa. There's no oil to fight over."

"You're preaching to the choir," warned O'Leary. "Why is Porton Down suddenly so interested in the Congo?"

"Because we need each other, Stephen. We want to join forces on this one," confirmed Major General Phillips.

"You know full well this isn't my expedition, Tom. If it was up to me..."

"An extra team member should be relatively straightforward for the institute to organise."

"We leave in three weeks. The visa applications alone took months."

"The Foreign Office is working on fast-tracking the applications as we speak."

"So it's already decided?" challenged an exasperated O'Leary.

"Look, for us to mount our own expedition to the Congo would take months to put together. We simply don't have the resources in Africa for something on this scale. Which makes your expedition our best chance of getting in there before Christmas. All I'm asking is that Littlejohn tags along as part of the British contingent."

"Changing the team now would be near impossible. The French have the lead on this one."

"I've spoken to the expedition leader, Leclerc. He's formally agreed to our request."

"I see. Then you don't need my blessing at all."

"We came here as a courtesy, Stephen. I owed you that."

"Fine. But, if this thing blows up in any way..."

"I guarantee your operation will not be impaired. You're fully insulated."

"If this gets out, it could jeopardise the institute's entire mission in West Africa."

"The department is prepared to make a generous donation to the institute to compensate you all. Enough to fund your research programme for this year and next."

The professor shrugged his shoulders in resignation. "Then it seems I have no choice."

"Good, then it's settled."

"For Queen and Country," toasted Littlejohn with a sip of cold coffee.

CHAPTER 12

Addis Ababa, Ethiopia
30 October 1998

The flight from Addis Ababa to Kisangani was an eventful five hours in what Alice could only describe as a rust bucket. In reality, their aircraft was a Fokker F27 with twin turbo-prop engines that looked like they had outlived their serviceable life by some years. Kept flying through love and money by Ethiopian Airlines, the Fokker was the only aircraft large enough to transport the bulk of the WHO party in relative comfort. Leopard-skin seat covers and floral carpets spoke of a more colourful period of private ownership. They had crated up the rest of their equipment and shipped direct via a United Nations C-130 Hercules, the ageing workhorse of the NGO.

Alice, Professor O'Leary and the new addition to the British team, Doctor Littlejohn from Porton Down, now masquerading as one of the scientists from the institute, had rendezvoused with the rest of the forty-five-person expeditionary group at the WHO headquarters in Geneva before their tortuous journey over Europe to Ethiopia, refuelling in Addis Ababa for their onward leg to Kisangani.

Alice slept somewhat fitfully, vivid dreams of lush forest and waterways she had seen in photos or videos. The professor nudged her awake as they crossed what he said was the border into the Democratic Republic of the Congo, though there was disappointingly little evidence of a border below.

While the rest of the team grabbed some much-needed shut-eye, Alice stared out of the window transfixed at mile after mile of verdant forest that stretched unbroken over hill and valley to the horizon. To her left she could see lakes and farms, a rich tapestry of colour from green to brown. When she thought of Africa, she imagined an arid dust-bowl or drought-starved land of red soil, but what she found was a landscape teeming with life.

At some point, she must have succumbed to fatigue, head slumped against the window frame. Now and then, she was unceremoniously shaken awake as the plane lurched without warning at each successive pocket of turbulence. Alice grabbed hold of the professor's arm as the aircraft began to judder. He cracked one eye open and patted her shoulder before settling back to sleep.

The decrepit fuselage adopted a persistent, bone-rattling vibration, stirring even the most seasoned of travellers in their metal seats. The plane passed through dark clouds, rain hammering against the window, streaking the glass. The pilot opened the cockpit door and shouted something to the cabin crew. From the tone of the announcement that followed in French, she assumed it was intended to reassure the passengers. For Alice, it had the opposite effect.

"How does anyone put up with this?" shouted Alice, gripping the armrests, her voice shaking.

"This is luxury travel by African standards."

The Fokker re-emerged from the clouds. Below them, undulating tree-covered hills seemed that bit closer. They were losing altitude. Perhaps the pilot was trying his level best to stay under the weather. Or maybe there was a problem with the engines, worried Alice. Only two weeks before they were due to depart, Tutsi rebels had shot down a Boeing 727 airliner operated by Lignes Aériennes Congolaises airliner over rebel-held territory, but the professor had assured her their route would keep them well clear of danger.

Just as soon as the shaking had started, the turbulence abruptly passed, much to Alice's relief. She stared at the featureless forest canopy below, dissected now and again by an undulating brown river basin that weaved left and right out of view beneath them. They followed the path of the great river that rose and fell, crashing over a waterfall to the valley below before collecting in a swollen lake. Huts dotted the shoreline, children playing outside, squinting up into the sunlight at their passing.

After another hour of fitful sleep, Alice gripped the armrest as the Fokker began another steep descent before turning northwest, following the track of the great river set out below them.

"I had no idea the Congo River was so vast."

"Second longest in Africa. The only river to cross the equator twice," answered the professor, stirring once more, perhaps sensing they were approaching their final destination.

Alice grunted her acknowledgement. The professor was full of facts from a lifetime of travel.

"I expect we'll be landing soon," he added, noticing the change in engine noise.

"How can you tell?"

"Because I just saw the pilot put on his parachute."

Alice's eyes widened, sitting up straighter, before realising the joke.

"Hilarious," she whispered, digging an elbow into the professor's ribs, laughing at her own naivety.

CHAPTER 13

Kisangani Airport
Democratic Republic of the Congo
1 November 1998

The WHO team sheltered from the searing heat in the midday sun as dozens of military storage containers, giant trunks containing all the field equipment they would use on the expedition, were unloaded from the C-130.

Francois Leclerc, the expedition leader, checked off each crate, clipboard in hand, noting the serial number and contents of each container. The manifest listed specialist medical equipment in short supply in the country. Personal protective equipment, gloves, face masks, scrubs, medical kits for dissection, sampling kits, decontamination material, and medicines, together with a limited supply of what the French referred to as Racal suits, laboratory-grade positive pressure suits for work with dangerous pathogens they might encounter on their trip.

In the briefing back in Geneva, one of the French laboratory workers had demonstrated the Racal suits' safe use. In the last few weeks, the professor had insisted Alice train day after day, wearing one, following WHO-set safety protocols, as she carried out her duties in the lab. It was one thing to wear the suit in an air-conditioned laboratory, temperature-controlled to twenty-two degrees Celsius, but not in a tropical country, like the Congo. She could barely imagine wearing plastic in this heat. The battery-powered Racal version had an electric blower to inflate the suit and circulate air, but not to regulate temperature.

A waiting coach took the scientists to their lodgings at the Hotel Congo Palace de Kisangani. It wasn't much to look at from the outside, a modernist building of concrete and glass, but the beds were firm. Alice would share a room with Maxine, a female scientist from Marseille who was monosyllabic and spoke little English.

After a quick change, splashing water on her face from a basin with a sponge, Alice was driven to the French ambassador's reception, at a grand colonial-style building beside the river, surrounded either side by a maze of temporary housing, row upon row of green plastic tents, erected by an emergency response team or NGO. Children sat outside, half clothed, undernourished, playing in the dirt.

They parked up outside the crumbling building, once the stately home of a Belgian colonialist and adventurer, built a century ago. The peeling, whitewashed exterior desperately needed a fresh lick of paint. However, inside, their hosts had done what they could to make the venue presentable: red carpets, colourful drapes, trays of cold drinks. Somehow she half-expected champagne and delicious chocolates, a mental image sourced from adverts set in grand receptions.

The French ambassador greeted them each in turn, flanked by a local in a poorly fitting suit one size too small for him. As soon as the brass band had finished butchering what Alice took to be the national anthem, the ambassador tapped his glass with a fork and waited for the room to fall silent once again. He spoke for several minutes in rapid French before remembering the English-speaking contingent from the United Kingdom, USA and Canada, who were the recipients of a more muted welcome. The ambassador handed things over to a local man he introduced with some reverence as Alain Beaumont, the government minister for health.

"Welcome to Kisangani, capital city of Orientale Province," boasted the minister. "The most important inland port on the Congo River."

He explained that Kisangani city was home to some half a million people. From the sprawling shanty towns they had passed on the outskirts of the city, Alice would have guessed Kisangani much larger than its population suggested.

Beaumont turned to the French ambassador and Leclerc. "We are grateful to our friends at the World Health Organization. Their mission here is very important to us. But this is not an easy time for my country. There has been too much fighting, too much bloodshed. But, please, do not worry. My government has stationed two thousand brave soldiers in and around the city and a further one hundred and fifty United Nations soldiers who will follow you wherever you go. You have my word you will be safe here in Kisangani. And my representative, Corbus Koch, will oversee the entire security operation."

Beaumont pointed to what Alice took to be a park ranger. A tall white middle-aged man with skin like leather, piercing blue eyes, thin expressionless lips and dressed head to toe in khaki. Alice pictured him posing next to his kill, a bull elephant collapsed in defeat, slaughtered for game.

"If you have any questions during your time here, let Mr Koch know. Now, please, relax, enjoy yourselves. Our work starts tomorrow," he implored to polite applause.

Alice wandered between diverse groups speaking in French, searching for her American and Canadian colleagues, though she didn't feel in the mood for small talk. She found the professor hobnobbing with the VIPs, Beaumont and Leclerc. Alice stepped aside to make way for a passing waiter and almost knocked the glass from a guest's hand. Spinning round to apologise, she found herself face to face with the ranger, Corbus Koch. She attempted to wipe the liquid from his shirt before it could stain.

"I'm so sorry. How clumsy of me," she said.

"Leave it," he said, brushing her hand aside. "Things dry quickly here."

It quickly became clear that Koch was a man of few words. Alice's good manners compelled her to make conversation, to atone for her error.

"So, Mister Koch, how long have you worked here?"

"Since 1989."

"Good heavens. That long. But I take it from your accent you're originally from South Africa?"

He inclined his head in acknowledgement, half-wincing at the insinuation that he had an accent.

"And what is it you do for the minister?"

"I fix what needs fixing."

He didn't seem overly keen to elaborate.

"I see. And what did you do before the Congo?"

"I was in the Recces." He seemed to be expecting some sort of reaction. Alice waited for him to explain. She had no idea what he was talking about. "Like your SAS."

He stared at Alice unblinking, as if further questions were unwelcome. She drained her glass and made her excuses. Anything to get away from him.

The professor waved Alice over, eager to introduce her to Alain Beaumont, the Congolese minister.

"Enchanté, mademoiselle," said Beaumont, taking Alice's hand and kissing it. "Professor O'Leary has told me so much about you. But he did not say you were beautiful as well as brilliant," he added, enjoying Alice's blushes. "How do you feel about your first trip to the Congo?"

"A little nervous, if I'm honest."

"I'd be worried if you weren't," he joked. "Most scientists who visit this corner of Africa do not know what to expect. Trust me, when they see first-hand the poverty in my country, I've seen experienced doctors get on the next plane out."

"The professor has prepared us well."

"I'm sure. And what made you want to come here in the first place?"

"Doctor Bishop's Master's thesis focused on the impact of early disease detection on saving lives," explained O'Leary.

"I see."

"I wanted to see for myself. To study viruses in their natural habitat. You see, our institute in Oxford is one of the WHO's Collaborating Centres. We handle hundreds of samples from all over the world, including those from the Congo."

"And why do you believe this region has become such a hot spot for new disease?"

Alice hesitated, remembering the hard-hitting conclusion in her thesis. She had been highly critical of the role of the government. Perhaps the minister was setting a trap. "I'm afraid you may not like my answer."

"I'm a politician. I have a thick skin. Try me."

"That government policy has accelerated the natural process."

"Which government policy are you referring to?"

"The systematic destruction of natural habitats."

"So you're an environmentalist?"

"Only in the sense that I believe deforestation has resulted in the decline of many species of birds and other animals. It's made the area around Kisangani a perfect breeding ground for disease."

"'A perfect breeding ground for disease'. We should use that in our advertising. It might boost our tourism industry," mocked the minister, to the laughter of those around him.

"In academia, we encourage forthrightness, bold thinking. I'm sure Alice meant no offence," explained the professor.

"Of course she didn't. Here in the Congo, we like plain speaking."

"I meant no disrespect. I apologise, Minister."

"Doctor Bishop's research looked at the impact of deforestation in several other countries, too. Viruses have been lurking in the jungles and rainforests for centuries, perhaps since the very dawn of time."

"But the Congo is not like other countries," corrected the minister.

"Correct. And that's why we're here. The Congo is one of the largest reservoirs of disease in the world. One of only a handful of places on earth likely to produce new pathogens."

"So you British are the equivalent of disease tourists? Come to watch my people suffer?" challenged the minister.

"On the contrary. Providing we identify cases early enough we can isolate them, quarantine affected villages, contain any outbreak. We are here to save lives."

"The villages around Kisangani are like canaries in a coal mine," added the professor.

"And I suppose you blame my government's policies for the civil war too?"

"I don't claim to know much about Congolese politics," Alice apologised. "I'm just a scientist."

"Just a scientist," repeated Beaumont, with growing irritation. "But I'm sure you have a view."

Alice ignored the professor's stare, warning her to tread carefully. "Minister, I believe war is responsible for massive displacement of people, refugees arriving in already crowded areas. These are the perfect conditions for an outbreak."

"What would you have us do, Mademoiselle?" he replied with growing irritation.

Alice wished she had the answer, and kept silent.

"Scientific progress should not be at the expense of Congolese interests. My people are not lab rats."

"No, of course not..."

"Alice has much to learn, Minister," interrupted the professor, keen to avoid a full-blown diplomatic incident on their first day.

"Now, if you'll excuse me, I have other guests to attend to."

Alice watched the minister walk away, crestfallen at her clumsiness.

"Well, that went well," concluded the professor with heavy sarcasm, keen to dispel any thoughts that Alice might have imagined the minister's displeasure. "What you need to understand is that these are proud people, Alice. The WHO cannot operate without Beaumont's support."

"I know. I'm sorry."

"Look, local politicians are prickly at the best of times..."

A hollow laugh from behind Alice interrupted their conversation. "I see you met the minister," said the local man in the tight-fitting grey suit, fixing Alice with a broad smile.

"Thierry," exclaimed O'Leary. "How good to see you again. Alice, this is Thierry Deschamps, the Chief Medical Officer from Kisangani Hospital I was telling you about."

"Delighted to meet you, Thierry."

"Whatever Beaumont said, I'd take with a pinch of salt. At least we at the hospital are thrilled to have you here. Beaumont's administration is under pressure right now. Best to ignore him."

"I will. Thank you," replied Alice, warming to the Chief Medical Officer. "We're looking forward to getting started in the morning."

"As are we. My hospital is full of patients. We could do with your help."

"Is that normal for this time of year?" asked Alice, already intrigued.

"Oh no. This year has been off the scale. That's why we petitioned the WHO to bring forward the expedition."

"As they say here in Africa, when you see a rhino ready to charge, you do not wait until it is close before making a decision," joked O'Leary.

"Except we do not have many rhino left, Professor."

"More's the pity."

"I saw you met Mister Koch too. What did you make of him?" Thierry asked Alice.

"I don't think he likes me very much."

"He doesn't like anyone very much. He's old school. A gun for hire. Kisangani has always attracted mercenaries and swindlers like him. If you know what's good for you, you'll stay well clear. Be careful not to over-promise or under-deliver. He can be uncompromising, even heavy-handed at times."

"I appreciate the warning."

"You'll discover people around here don't like him very much."

"Noted."

"But you will find there is much to like about the local people of Kisangani."

"I look forward to meeting your team."

With that, Thierry excused himself, leaving Alice feeling a little better about her earlier faux pas with the minister.

CHAPTER 14

The following morning, after a restless night's sleep in the cramped hotel room, listening to Maxine's incessant snoring, Alice was up early, eager to get started with the job in hand. Maxine had come in late, reeking of booze. Some bootleg concoction the locals called pétrole, brewed right here in Kisangani. It took one sniff of the potent moonshine thrust under her nose at the after-party to put Alice off, but there was no stopping Maxine. Her fun-loving room-mate had hit it off with the Congolese staff. *Travailler dur, jouer dur*, as Maxine was fond of saying. Hard-working Marseille scientist by day, life and soul of the party by night. Alice couldn't help but feel a little jealous, struggling to follow the conversation in rapid French. Stuck talking shop with Littlejohn again. Fun could wait until she got home, she told herself. Always the bridesmaid, never the bride.

Down at the breakfast buffet in the hotel restaurant, decorated with colourful murals depicting a tribal dance, a swirl of colours and half-naked figures, Alice found the professor talking to a tall Westerner she didn't recognise from last night's reception. Strikingly handsome with a closely cropped beard, she guessed him to be in his early thirties. O'Leary introduced him as Jean-Philippe, the French Head of Security.

"Please, call me JP." There was something mischievous about the way he maintained eye contact. A roguish self-confidence, proud aquiline nose, high cheekbones. "Is this your first time? In the Congo?" There it was again. Alice was definitely not imagining it, as if he was daring her.

"First time in Africa, yes."

"Alice and I were in Hong Kong earlier this year," added the professor. "Second UN expedition."

"The Congo is very different to Hong Kong," warned JP. "There are dangers here you should be aware of."

"So people keep saying."

"But, try not to worry." He rested his hand, momentarily, on her forearm. "You'll be well protected. I'll be with you day and night." Alice couldn't decide whether he was patronising her or just doing his job.

"What's the latest on the rebel advance?" asked the professor. "The ambassador said more foreign fighters had crossed the border from Uganda and Rwanda in the last few days."

"There's really nothing to worry about," reassured JP, perhaps for Alice's benefit. "That's hundreds of miles away."

"Things change quickly in the Congo, n'est-ce pas?"

"Not that quickly, Professor. My team will continue to monitor the situation. Shadow you wherever we go. Don't worry. I'll keep you out of trouble," he added with a boyish grin. Alice felt her cheeks redden. "You'll be long gone before the rebels get this far from the border."

"With any luck," admitted the professor, keen to bring the conversation back to the matter in hand.

"So, when can we get started?" asked Alice, impatient to get to the WHO field office and meet the rest of her team.

JP checked his watch. It was only half past seven, still early.

"Not for another hour and a half, but Philippe and I can show you around town if you like." He gestured towards the Congolese guide standing at a respectful distance, and waved him over.

Alice nodded her agreement, eager to stretch her legs after the long flight.

"You'll need your headscarf," said JP.

"Of course. Sorry." Alice had nearly forgotten the custom for women here in Kisangani, fishing a black shawl out of her purse and wrapping it round her head.

Alice, JP and Philippe made their way down to the bustling waterfront where dozens of boats were already unloading their cargo, sacks of grain, drums of vegetable oil, cut timber, as JP pointed out several landmarks, buildings she recognised from photos as colonial influences. Belgian settlers had built much of Kisangani's old town more than one hundred years ago. The sights, sounds and smells of the port assaulted her senses.

As they exchanged small talk, she asked their local guide, Philippe, about life in Kisangani. He explained in fluent English how he had lived there for almost fifteen years. Long enough to form a strong attachment to the area. He referenced the residential districts they had driven through from the airport upon arrival, pointing out botanical gardens, brownstone townhouses, European-style villas with red brick walls, tiled roofs dating from the early 1900s, much in contrast to the simple thatched roof dwellings and crumbling concrete apartment blocks she had seen in other quarters.

"How about you, JP? What's your story?" she asked provocatively.

"Almost three years in the Congo. Two in Kinshasa, one here in Kisangani."

"And before that?"

"Rwanda, Somalia. Before that, France."

"How many years working for the UN?"

"You ask a lot of questions."

"I'm sorry. Force of habit. It's my job to be curious."

JP laughed. "Makes sense. My old job was evacuating French nationals from crisis zones. Those caught up in other countries' civil wars. It's becoming something of a speciality." He frowned.

"You think that could happen here?"

"We'll see. Hopefully, it won't come to that."

Alice fanned herself with the guidebook she was carrying, trying to cool herself down. Her back was already damp with perspiration. "It's so humid here."

"This is nothing. You should try being here in summer."

"Does it rain a lot?" said Alice, noticing how green everything was.

Philippe laughed into his sleeve, amused by her naivety. "More than you'd think. But mostly in monsoon season."

As they reached the market, they found traders setting up their stalls, unloading farm produce and replica football shirts from vans and carts. Alice listened absent-mindedly to their lively conversations, refusing what she took to be an invitation to inspect their goods.

"Does no one speak English?" complained Alice in mock frustration.

"A few, but not many. Most people speak French or Lingala. Some Swahili."

"What's that over there?" asked Alice, pointing to a sports stadium in the distance.

"Stade Lumumba where the local football team play, AS Nika," replied Philippe with obvious pride.

"They're surprisingly good," added JP. "It's not quite Stade de France, but you should hear the crowd on a weekend. I'll take you one evening."

"Thanks, but I'm more of a rugby girl."

"Hmm. I've never met an English person who didn't like football."

"Not me. Too many hooligans."

"In Europe, football still has an image problem," JP explained to a puzzled Philippe. "Even in Lille, where I come from, people have long memories of fighting on football terraces."

JP stopped next to a ramshackle food cart and shook hands with a toothless old soul Alice took to be a friend. After a rapid exchange in heavily accented French, the trader produced half a dozen wooden skewers from a cool box loaded with shelled prawns in a sticky sauce which he positioned on his already hot plate warmed by a gas burner. He flipped them over a couple of times to warm them through and handed them to Alice in a serviette, waiting for her approval.

The prawns smelled of garlic and chilli. She blew on them twice before dissecting the first two prawns. They were nothing short of delicious.

"The best prawns you'll ever eat," claimed Philippe.

"Cossa cossa," confirmed the trader.

"His cousin catches them right over there."

JP paid the stall holder, and they continued through the market, dodging the many bikes and mopeds, enjoying the sights, sounds and smells of town. They stopped to listen to an African jazz ensemble warming up, playing what Alice recognised as a Miles Davis song. They weaved between the assembled throng, trying to get closer, and Alice tossed a couple of coins into a hat left out for donations.

"Careful. With generosity like that, you'll attract every kid in town," warned Philippe.

They continued beyond the café as far as the crashing roar of the Tsoppo River on the far side of town, where Philippe pointed towards the hydroelectric dam north of the city with noticeable pride, explaining how it powered much of the local area.

Despite the headscarf JP insisted she wear, Alice began to attract the attention of a group of local men, pointing and shouting at Alice, commenting on her fair skin and the locks of blonde hair that had tumbled free. JP visibly straightened at the implied threat, lifting his jacket to show them the 9mm pistol tucked into his jeans.

"I'm sorry," Philippe explained. "The locals don't see many Westerners here."

"Let alone attractive blondes," added JP, with a raised eyebrow.

Alice found herself blushing again. "What were they shouting?"

"You don't want to know," said Philippe. "Westerners are not very popular here right now. They have long memories. We've never much liked foreign meddling."

"But the United Nations is here to help."

"Yes, but you have to remember, most people are uneducated. They still remember when this place was thick with jungle, swamps and rainforest. This entire region was totally impassable."

"When did that change?"

"They built the Kinshasa Highway in the 1970s. Before that, the fastest way to travel was by ship. When they opened up the Kisangani to Bukavu road, everything changed. For the first time, whole swathes of the country became accessible to traffic. Fast-forward twenty-five years and this is what you get. Thousands of immigrants looking for work. Kisangani has become a melting pot. Every race and creed you can imagine. Greek, Chinese, Indians. Muslims, Catholics, Arabs."

"The locals blame the new arrivals for taking their jobs, spreading disease," added JP.

"Migrant labour is notorious for bringing in common infections from the cities. It's well documented," said Alice.

"You're saying the locals are right to blame immigrants?" asked Philippe, intrigued by Alice's scientific viewpoint.

"Take those dock workers back there, unloading the boats. They're carriers for diseases some locals will never have encountered before. The unlucky ones will have no immunity at all."

"The villagers around here are God-fearing people. Whenever there's an outbreak of disease, or a crop fails, sometimes even just plain bad weather, the elders tell their people God is punishing them. Communities are suspicious of outsiders."

"Most of the time it's more convenient just to blame the UN," JP admitted with a laugh. He checked the time. "We should get going. The traffic is terrible at this time of day."

CHAPTER 15

The WHO scientific team assembled at nine o'clock sharp at the animal testing centre to meet Samuel Ntumba, the senior veterinarian responsible for the entire Tshopo province. Ntumba spoke fluent English. From the outside, the facility appeared run-down, a dilapidated warehouse building with whitewashed walls and a corrugated iron roof.

"Where's the professor?" Alice asked Doctor Littlejohn, noticing O'Leary's absence.

"Called away on some other business. Corbus Koch picked him up straight after breakfast."

Alice wondered what could possibly be more important than their first official appointment.

Inside, the facility appeared more modern, as if someone had designed the exterior to deter local interest. Alice had to breathe through her mouth to avoid gagging. The stench from the cages housing the monkeys quickly became overpowering.

The senior veterinarian made a joke in Congolese at Alice's expense as she pinched her nose. The other staff members seemed amused by the presence of women on the WHO team.

"So, Doctor Bishop, have you worked in an animal testing laboratory like this before?"

"Not one this large, but I've visited several in the UK and Hong Kong."

Ntumba seemed satisfied with her response.

"How many animals do you have here?"

"One hundred and seventy-four. Mostly marmosets. Some macaques."

Alice nodded. "We use marmosets too. Easier to work with."

"Don't be fooled," he cautioned, alarmed by what he interpreted as sentimentality. He addressed his comments to the entire WHO group. "These animals may look like something out of *The Jungle Book* but, please, underestimate them at your peril. These are powerful animals, despite their diminutive size. Their speed can be deceptive."

"We'll be sure to keep our distance," said Littlejohn.

"Avoid eye contact," Ntumba continued. "Anything that might suggest a challenge or a threat."

"WHO protocols require the wearing of protective suits at all times," reassured Leclerc, the expedition leader.

"Even with a helmet, an attack can still be deadly. A suit offers limited protection to a wild animal. Once a marmoset wraps its tail around your neck and starts clawing at your face..." His voice faded away. The mental image resonated with Alice. "Only last month, an animal attacked one of my workers. Needed a dozen stitches around his eyes and nose. His skin was literally shredded."

"Every member of the team has received rigorous training, Samuel," insisted Leclerc.

"One more thing. These animals have a habit of spitting. They'll aim for the eyes and face, any unprotected skin. That's normally how workers here contract disease."

"I appreciate the warning. My team will wear full-face masks. Thank you."

The veterinarian held open the door to the staff changing room. "Shall we?"

Inside, Alice discovered there were no separate changing rooms for male and female staff. After an awkward stand-off, they allocated the women their own corner, affording at least some privacy from the stares of their guides.

Alice stripped to a T-shirt and underwear and helped herself to some latex gloves from a box and one of the Racal suits hanging from a hook. She climbed into the one-piece suit, sweat already beading on her top lip from the effort. She tied back her hair, took a breath and inserted her head into the oversized helmet. Arms extended, she waited as her colleague checked the fitting of the suit and turned on her air supply. It took a few long seconds for the air to begin to circulate and the suit to inflate. It was already impossibly hot and claustrophobic inside. Her hands felt clammy, clumsy with the additional protective layer, but after the safety briefings, they all accepted the precautions were necessary.

Inside the animal holding area they found rows of cages, perhaps one hundred in total, most of them occupied by a single marmoset monkey. The animals were strangely subdued, perhaps dehydrated from the heat, but otherwise healthy. None of them displayed any obvious external physical symptoms beyond lethargy. Alice felt self-conscious being watched by man and monkey as the team progressed from cage to cage, recording their observations on notepads.

"How long have you been at this facility?" she asked Ntumba.

"Three years," he said. "Ever since the WHO designated Kisangani as one of its key monitoring stations in Central Africa. We send regular samples back to Geneva for analysis."

"That's right. My institute in the UK is one of the other receiving centres."

"I see."

"The earlier we detect new strains of virus, the faster we can respond should there be a fresh outbreak."

The vet grabbed what looked like a long-handled cattle prod with a needle attached to one end. He selected one monkey and while his colleague pinned the frightened animal to the back of the cage with a Y-shaped stick, Ntumba jabbed it with a sedative. Two minutes later, the animal sank into a deep sleep, unconscious to the naked eye. The vet waited a further minute to make sure.

The handler took appropriate precautions, looping a collar around its neck before reaching in to drag the monkey on to the stainless-steel trolley by its feet, ready for transportation to the laboratory. They repeated the exercise several more times until four of the animals were sedated.

"Even a bite from a sedated animal can prove fatal," warned Samuel, opening the subject's mouth to reveal sharp teeth that could easily puncture the suit's protective layer.

The Congolese team went through a well-rehearsed procedure, taking blood samples, cheek swabs, carefully recording measurements and taking photos until everything was catalogued before moving on to the next specimen.

One animal displayed symptoms of infection and was put down. They prepared the animal for autopsy, placing its limp body on a trolley to be wheeled through. The duty pathologist had already laid out his tools on a stainless-steel tray, each labelled and numbered so that his trainee assistant could pass the correct implement without explanation or interruption.

Once everyone had taken their positions to observe, the pathologist made a long incision before cracking the ribs and exposing the chest cavity. He wasted no time in skilfully removing the heart and lungs, weighing each organ as his colleague photographed and recorded everything, noting some discoloration. The distended belly was filled with a viscous liquid that resembled blood. The whites of the eyes were yellow and bloodshot. Alice noticed streaks of dried blood from its nasal passages. All signs pointed to internal haemorrhage, thought Alice, leaning forward to get a closer look at the internal organs.

The pathologist stepped aside, deferring to the WHO team, inviting Alice to take over. He held out the scalpel on the palm of his gloved hand. Alice hesitated, the glint of steel reflecting in the overhead light. Most pathologists worked alone to minimise the risk of accident. A single suit tear or slip could be fatal. In the wrong hands, even a hospital-standard scalpel could become a lethal weapon, particularly where pathogens were concerned.

Over the last few weeks, Alice had performed half a dozen autopsies prior to the expedition under the professor's watchful eye and been inoculated against more than a dozen viruses she might be exposed to on her trip. Every vaccination made her poorly and she had lost several days in bed with fever, but in her line of work, inoculation was compulsory. Between her trip to Asia and now Africa, her vaccination record read like an infectious disease greatest hits. Rabies, influenza, Q fever, yellow fever, even anthrax. But as every infectious diseases specialist knew there were no vaccinations against some of the more deadly pathogens. Direct contact with haemorrhagic fever might prove deadly. Safety protocols were everything.

Alice set to work, dissecting the lungs, heart, liver and pancreas, watched closely by the pathologist, his arms crossed, waiting for questions as he scrutinised her handiwork. While she had conducted many autopsies before, both animal and human, in the heat and claustrophobia the suit made Alice uncomfortable, fighting to keep her hands from trembling.

The pathologist watched Alice's hands closely as she worked. It was possible he had never seen a woman perform an autopsy.

"Are you married?" asked the pathologist, as if sensing her sudden attack of stage fright. An autopsy of an infected animal was hardly the place for idle conversation. However, on this occasion, she welcomed the distraction, giving her something else to think about as she worked.

"Engaged."

He didn't seem to understand.

"To be married."

"Ah, yes. And you hope to have children?"

"One day, yes."

"Good. Then I hope you will not mind me giving you some advice. This is no job for a woman. Certainly not one who wants children."

"In the UK, there are lots of women in my profession. Career comes first."

"I admire your dedication. But have you noticed there are no female doctors or pathologists here in Kisangani? Only female nurses. Did you ever ask yourself why?"

"The thought did occur to me."

"Trust me. I've seen too many European doctors come here wanting to make a name for themselves." Alice wondered if he was referring to the professor. "If you have any sense, you'll put your family first. When you're done here, please return to your home in England and never come back."

Alice considered his honesty well-intentioned. Her attention remained focused on the task in hand. "You see, preventing outbreaks here in the Congo helps keep other countries safe, too."

"If you'll take advice from an old man," he leaned closer so that Alice alone might hear his words, "you'll get out now while you still can. Don't wait too long. One slip of concentration is all it takes."

"I'll bear that in mind," she responded, with a raised eyebrow.

"Believe me when I tell you that until you have seen the consequences of infection up close, you can't begin to understand. Photos do not do these viruses justice."

Alice paused, looking up at the pathologist's downcast expression. She realised he must have suffered some personal tragedy or other.

"I've lost too many to count. Before I moved into animal pathology, I worked at the local hospital."

"Then you saw victims with Ebola?" she asked, encouraging him to continue, excited to be talking to someone other than the professor with first-hand experience.

"May you never have to see what I saw. Victims gasping for breath like fish out of water, lungs drowning in fluid. I have seen children, too young to articulate their pain, clawing at lesions on their skin. Bleeding from every orifice. In one case, teeth falling out, one by one. Entire families dying, one after the other. You can never unsee such horror."

Alice tried to imagine the carnage wrought by Ebola, her mind wandering momentarily from the dissection. A doctor could wait an entire lifetime to treat a single case of Ebola, and here was someone who had seen dozens.

A sharp intake of breath made her pause in her work. The pathologist was pointing at Alice's left glove. For a moment, she was unsure what he meant, then she saw it too. A tiny nick in the rubber. With mounting panic, she placed the scalpel flat on the stainless-steel trolley and stepped back from the autopsy table, her breathing rapid. With a cloth, she wiped excess liquid from the affected area, staring at the now obvious tear, terrified both the protective layers might be punctured.

How on earth had she been so stupid? All that training only to be distracted by a well-meaning local. What would the professor say? She had been so careful, hadn't she? Her mind was playing tricks on her. Her fingers sensed wetness within the inner glove. Oh God. Oh God. She ran to the decontamination area, as her colleague sprayed her glove with disinfectant, eyes wide with concern, waiting to be hosed down.

Once she had removed her suit, she tore off the inner glove, inspecting the skin of her index finger, the nail, nail bed, searching for a cut, however minor. Her breathing drowned out her other senses, her heartbeat pounding in her head. Her colleague was giving her instructions, but she could not hear.

To her immense relief, there appeared to be no liquid in the inner glove. Her skin was intact. Her breathing slowed. For good measure, she squirted handfuls of powerful disinfectant gel into the palms of her hand and worked it through her fingers, scrubbing her nails with a brush to remove any chance of infection until her hands were red raw and she was finally satisfied there was no contamination. No cut, no lesion in the skin's barrier. More through luck than judgement, she was going to be fine.

Alice stared at herself in the mirror. Perhaps the pathologist was right after all, she admitted with a heavy sigh. This was no profession for a young woman. She had her whole life ahead of her, didn't she?

CHAPTER 16

At dawn the following day, the UN convoy arrived at their hotel, blue flags fluttering, to escort the WHO team far beyond the organised bustle of the city to visit the village where isolated human cases of a mystery virus had been reported.

Two open-top United Nations armoured trucks carried an entire company of more than thirty uniformed soldiers sat facing each other, rifles between their knees. JP explained their role was to ensure the scientists and medics were allowed to collect samples from volunteers, unhindered by the somewhat ambivalent tribal elders. After days of sentry duty, a field trip outside the city appeared most welcome for the young soldiers.

The vehicle convoy weaved its way through endless slums on the outskirts of town, ramshackle corrugated lean-tos, green disaster-relief tents housing hundreds of refugees. The stench from the hastily dug latrines that ran along the roadside was overpowering, taking raw effluent towards the river. A dense cloud of flies and insects swarmed around piles of black garbage sacks, and two emaciated dogs fought over rotting scraps. Alice noticed the carcass of some colossal beast, possibly a cow, almost unrecognisable, its skeleton picked clean.

"I hear you had a nasty scare yesterday," said Littlejohn, leaning in so he could make himself heard over the noisy diesel engine.

"Please don't tell the professor, Ben, he'd only worry."

"Don't worry. It's happened to all of us. That's why we work in pairs at Porton. We watch out for each other."

"It won't happen again."

"I told you it was dangerous in the Congo," said JP with a smile. Alice hadn't realised he was listening. "My grandmother used to say, 'be ready for surprises and you will not be surprised'."

Alice smiled. "I like that."

"A single lapse of concentration is all it takes."

"What could a man like you possibly have to fear?" asked Alice, half-mocking the ever confident Frenchman.

"No one who values their life gets used to working here."

"You surprise me," joked Alice.

"Trust me. You only have to take your eyes off the road for a second. I've seen cars disappear into a sink hole, drive off the road, over a precipice even. If you fall down a ravine here in the Congo, you're never seen again. So yes, that's what I have nightmares about," said JP.

He gestured towards the dark clouds gathering above them. As if on cue, after two days of settled dry weather, the heavens opened. The dirt road baked hard in the sun was quickly transformed into a raging torrent of muddy water cascading across the road, creating deep gullies and grooves to catch out the unwary. The convoy's progress slowed to a crawl. On the road ahead, an entire section had been washed away, leaving a waterfall crashing down into the forest below.

Alice assumed they would have to abandon the trip and turn back but, just as quickly, the rain slackened and the clouds parted once more to make way for bright sunshine. The humidity became unbearable. Alice soaked her headscarf in water from her flask, as recommended by her guidebook, but it made little difference. She checked herself in a vanity mirror and decided she liked the new look, even though humidity was playing havoc with her normally straight hair, now covered once more by the headscarf.

After some debate, the lead vehicle, an open-top Land Rover, navigated to the extreme left-hand side of the road, furthest from the drop, bumping and sliding, fighting for traction before safely navigating what remained of the narrow track.

Alice's driver appeared less confident, mumbling something under his breath, perhaps a prayer or telling himself he could do this. The wheels slipped in the slick of mud, fighting for grip, with their heavy load of medicine and supplies. Despite the driver's best efforts, revving the overheating engine, he finally shifted into neutral, admitting defeat. It appeared they were stuck fast in a gully.

JP ordered the passengers out and after much shouting in French, a squad of soldiers surrounded the rear axle, putting their backs into rocking the truck backwards and forwards. The driver shouted for them to stop as Philippe, their guide, reappeared carrying several tree branches, freshly cut with his machete, and placed them beneath the back wheels to provide extra purchase. The assembled group redoubled their efforts until the tracked tyres gripped and, much to everyone's relief, the truck roared free.

Just as suddenly as the rain had arrived, within a couple of hours, all traces of the downpour had disappeared, completely evaporated in the oppressive heat. All that remained was a viscous mud layered with a thin crust. Fearing another scare, the convoy proceeded at walking pace until they were on the far side of the hill.

Rounding a blind corner, the driver jammed on his brakes to

avoid ramming the stationary truck in front. Alice couldn't immediately tell why they had stopped until she heard the commotion from the lead vehicle.

"Wait here," shouted JP, jumping down and unclipping the strap securing the Glock sidearm in the holster on his hip.

The other two French security specialists followed, quietly taking up defensive positions. One shielded behind the open passenger door, the other kept his semi-automatic long-barrelled weapon hidden behind the bonnet of the UN truck. Alice craned her head out of the window to see what was happening.

Two jeeps blocked the road. Four uniformed militia trained their weapons on JP and Philippe, as they moved purposefully towards the blockade, hands raised, nervously watching the tree line for movement. She could hear Philippe talking to the militia, perhaps explaining how they were delivering medicine to the surrounding villages, that they had no interest in any territorial dispute with government forces. He pointed to the United Nations flags. They were here to save lives. The militia commander's eyes lingered on the two squads of United Nations soldiers looking on from the trucks, ready to disembark at a moment's notice. The commander barked an order at his men who jumped into each of the jeeps and reversed them clear.

"Who were they?" asked Alice as JP climbed back in.

"They weren't local, that's for sure. Anti-government rebels, probably. I think I heard Philippe say the uniforms were Rwandan."

"This far from the border?"

"The ambassador received a report this morning saying thousands of soldiers were marching east," admitted JP. "They plan to overthrow Kabila."

"What does that mean for our expedition?" asked Littlejohn.

"I'm not sure. But if they march on Kinshasa, Kisangani is

right in their path. The ambassador said there were reports of an attack against UN peacekeepers," said JP.

"Yeah, but it's a long way east of here," said Alice. "Why would they attack the UN?"

"Memories live long here." JP sighed. "Local people still distrust Westerners at the best of times. Claim the UN is some occupying force. That's just the way it is, not just here, but most of Central Africa. They maintain that European settlers stole their country's riches. Who's to say the UN will be any different from the last lot who invaded their country."

After almost thirty minutes of rapid progress the convoy slowed once more as they attempted to navigate a fallen tree, bumping along rutted tracks carved through dense jungle, branches that seemed to reach down to caress the side of their vehicle as they passed. Eventually the forest of trees and foliage abruptly ended, giving way to farmland and scrub.

A half-naked herder stepped into the road, forcing the driver to jam on his brakes. The herder barely looked up, driving his pigs towards an enclosure on the far side of the road where a farm hand in tall leather boots was shovelling stinking slop into shallow steel troughs for the animals to eat. From the stench it was most likely waste from the local village but the pigs didn't seem to mind, jostling for position, their bulging bellies packed into narrow pens with a corrugated iron roof.

The lead Land Rover came to a halt near a cluster of wooden huts where a gaggle of villagers stopped and stared, shoulders slumped, thin and emaciated. The trucks' diesel engines fell silent. Philippe invited the WHO scientists to unload their equipment, beckoning Alice towards the nearest of the village huts.

Inside, the occupants had crudely divided the dirt floor between a living area where bare mattresses covered one end. Pots and pans were set upon a smoking fire ringed with stones.

Damp clothing drying in piles and peeled vegetables floating in a bucket of water. From a darkened corner, a sow and three piglets kept at bay by a horizontal wire snorted their excitement at the visitors. On the far side of the enclosure came the raucous clucking from a henhouse.

Seeing how the villagers lived cheek by jowl with their farm animals, it was easy for Alice to understand how disease might jump between species. With the permission of the homeowner, she snapped some pictures for her records on a portable SLR camera, hoping the dim light was sufficient for her purpose.

She had seen the same unsanitary living arrangements in the high-rise slums of Hong Kong. The professor had called humans co-habiting with farm animals like this a "genetic soup". She smiled at the choice of words. Conditions such as these, where contaminated droppings from birds were fed to the pigs, would inevitably give rise to cross-species spillover. Virus mutation was as certain here as night follows day. Depending on Mother Nature's whim, the resulting strain could easily incubate in pigs before jumping to humans when circumstances allowed.

Alice asked several questions of the farmer, waiting for Philippe to translate, her pencil poised to take notes in her pocketbook.

Continuing on their tour of the village, they arrived at what appeared to be a nineteenth-century Belgian church. In the steeple's shadow was a makeshift orphanage with whitewashed concrete walls. Villagers had come from miles around to queue for the chance to be seen by a visiting doctor from the hospital. Philippe introduced Alice to a volunteer, a French nun named Sister Francine who was administering jab after jab of vaccine. Alice noted that after each patient the sister dipped the needle in a jar of disinfectant. Reusing needles was unheard of in the West and yet there was no alternative here in the Congo.

"Salut," said Francine with a smile, inclining her head,

barely pausing in her vaccinations to acknowledge the visiting doctors.

"We've brought you the supplies you asked for," added Philippe, gesturing towards several medical crates the soldiers were unloading.

"Philippe, I'd marry you if I could."

"If you hadn't taken a vow of celibacy," Philippe joked. "Is there anything else you need while we're here?" he asked, noticing how many people were waiting to be seen.

"I'll take all the needles you can spare. Also, syringes, bandages, painkillers. All medical supplies are welcome here," Sister Francine added for Alice's benefit.

"So many have come," observed Alice.

"We are the front line. We do what we can. Preventative medicine, mostly."

"Have you seen any patients with unusual symptoms in the last few days?" asked Alice.

"Unusual in what sense?"

"Fever, coughing, sore throat, vomiting, diarrhoea."

"You mean seasonal flu?"

"We think it could be more serious than that."

"Should we be worried?"

"That's what we're here to find out. Where would you say most of the patients are coming from?"

"I treated several children from the next village further east of here earlier today." Sister Francine leaned closer. "You don't think this is a new *épidémie*, do you?"

"We don't know."

"I try to reassure them as best I can."

"Look, if we find anything out, you'll be the first to hear."

"We should move on," said JP, noticing the crowd of children gathered at the door to the orphanage, pointing and staring at Alice as she spoke with the sister.

"Why do the children stare so?"

"They say you're a princess," explained the nun, much to Alice's amusement. "They've never seen a woman with blonde hair before."

Alice smiled awkwardly and waved at the children who giggled and waved back. "Why are there no men in this village?" she asked, noticing only children, women and tribal elders.

"Once the boys become teenagers, they go and fight in the youth brigades. Vigilantes mostly, raiding other villages, setting fire to properties, driving families from their homes. It's a massive problem."

JP encouraged the scientists back to their vehicles so the convoy could continue on to the next village where the visiting doctor from the hospital had identified the first case earlier in the week. Alice knew from bitter experience that where there was one case there were dozens more without symptoms. She swallowed hard, marshalling her thoughts. She felt a curious mix of excitement and dread at what she might find. Being in the right place at the right time could change the course of her entire career. Everything that had gone before, all those years of study, to prepare her for this very moment. Alice had never felt more alive.

CHAPTER 17

As they drove into the next village, some three miles east, it was immediately clear that the initial reports of so-called "isolated cases" were hopelessly out of date. The village was a ghost town. Normally busy communal areas appeared deserted. Upon the instructions of Leclerc, the WHO expedition leader, the entire medical team suited up as a precaution before exploring the village.

They were immediately grateful for that decision. In the chicken coop between the villagers' huts, a sickly bird pecked distractedly at its food. Without warning, it fell on its side and lapsed into spasm. Alice stepped over the low wire and gingerly approached its still twitching body. The bird's wattle had turned pitch black and a viscous liquid dribbled from the beak. Beyond the coop she noticed more carcasses, dead chickens piled three feet high, against the wall of the hut.

"Right," said Alice, recognising the symptoms of an avian flu outbreak when she saw it. She had witnessed first-hand similar sickly birds in Hong Kong. "We're going to need to isolate these villagers immediately," she whispered, keeping her voice steady, trying to marshal her fear.

The soldiers set to work banging on the doors of the nearest dwellings, but received no answer. A cross was chalked in the wood of one door, perhaps a warning to others not to enter. The commanding officer gave the order to force entry, before stepping aside to allow the scientists to do their jobs.

Inside, the stench of decomposition hung in the air. A scene of pitiful suffering. Blood stained the straw mats stretched across the earthen floor. Laid out in the corner were five bodies, two adult males, two females and an adolescent girl. A few feet away, slumped against the mud wall of the hut, was a prepubescent boy, eyes bloodshot, blood streaming from his nostrils, his emaciated body wracked by coughing.

They carried the boy to a deserted school house designated as a temporary treatment centre to care for those still alive. The boy was no older than twelve, his bare chest heaving, as if the effort of breathing required every ounce of strength. During a moment of lucidity, he confirmed that both of his parents were dead. The others in the hut were his uncle and aunt. His other brother and two sisters were missing. Perhaps they had got out while they still could.

Listening to his laboured breathing through a stethoscope, Alice's room-mate, Maxine, one of the French doctors, confirmed the boy's lungs were filled with what she said was fluid consistent with cases she had read about in other local autopsies. Within barely forty-five minutes of monitoring him, his condition deteriorated. His face and hands turned a bluish colour, which Alice knew was consistent with acute respiratory distress where patients literally gasp for oxygen.

Alice had seen this condition before. Patients in Hong Kong suffering from severe cases of influenza. The difference being, here in the Congo, they had none of the equipment to ease the patients' suffering, nor ventilators to assist their breathing. Alice set to work examining the boy, discovering reddish marks and bruising across his abdomen. His belly appeared distended, like the marmoset monkeys back at the testing centre. There were lesions on his back, several of which were oozing liquid. His boyish skin appeared to sag as blood and fluid filled the space beneath its surface.

Alice opened her rucksack and removed a sampling kit, drawing blood from a lesion and repeating the process from two other patients laid out on the floor. She packed the test tubes in a plastic case and made each person as comfortable as she could with their limited supplies. The victims were too poorly to manage much more than a muted response.

Returning to the boy, she noticed the terror in his eyes for the first time. For most of the examination, he had remained brave and lucid, eyes expressive, imploring Alice to make the pain go away. The next time she checked on him, he was noticeably less responsive, staring up at the ceiling, pupils dilated, perhaps lost in private suffering. Forty-five minutes later his entire body began to convulse. After that, nothing more could be done for him. Death came quickly. According to one of the village elders watching nearby, in less than fourteen hours the boy had succumbed to the virus.

By the time the UN soldiers had rounded up all the remaining survivors, there were four adults and twenty-two children rescued alive from the village. They found some of the younger kids clinging to their parents' lifeless bodies, refusing to leave their sides. An infant sat half-naked in the semi-darkness of a hut, shivering despite the unrelenting heat outside.

As for the bodies of the deceased, they advised the soldiers not to handle the infected without proper protective equipment. A clean-up crew would return another day, their commander insisted. Alice could only imagine what the heat would do to their already decomposing bodies.

"If the animals don't get to them first," admitted Littlejohn.

"Or the rebels," added Philippe, numbed by these scenes of horror.

"Why would rebels interfere with their bodies?" asked Alice.

"For their clothes, for their jewellery. We often find bodies mutilated," said Philippe.

"Dear God," whispered Alice.

"Some tribes still practise cannibalism." Alice couldn't be sure whether or not Philippe was joking. It seemed a strange time for humour. "I'm told human flesh is like pork, unequalled in flavour and texture."

"Gross," replied Alice.

"Really? In Europe, you think nothing of eating white meat. Sometimes we find human bones picked clean. Used for decoration," added Philippe, who seemed fascinated by the macabre.

JP laughed at such tales of cannibalism. "Philippe, these are stories to frighten tourists. Nothing more."

Philippe shrugged his shoulders. "I'm only telling you the truth. We should leave a squad of soldiers overnight to keep watch over the village."

"Agreed," confirmed JP. "There will be no stealing from the dead tonight."

"May God punish them if they try," said Philippe, shaking his head. The outbreak alone was sufficient cause for concern without the threat of rebels mutilating victims' bodies.

"We'll need to quarantine the entire village," insisted Alice. "Stop anyone else from leaving."

"We both know it's too late for quarantine, Alice," challenged Littlejohn. "You saw for yourself, there were people from this village where we've just come from. Sister Francine said so herself."

Alice knew Littlejohn was right. How on earth were they meant to contain this virus if they couldn't stop villagers from leaving? She wished the professor was here. He would know what to do. The WHO team's worst fears risked being realised. If the virus was allowed to take hold, it would take a miracle to prevent wider spread. If that happened, all they could hope to do was to contain the outbreak and pick up the pieces afterwards. First, they needed to get the samples back to the lab as soon as possible to see what they were dealing with.

CHAPTER 18

Back at the field office in the suburb of Kisangani, Alice shuffled through recently developed photos of dead chickens and ducks. Their wattles had turned green and black, almost unrecognisable from the farmyard animals she had grown up with back in England. She referred to the handwritten notes in her contact report, together with her colleague Maxine's interviews with victims' surviving family members, searching for any clues.

Slowly but surely, she built a picture from the fragmentary inputs, listing the missing pieces and questions as they arose. Had there been any visitors to the village in the last few days? Who had fallen victim first? She grimaced at the unnatural image of treacle-like saliva coating one bird's beak. Post-mortems of their carcasses had revealed multiple blood clots and deformed eggs with no shells.

In all but one of the recorded cases in the affected village, victims had been in direct contact with live chickens, either on farms or in marketplaces in the days preceding the initial onset of symptoms. There was no indication that human-to-human transmission had taken place. That was the good news.

The WHO research centre in Geneva had already been in contact to request samples be sent to them for further analysis. They had placed an entire team of specialists on standby pending the arrival of the samples. The professor instructed Alice's team to work through the night to complete further autopsies. They would need to prepare tissue samples, double-bagged and sprayed with a toxic bleach to kill any external traces of virus, before sealing them in a biohazard airtight shipping container to be picked up later that day.

"I need to get these samples express shipped to the WHO centre in Geneva. And this one goes to the Centers for Disease Control and Prevention in Atlanta," instructed Alice.

"You want me to FedEx them overseas?" asked her Congolese assistant in disbelief.

"It's perfectly safe. I've done it dozens of times. Standard operating procedure."

There was a knock on the door and the centre receptionist appeared. "Sorry to interrupt, Doctor Bishop, but the professor is asking to see you."

She found O'Leary in his office, reading her preliminary field report.

"Talk to me, Alice. What am I looking at?"

"We won't know for sure until tomorrow at the earliest."

"What's your gut telling you?"

Alice blew out her cheeks. "Initially, I assumed it was bird flu, but now I'm not sure."

"Why would you doubt the facts?"

"Have you seen the photos?"

"Some of them."

"I've never seen anything like it," said Alice, shaking her head. "It's no wonder this thing is spreading. Multi-generational families living in huts in close proximity with birds and pigs."

"Just like we saw in Asia."

"It's a real—"

"Genetic soup?" he interrupted, anticipating her response with a laugh. "A living arrangement irresistible to novel viruses."

"Except, this Congo variant kills much faster."

"I doubt the virus is doing this level of damage. It has to be an immune response; the body overreacting, encountering this virus for the first time."

"We can't be sure."

"You said so yourself. The healthier the patient, the more likely they are to die. That suggests a cytokine storm. Reminds me of our old friend Ebola."

"Except this thing is more contagious."

"We need to know the vector, Alice. How is this spreading so fast?"

"Doctor Littlejohn is working on that now."

"I saw your report. Multiple eye witnesses described a recent plague of rats scavenging for food, driven out of the forest by something. What's your hypothesis?"

"It can't be rats. The distances involved are too large. Birds seem the most logical vector."

"Remember what we saw in Hong Kong? Human and avian viruses combining, exchanging genetic material. Viruses jumping from bird to pig and pig to human."

"And back again."

"The normal barriers between species had collapsed. Pigs were the common link."

"But Professor, we tested the pigs. There was no trace of infection."

"They're likely immune to the virus. An incubator, like we discussed."

"But the range of symptoms is still too broad. There must be something else we're missing."

"Have you considered bats as the vector?"

"We looked at the historical data. I traced most bat-related infections to cave visits themselves. They don't explain the scale of the current outbreak."

"Okay, but we know bats host several viruses capable of infecting humans. And there are several cave systems and disused mines near Kisangani housing vast bat colonies. Tens of thousands of them. The same was true of regions in China we looked at prone to new strains of viruses."

"Yes, I remember."

"You said yourself, local bat populations are in decline from the growing use of pesticides."

"That's right. Human activity continues to disrupt bats' natural habitats and impact biodiversity. But, again, bats alone don't explain the range of case data we're seeing."

"I'm not suggesting bats are solely to blame. There are undoubtedly multiple factors at play here. But are you not intrigued by the bats' role?"

"I'm certainly not dismissing your bat theory, but cases of direct contact are a tiny minority."

"Infected bat meat, then?"

"Excuse me?"

"Villagers round here eat bat meat."

"People eat bats?" Alice found the thought repulsive.

"You're kidding? You really think starving people would balk at eating bats? Remember, we saw the same in Hong Kong and China. I'm told bat meat is a local delicacy."

"What does Littlejohn say?"

"I'm speaking to him next."

Alice nodded, wondering why the professor saw fit to keep the meetings separate. "So what happens now?" she asked.

"Oh, the WHO has detailed protocols for situations like this. Leclerc will ask Beaumont to declare a state of emergency. They'll send additional resources; the military will secure the area; the affected villages will be placed under quarantine; strict lockdowns will follow; no one in or out. We contain it and move on."

"And if that doesn't work?"

"The WHO has protocols for everything. Right up to stage five."

"Stage five?"

"Trust me, it won't come to that." Alice would not take no for an answer and stood, hands on hips, waiting for O'Leary to explain. "Typically, if civilian organisations lose control, the military has a whole range of measures, depending on the severity of the situation. They have tactical teams trained to eliminate infection."

"What could they possibly do that we can't?"

"Alice, you don't want to know."

"Tell me."

"Worst-case scenario, they sanitise the entire area. Wipe out all traces of the virus."

"How?"

The professor shrugged his shoulders. "A tactical nuke is a last resort."

"You are joking."

The professor was giving nothing away. "Like I said, these are tactics of last resort, Alice. They expect collateral damage."

"You can't be serious?"

"I told you. The military has a plan for every eventuality."

Alice remained convinced this was some elaborate practical joke designed to make her look foolish, and if she was right it was bad timing on the professor's part.

"But, Alice, this stays between us."

"Of course."

"Now you know what we're up against. You're on the clock now. We've got to get ahead of this thing."

"I'll do my best."

"There's a team heading to the hospital first thing tomorrow. I want you to brief Thierry. Let his team know the symptoms to watch out for so they can isolate patients as quickly as possible when they present. And Alice, don't take any chances. Wear the suit. I don't want anything to happen to you."

CHAPTER 19

The line of vehicles queuing to reach Kisangani's main hospital stretched all the way back to the main road through town, car horns blaring in the sweltering midday heat. The commotion reached Alice and the WHO team long before they rounded the corner in sight of the main building. The Racal suits they wore made the temperature unbearable.

An animated throng of humanity gathered at the front entrance, waiting impatiently for news of loved ones. The armoured truck at the head of the convoy forced its way through the crowd, its driver leaning on the horn. Once the locals noticed the WHO team in their bright orange space suits, people stepped aside, staring open-mouthed in a mix of curiosity and fear.

Inside the grounds of the hospital, it was even worse than Alice had expected. Porters stretchered newly arrived patients to wherever there was shade, left propped against the wall, or covered by a blanket in the dirt. The victim nearest Alice was bent double, wracked by a fit of coughing she seemed unable to stop. No more than twenty years old, the young woman wiped a languid hand across her thighs, smearing blood on the grubby fabric of a floral dress. The persistent cough echoed by others nearby who joined the noisy chorus.

Beyond the chaotic reception area, each doorway and corridor revealed similar scenes. “S’il vous plaît,” shouted a nurse in uniform, a strained tension in her voice as she fought to get past, bustling from patient to patient, checking each for the telltale signs of infection. Alice pressed against the corridor walls to let the nurses pass, seemingly invisible to the preoccupied staff, like visitors from another planet in their suits.

Further down the hall, brow-beaten orderlies attempted to lever an unresponsive figure on to a gurney to be carted away. The swing doors provided a glimpse of an open-sided disaster-relief tent in military green pitched at the back of the hospital in the car park, away from prying eyes. Alice assumed they were using the tent as an overflow ward.

Alice and the WHO team battled their way towards the hospital administration wing, squeezing between beds and recumbent bodies. As they brushed past a deceased victim covered with a stained sheet, Alice’s medical bag caught the fabric, exposing a discoloured head and shoulders, a limp arm, and a leg woven with varicose veins snaking towards the foot. Alice bent to have a closer look, prodding the wrinkled skin of the left arm with a gloved finger. There was little or no muscle tone at all, no skin tension, almost as if the tissue and muscle had liquified, leaving just a bag of bones.

She checked the patient’s chart at the foot of the bed, puzzling at the time of death. The scribbled notes from a doctor confirmed the patient had died within the hour. The speed of decomposition terrified Alice. No virus worked this fast. She dismissed the information as a clerical error. Mistakes happened, especially under this kind of unrelenting pressure.

They forced their way into the staffroom still searching for

Thierry. Despite the supposedly airtight protection offered by her suit, Alice noticed an overpowering stench of rotting fish.

"What is that smell?"

The nurse wore a gauze mask and mocked Alice for her squeamishness, noticing her wrinkled nose. "We call it juji." She grabbed a small bag hanging from a hook near the door and handed it to Alice.

"Juji?" Alice repeated, as she studied the sack, which appeared to contain the offending putrid concoction. "What in God's name is it?"

"Fish guts. We use it to ward off evil spirits."

"Interesting. Does it work?" Alice asked, humouring the nurse.

"Well, it certainly helps people keep their distance, if nothing else."

"No kidding." Alice laughed at the gallows humour.

"You find juji in other African countries," added Maxine. "They just call it something else. Asafoetida, I think."

"Well, it stinks, that's for sure." Alice handed back the sack of rotting fish for the nurse to hang on its hook.

The nurse led them to the wooden door emblazoned with the sign "Chef du Service Médical", knocking curtly before entering.

Inside, Thierry Deschamps, the white-haired head of the medical faculty, stared blankly out of the window, his face ashen, as if in a state of shock at the scenes unfolding at his beloved hospital.

"These people are from the World Health Organization," the nurse announced.

He nodded solemnly, without turning to greet Alice and Littlejohn. "Thank you for coming so quickly. Do you know what we're dealing with yet?" he asked in a childlike voice, staring off into the distance, visibly shaken to the core by the scale of the outbreak sweeping over his normally quiet hospital. "So many have c-come," he stuttered, surveying the number of patients covering every available inch of the hospital grounds.

"This is just the beginning, Thierry. There are many more to come."

"What should I do?"

"You need to close the hospital immediately," said Alice.

He nodded, barely registering the seismic consequences this decision would entail for the surrounding communities.

"The minister will need to issue a stay-at-home order. Full quarantine protocols."

He gestured to his assistant to do as instructed. "Do we know how it's spreading?"

"Not yet. We're still waiting for the test results."

Thierry seemed to stir from his reverie. "What else do you need from me?"

"Doctor Littlejohn will need full access to patient records."

He nodded. "Of course. Nurse, can you show him where to find them?"

"Bien sûr."

"In the meantime, I'd like to talk to the doctors and nurses treating the victims," said Alice.

"I'll take you," replied the nurse.

In the children's wing, there was barely room to stand, all available floor space filled with newborn infants wriggling in their blankets, faces puce, eyes screwed shut, bawling for their mothers. Toddlers and the very young in the next ward, separated from their parents, sobbed into their blankets. In most cases, all available beds and mattresses contained not just one wriggling form but two, grey sheets thrown back in the heat.

Ward after hospital ward resembled successive visions of hell. The coughing, the fug of human decay, the abject suffering. What struck Alice most was how young many of the patients were. Consistent with her preliminary findings, most were adolescents in the prime of life. Sometimes, pneumonia was reported to have choked the lungs. Nurses recorded patients literally drowning, gasping for breath. A fever had struck down what should have been the healthiest, the very fittest members of society. If Alice and the WHO team were unable to come up with answers quickly, things could get worse, much worse. Where was the professor when she needed him?

The nurse led Alice and Maxine to the bedside of a feverish patient, a woman in her early twenties, forehead bathed in sweat, eyes flicking around the room, struggling to focus on the doctors in their space suits. Dried tracks of blood from a recent nosebleed were smeared around her mouth, across her chin, though she didn't appear to notice. Alice struggled to remain professional, fighting back her own tears. Detachment did not come naturally to Alice, particularly when observing first-hand a patient's tentative grip on life. There could be no words of comfort for the victims. The nurse grasped the patient's hand, ignoring the advice of the WHO doctors, whispering soothing words in Lingala. It was already too late for this one. The group moved on.

Inside her helmet, Alice let out a low sob, unable to wipe away the tears cascading down her cheeks. The nurse squeezed Alice's arm, noticing her distress.

"Doctor, they're watching us," she implored. "We must be strong. Your presence reassures the patients. We are their last hope." Alice nodded, struggling to master her emotions.

The nurse led them outside to a temporary mortuary where orderlies delivered another body as they watched. They had already given up laying the deceased side by side, instead stacking them where space allowed, despite the protests of the families watching through the fence.

They returned inside, continuing on to the next hospital

wing. Alice had asked to see the most recent patients, those being triaged by overworked nurses. Alice watched as the staff went about their duties, moving from patient to patient, asking them about their symptoms in French.

"What did he say?"

"That the lining of his lungs feels like it has been ripped out," said the nurse. "This one says he has the worst migraine ever. His wife said he is quiet now but two hours ago he was feverish, shouting names as if possessed by the Devil himself."

The patient began to cough, blood streaming from his nose as he began to haemorrhage. Alice asked the nurse to lift the patient's arms, revealing dark swellings as if filled with blood. The pustules reminded Alice of the bubonic plague, medieval in nature. Further investigation revealed blotches on the thighs and arms, like a victim of the Black Death. The patient's abdomen and chest were discoloured, the belly appeared distended, as if inflated like a balloon, and his fingers and toenails were blackened. If Alice didn't know better, she might have said the body was already beginning to decompose before the patient had even died.

They moved on to the next patient, who the nurses had seen fit to physically restrain, hands and feet tied to the bedposts, as he presented a potential danger to themselves and to others. The nurse explained that some patients had already taken matters into their own hands, realising what was coming. Others had refused treatment, preferring to accelerate the process. Suicides were not uncommon, the nurse explained.

Afterwards, Alice would struggle to reimagine these scenes if she hadn't seen them for herself. Nurses and doctors wearing the most basic of protection trudging between tightly packed rows of beds, each containing a patient, their chests heaving, gasping for breath, a brittle rasping or crackling sound emanating from clogged airways. A cleaner with a bucket and mop busied himself between beds, clearing up the mess, engaged in an endless Sisyphean task. The linoleum floor of the makeshift ward had become slick with bodily fluids. No amount of disinfectant could mask the stench.

A low moan filled the air as another victim gave voice to their private anguish. Occasionally, one would scream or shout out but most lacked the breath to articulate their private pain. Fortunately, for many, the suffering did not last long. The stretcher bearers were fully deployed in tagging bodies and carrying them outside to make way for new arrivals. The surviving families of victims had taken to pressing themselves against the fence separating the car park, watching in tears as the chaotic scenes unfolded, despite the protests of staff.

"Have you ever seen anything like this before? Regardez," implored the nurse, pointing at the cyanosis spreading over one victim's lips. In patches, their face appeared mottled to the extent that the patient's normal skin colour was no longer clear. "What causes this?"

"Cytokine storms," explained Alice. "It's an immune response where the body literally attacks itself. Once we have the test results, we'll know how to fight this."

"And until then?"

"We need to close the hospital. Send people home."

"Send them home? But this is a hospital. Where else can they go if not here?"

"Staying open will only make matters worse. We need to tell people to stay indoors and avoid contact with others."

"How could things be any worse?" asked the nurse in despair.

"Believe me, things can get much worse."

There was a commotion beyond the fence. Raised voices confirmed the arrival of another detachment of soldiers at the main entrance. The crowds were already beginning to disperse.

In a few hours, once curfew came into effect, the streets would be deserted, as soldiers enforced strict quarantine measures. At least it should keep everyone indoors. That was the only way they were going to beat this thing, to buy themselves time. Those test results could not come soon enough.

PART III

FALL OUT

CHAPTER 20

Baghdad, Iraq
4 November, 1998

Blake Harris was buying fruit and vegetables in his local Baghdad market of Bab Al Sharqi in the Al Shorja district when his trusty Motorola pager began buzzing. He snatched the black plastic communication device from the clip on his belt. The telephone number to call that flashed up on the one-inch monochrome screen was one he recognised as an emergency contact. That was a first.

Harris found the nearest payphone outside the old post office and called the number. There was a digital hook-up as the call was routed through an encrypted exchange. Brokenshire picked up immediately.

"How fast can you get to the safe house?"

"Which one?"

"Baghdad south-east."

"Rush hour traffic? Forty minutes."

"I can make that work. If you're not here by the top of the hour I'll start without you."

Start what, thought Harris. The safe house was on the other side of town, near the Iraqi military academy in Rustamiyah, six miles south-east of Sadr City. It was one of three they used on a semi-regular basis. Home from home for visiting military personnel with a secure comms station, satellite link-up and an armoury containing standard-issue semi-automatic weapons, a sniper rifle, grenades and a range of explosive ordinance. From the urgency in Brokenshire's voice, Harris could only imagine a high-value target had been brought in for questioning, someone Brokenshire needed Harris to meet.

Harris accelerated the rusting Jeep through another busy junction, jumping a red light, sending pedestrians scurrying out of his way as he sounded the horn. He made it across town in thirty-seven minutes. Brokenshire was watching out of the blast-proof windows, waiting for Harris's arrival. He hurried him inside and bolted the door behind them.

"Follow me."

They had configured the basement of the safe house as an interrogation suite, with an interview room connected to an adjoining observation area where intelligence officers could watch proceedings through a one-way mirror. Recording equipment cluttered the counter. A video monitor displayed a live black-and-white feed of a plastic chair facing the door, an Iraqi officer wearing the khaki green uniform, gold epaulettes and claret beret of a General in Saddam's Republican Guard. The officer checked his watch, no doubt eager to get back to wherever he had just come from. He stared directly at Brokenshire or where he assumed those in charge were behind the one-way mirror and tapped his watch. Harris didn't recognise the face.

"Who is he?"

"This," announced Brokenshire with a flourish, "is General

Amir Abdallah Al-Rahi. The source I've been cultivating for the last six months."

"What have you got on him?"

"An unfortunate incident he'd rather his wife knew nothing about."

The two men exchanged a mischievous grin.

"Where do you want me? In here or with you?" Harris said.

"In here. You're an observer on this one."

"What about an interpreter?" said Harris, noticing there was no one else present besides the technician.

"His English is surprisingly good."

"Let's see how long that lasts."

"Trust me, I know how to play this guy. Grab yourself a drink and enjoy the show. There's coffee in the pot. We'll get started in five."

The Iraqi general stubbed out his cigarette in a souvenir airport ashtray decorated with Saddam's face, helping himself to a glass of water from a two-litre bottle. He lit another cigarette in feigned annoyance.

Looks like he's ready to talk, thought Harris.

CHAPTER 21

Harris watched the early exchanges between Brokenshire and the Iraqi general with disinterest. In his experience, men like Al-Rahi remained tight-lipped, guarded at the best of times. They would go through the motions of betrayal without giving away anything substantial. The intelligence gathered would be treated with caution and scepticism, used for context, background, scene-setting. Brokenshire claimed such sources were important for what he called "fragmentary intelligence" in building a more detailed picture, validating what they already knew.

The general leaned back in his plastic chair with a dismissive wave of the hand. "I used to believe that the UN was this untouchable guardian of international standards. Infallible, resolute, noble." His English was even better than Brokenshire had suggested. Educated overseas, Harris imagined, perhaps his linguistic skills would fail him when the questions got harder. "After all, what they say is unquestionable. How could the UN possibly be wrong about anything?" claimed the general, his sarcasm undeniable.

"What did you expect?" responded Brokenshire, dead-eyed.

"The UN is just as fallible, biased and compromised as any other regime. Is your government really so different?"

"Then you admit that the UN inspections are a front for military intelligence?"

"That's a serious allegation, General. You're talking about *the* United Nations," challenged Brokenshire with a glint in his eye.

The general snorted in derision. "Then do you also deny that the intelligence you gather about Iraq's industrial facilities will be used as a hit list in the coming air war?"

"If Iraq complies with the UN mandate, as your government claims, there will be no grounds for war."

"Intelligence gathered in the name of peace and disarmament," Al-Rahi continued, shaking his head in disgust. "You realise the consequences of an American bombing campaign could be catastrophic?"

"Catastrophic, how?"

"By destroying our factories and research facilities, you risk an environmental disaster for the Middle East." He banged his fist on the table in a show of frustration. "And you claim we are the bad guys?" Brokenshire stared back at the general, waiting for his indignation to subside. "What the United Nations amusingly calls 'spin', we call lies."

"And Saddam wrote the book on that topic."

The general visibly reacted but did not respond, continuing with his diatribe against the allies. "Once again, history will be rewritten." He clicked his fingers. "Past failures will be forgotten."

"Only if you believe Iraq is the victim not the aggressor."

"Do not mock me, Sir. We both know winning and losing are irrelevant to Saddam. This all plays well for him."

Harris was beginning to like this guy. He was a match for Brokenshire, at least.

"Saddam has a chance to avoid war. There's still time."

Al-Rahi stared at Brokenshire, perhaps wanting to believe that outcome was still possible. "We both know Saddam will never back down. Every time he stands up to Bush's threats, his support in the Middle East grows. To other countries, Saddam is a hero."

It was Brokenshire's turn to mock. "A hero?"

"We all believe what we want to believe," admitted Al-Rahi.

"Perhaps. But whenever we place too much blind trust in our leaders, our faith is destroyed, little by little, no?"

"We are all more malleable than we give ourselves credit."

"Malleable, yes. Capable of credulity, naivety? Trust me, in my experience, it doesn't take much to burst the bubble," countered Brokenshire.

"We have all been deceived by our governments' lies."

"You and I, we are both patriots. I love my country. You love yours."

Al-Rahi took another long pull on his American cigarette and directed the plume of smoke towards his inquisitor, legs crossed. He appeared to be enjoying their exchanges. "All I ever wanted was to keep my country safe from its enemies."

"What patriot wouldn't?"

"But my first loyalty is to science."

"Of course. My mistake," corrected Brokenshire with a wry smile.

"The last few years have been much harder than you can imagine. Sanctions starved us of contact with our counterparts in the West. We were left isolated, under-funded, marginalised."

"Until the Haboob Project?" challenged Brokenshire.

Haboob Project, thought Harris. Now we're getting somewhere. In Arabic, haboob referred to an intense dust storm that blinds and incapacitates anyone unlucky enough to be caught in its path.

"When one's country faces the threat of invasion, annihilation even, it is amazing what can be achieved in a short period. Innovation on an unimaginable scale."

"Compared to what? You said yourself Iraq was isolated."

"Experiments that only a handful of scientists in the world could comprehend. Haboob gave us a new purpose."

"Or were those more lies to massage Iraqi egos and boost productivity?" challenged Brokenshire.

"Is it so hard to acknowledge that Iraq is a world leader?"

"It's hard to know. So little is known about Haboob."

Here it comes, thought Harris.

"Our intent was to explore the limits of possibility. A breakthrough that might inspire the world and give us an overwhelming advantage over the West, a deterrent to stop the American troops crossing the border again."

"And you never doubted you were doing the right thing?"

"You misunderstand," said Al-Rahi. "Our job as scientists is not to dwell on morality. Whether an experiment should or shouldn't be undertaken. That is for politicians to decide."

Why is he making so many excuses, thought Harris, unless there is underlying regret? Al-Rahi had a conscience. Perhaps that was the general's weakness, one Brokenshire aimed to exploit.

"Did you never stop to think about whether these programmes would actually increase the risk of war?" asked Brokenshire.

The general smiled at the suggestion. "Did your scientists in the West? Of course not. Iraq was hardly the first to develop such weapons. We simply took what already existed and made it better."

"Better or deadlier?"

"Is there a difference? If my team had not taken this on, Saddam would have found someone else."

"So what was the focus of Haboob?"

The general lit another cigarette, staring at Brokenshire through the plume of smoke. Cold and calculating. "To develop a deterrent that would be impossible to detect, let alone stop."

"Deadlier than nuclear?"

Al-Rahi laughed dismissively. "We gave up on nuclear years ago. Much too expensive. Too easy to detect. No, we were tasked with creating a deterrent greater than any man-made army."

"Chemical then?" asked Brokenshire, playing along, although he already knew the answer.

"Again, chemical weapons were much too hard to hide from your inspectors."

"Then what? Biological?" He loaded the question with a delicate balance of wonder and curiosity. There was no judgement.

"A triumph of imagination. A scientific programme the West could only dream of with all your rules and regulations," the general boasted.

"Is that how you see your counterparts in the West? Tied up in red tape?" Brokenshire shook his head at this Iraqi propaganda. "Once you're force-fed enough lies, the truth becomes lost."

The general grinned, revealing tobacco-stained, yellowing teeth. "You think destroying our laboratories will stop us?"

"Don't you?"

"Scientific progress cannot be undone. One cannot unlearn what one already knows."

"I seem to remember the Iranians saying something similar about their nuclear ambitions."

"Haboob is different," the general said, scoffing at the idea. "You can destroy our physical infrastructure, but you'll never disrupt our programme."

"Is that how you see your Haboob programme? As inevitable?"

Al-Rahi ran his hand over the table and collected some dust, which he allowed to fall from the palm of his hand. "Did you know it only takes a few grams of a biological agent to kill every human being on the planet?"

"Perhaps, but if it was that easy to weaponise, don't you think every terrorist on earth would have tried?"

Good, thought Harris. He wants so desperately to tell the world about his team's achievements. The secrecy is killing him. The general's flaw is pride. With a little encouragement, he can't help himself.

"The terrorist group, Aum Shinrikyo, proved what was possible in the Tokyo subway. Had they substituted sarin for, say, anthrax, the death toll would have been catastrophic."

"Then perhaps you weren't told the truth. The attack was a failure."

"You call five thousand injured a failure?"

"Thirteen people died," dismissed Brokenshire. "Aum Shinrikyo was shut down. All its members rounded up and locked away."

"By comparison to Haboob, Aum Shinrikyo's methods were primitive."

"Then your leadership supports terrorism?"

The general stiffened, eyes narrowed, spotting the trap.

"Of course not. The use of weapons of mass destruction can never be justified against civilian targets."

"Nor can the mass production of anthrax or any other biological weapon."

"Necessity is the mother of invention."

"Meaning what?"

"The threat of American bombs required a response. You think your countries alone should have the right to maintain a deterrent?"

"A deterrent we have committed never to use."

"And there lies the contradiction."

Harris was enjoying the back and forth. Did Brokenshire really think he could manipulate an educated, high-ranking Iraqi officer, close to Saddam?

"General, I congratulate you," conceded Brokenshire, with feigned resignation. "There's no question. You and your team have achieved scientific breakthroughs we in the West never thought you capable of."

Another backhanded compliment, thought Harris. The general inclined his head, accepting the praise at face value.

"Who knows what else would have been possible had Saddam granted the additional help you requested?"

The general's brow furrowed, his pride wounded by Brokenshire's assertion that the programme was somehow impaired.

"We've catalogued countless items of Russian laboratory equipment shipped to Iraq and installed in your facilities."

"Equipment bought, legally, on the open market."

Brokenshire smiled, pleased with the trap he had set. "There's no point denying it." The general feigned ignorance. "Your old boss was most helpful in filling in the gaps in our understanding."

Kamel al-Majid. The man with two humps, thought Harris, smiling. Former Minister for Oil. Married to one of Saddam's daughters. Defected 1995. Killed upon his return to Iraq in 1996.

"Kamel was a fool. A patsy. He had no detailed knowledge of Haboob."

"What about your new boss, Rihab Taha?"

"You best ask her yourself," said the general, crossing his arms.

"Oh, I intend to."

"Why does the West continue to underestimate Iraq?"

"On the contrary, our teams are scouring the country as we

speak. We intend to keep on searching until we find what we're looking for."

"You'll never find Haboob."

"Everything can be found. Eventually."

"Not by your hapless inspectors. And not when there is nothing left to find." The general corrected himself. The inconsistency would not have escaped Brokenshire. "Our programme has already served its purpose."

Harris knew the general was right. The truth was perhaps more terrifying than anyone realised. They could repurpose the industrial facilities he had seen with his own eyes towards weapons production in a matter of weeks, even days. Much of the equipment he had seen was on wheels, ready to be reconfigured.

"Interview terminated," said Brokenshire, checking his watch. "I'll ask the driver to take you back to your car."

It was clear, to Harris at least, the general would never tell them where the programme was hidden. The inspectors' task was like looking for a needle in a haystack. Trace quantities of viral or bacterial strains could be concealed anywhere, buried in hermetically sealed storage units in the desert. They were wasting their time searching for clues.

"What did you make of the general?" asked Brokenshire when they had the room to themselves.

"For someone so fiercely proud of his achievements, why is he really helping us?"

"Like so many patriots, he's deeply conflicted. The scientist in him wants to tell the world about his team's achievements, but fierce loyalty to Saddam demands his silence."

"As soon as we loosen Saddam's grip on power surely that position becomes untenable."

"Perhaps."

"Men like Al-Rahi will vote with their feet. Like they always do."

"I wouldn't be so sure. Loyalty runs deep with this one."

Harris was puzzled. "If he was never going to tell us where those storage bunkers are, why am I here?"

"Because we don't need him to."

"Wait, what?"

"Perhaps you weren't paying attention. He's already told us what we needed to know."

Brokenshire turned on his heels and took the stairs two at a time, leaving Harris to wonder what he had missed.

CHAPTER 22

Kisangani
Democratic Republic of the Congo
6 November 1998

By the fifth day of the outbreak, the stay-at-home order had slowed the tide of infection sweeping the region. None of the local staff supporting the World Health Organization team dared spend time together. In the last forty-eight hours even Maxine showed little interest in fraternising. A constant fear of close contact made everyone afraid to shake hands, to hug, to be human. Alice's colleagues buried themselves in their work, working around the clock, eager to finish their rotation and get on the next plane home.

As Alice shuttled between the hospital, the field office and the animal testing centre, she observed soldiers marking the front doors of infected households with a chalk cross to warn others from entering. It struck Alice as a macabre game of noughts and crosses. Too many times, she counted three in a row. In some blocks, there were more houses with infections than without. The only signs of human life were the steaming casseroles left on doorsteps by family members caring for their sick, too scared of infection to go inside.

Even at this early hour, the docks were crowded ten-deep with refugees desperate to escape. Captains of river boats who made a living plying their trade up and down the Congo River now refused to dock at Kisangani, preferring to anchor on a mooring, ignoring the shouts from those waiting ashore.

Thirty-seven villages in the surrounding area had reported cases of infection. The virus was spreading rapidly from family to family, village to village, leaving many dead and dying in its wake. Entire communities up and down the river had ceased all communication. No news came from these remote habitations. Tribal elders unilaterally imposed lockdowns, sealing off their villages from the outside world. Locals now viewed outsiders, particularly Westerners, with deep suspicion, questioning their motives. Trust had all but collapsed.

Many in the city had come to believe the outbreak something of a lottery; fate determined who lived and who died. The village elders, however, knew better. Death, they believed, soon followed the arrival of strangers. Those that survived did so by building physical barriers between themselves and the outside world.

Reports of violence towards migrant workers and ethnic minorities had come to light, both groups suspected of spreading disease. Everything Alice knew about the virus suggested it killed indiscriminately, without thought to colour or creed. The great leveller, she thought, but that didn't stop different tribes or factions blaming each other.

In her daily report to the WHO back in Geneva, Alice chronicled her observations. The stay-at-home order had undoubtedly slowed the spread of disease, though it was hard to stop people simply being human. Every time families hugged and kissed each other goodnight, or friends greeted each other in the street, the virus penetrated deeply into their lives. An unseen killer crept silently from person to person. Through bitter experience, people in towns and villages came to understand that all social contact spreads disease, but by then, it was normally too late.

The staff from other aid agencies still operating in the region did so at immense personal risk as local soldiers refused to accompany them to affected villages. Looting had become widespread. Everyone feared for those cut off by the spread of the virus.

At Kisangani's main hospital, still closed to new patients, the temporary morgue had filled to capacity. Body bags stacked several feet high, waiting for the next convoy of trucks to transport their grim loads to mass graves dug in wasteland just outside the city limits.

Each corridor and waiting room hosted yet another scene of suffering. Bloated, blackened corpses hastily covered by stained sheets, doused with chemicals. The powerful disinfectant they used here could barely conceal the stench of putrefaction drifting back over the hospital grounds like poisonous fog. Staff here referred to the stench as "la puanteur", or the ill wind, silently spreading among the settlements and buildings downwind of the hospital, infecting everything in its path. Nurses complained about the smell of death that clung to their clothing and hair, impossible to wash away at the end of a shift. Morale had all but collapsed for the hard-working team at the hospital, but still they came to work to ease the pain of those infected, with little thought to their own safety. The search for viable treatments continued, but the WHO team were facing an impossible task.

Alice appealed once more to Thierry Deschamps, begging

him to lobby the health minister, Alain Beaumont, for additional resources. Beaumont had met all her direct requests for an audience with an icy silence.

"Please," she implored Thierry at their next meeting.

"I've already asked," he said, throwing up his hands. "There's no point."

"Why would he refuse?"

"Because politicians don't like bad news. Perhaps things are different in your country. Men like Beaumont seek to control the message and the flow of information. No news is good news."

"But Thierry, people are dying. Why pretend otherwise?"

"Denial is easier than the truth. If I were you, I would get your expedition leader, Leclerc, to make the request through the official channels. In my experience, politicians like Beaumont only listen to other men with power."

"Fine," admitted Alice with an abrupt about-turn. She knew Thierry was right. Beaumont would never accept the word of a mid-level scientist, let alone a woman, regardless of whether she was right. She didn't like it, but she had little choice.

Three hours later, Alice and Professor O'Leary sat outside the health minister's department, staring at their watches. Alice was already regretting wasting time dragging the professor here. At the very least, Alice told herself, they had to try. Finally, after being kept waiting for almost an hour, time that would have been better spent in the laboratory, Beaumont's minder, Corbus Koch, opened the oak-panelled doors to reveal the minister sat behind his throne, in reality, a dark mahogany desk set with neatly organised piles of paper, a gold pen in his hand, to match the gold rings on his fingers, poised ready to sign some important document.

The minister rose and shook hands with the professor.

"I am sorry to keep you, Stephen." He nodded disinterestedly at Alice, but his eyes lingered, running the length of her bare legs up to her knee-length khaki shorts and up towards her buttoned blouse, taking in every line, every curve.

Alice's breath caught in her throat, suddenly self-conscious. She took her seat, crossing her legs, visibly blushing. Koch closed the doors and stood guard at the entrance, studying the two visitors.

"What can I do for you today?"

"Minister, we're grateful to you for seeing us. I appreciate you're a busy man." O'Leary paused, choosing his words carefully. "Our attempts to contain the virus have not been successful. We need additional resources if we are to avoid a humanitarian disaster in Orientale Province."

Beaumont seized on the admission of failure. "Kabila grows tired of your excuses. My government has given you everything you have asked for. And now you ask for more?"

"We must declare a state of emergency."

The health minister stiffened in his leather seat, eyes fixed on the professor. "A state of emergency? I see."

He reached for an expensive-looking walnut cigar box and offered one to the professor who declined. The minister took his time, clipping the end of a Montecristo Cuban cigar with a pair of gold scissors. Alice noticed a handwritten gift label signed Leo hanging from the ornate cigar box. The handwriting was distinctive. She had seen those same cursive letters once before. On cue, Koch leaned forward, gold-plated Zippo lighter, hand steady as he scorched the neatly clipped cigar until the tightly rolled leaves caught.

Through the haze of cigar smoke that drifted across the desk towards his visitors, the minister fixed O'Leary with a steely stare. "How would me declaring a state of emergency change anything?"

"It would allow federal agencies to act. And permit the CDC, the WHO and international aid agencies to mobilise additional emergency teams to come to your aid."

The minister nodded, a smile creeping across his lips. "Believe me when I say, Professor, that I would very like to be of service to you. I am not ungrateful for the important work your team is doing." He paused, taking another long draw on the cigar. Alice knew there was a "but" coming. "This is not a simple matter for my government. There's an election to think about. We are facing the threat of civil war once more. Declaring a state of emergency now would be an admission of weakness. It would embolden our enemies."

"Your people are dying, Minister," said the professor.

"Politics in my country is sometimes difficult for Westerners to understand. You see, voters have very long memories. No one wants to be remembered for overreacting. Legacy matters."

"Yes, but—" O'Leary began.

"Like I say, if I could help in some other way."

"At the very least, you could lift the blackout. Allow us to get word out to news outlets. To make people in the wider community aware of what symptoms to look out for."

"I don't want to start a panic."

"Start a panic?" replied O'Leary, unable to contain his frustration any longer. Koch was suddenly behind him. Remembering where he was, the professor relented. "With respect, Minister, if we don't contain this outbreak now, we lose the initiative."

"Yes, yes, I've read your report. The WHO does not have a monopoly on the truth. Other experts are divided on the best course of action."

"What other experts?"

"In Kinshasa. "

"Do your experts understand what will happen if this virus

spreads to other cities, to other countries? Viruses don't respect borders."

"You're exaggerating." The minister wagged his index finger, as if the professor was bluffing. "It was your team that issued the warning about Ebola, wasn't it? And before that, bird flu?"

"We were right on both occasions."

"But what if this outbreak fizzles out tomorrow? The people will remember how the government overreacted."

"Yes, but what if it doesn't?" countered Alice, unable to stay silent any longer.

Koch's cough was intended as a caution, but she ignored him.

"Please. No more of these scare stories. The last thing we need is more emotion and drama."

Alice had to bite her tongue at the blatant misogyny at her expense. "With respect, have you actually been to the hospital?" she said.

The minister dismissed her concern with a wave of the hand. "Stephen, I suggest the two of us continue this conversation in private."

"Alice is right," the professor countered. "The death toll is climbing every hour. Any further delays will be catastrophic."

"Thierry's team has the situation under control."

"This has nothing to do with blame, Minister. Our only interest is saving lives."

"If you're not willing to face the truth—" began Alice.

Koch placed his hands on Alice's shoulders. She could smell his stale breath on the back of her neck. "Careful, Princess," he whispered.

The minister waved Koch away. "The truth?" He laughed at her naivety. "We all believe what we choose to believe. I, for one, have put my faith in our local doctors." The minister studied their reactions, amused by Alice's indignation. "If you don't agree, then I suggest you make an official complaint to your superiors back in Geneva."

"Perhaps I should write to Jean-Marie Kasongo, the editor at *L'Avenir*, or Christophe Ilunga at *La Prospérité*? Their reporters are always calling the office on the hunt for stories like this."

"That's enough," shouted the minister, banging his fist on the table, infuriated at being spoken to like this by a woman. But the threat of leaking the story to news outlets seemed to have given Beaumont pause. He could threaten Alice, but did he really have the gumption to silence her? He seemed to soften a little, rubbing his hands together. "Leave this with me. I will pass this up the chain, speak to Kabila. Let him decide."

"Thank you, Minister."

"Now, if you'll excuse me. I have other matters to attend to. Mister Koch will escort you back to your laboratory."

"We have our own driver waiting downstairs."

"Oh, but I insist. I wouldn't forgive myself if something happened to you." There was just a hint of menace about his insistence, unless Alice was much mistaken.

"Thank you," said the professor.

As the doors closed behind them, Alice forced a smile at her minor triumph. If the minister was unwilling to help, then she was prepared to take matters into their own hands, whatever the personal cost. The alternative was simply too awful to contemplate.

CHAPTER 23

Baghdad, Iraq
8 November, 1998

Over an unstable video link, Brokenshire used his full allocation of fifteen minutes to brief Major General Phillips, the sole representative of the Joint Intelligence Committee back in Whitehall, about the progress, or rather lack of, being made by the UN team in their search for Iraq's illegal weapons programme.

"You said the inspections are entering a 'dangerous phase'. Perhaps you can explain what you mean?" asked a voice the MI6 officer struggled to identify over the crackly feed.

"Sir, the UN inspectors still cannot issue Iraq with a clean bill of health, nor are they able to provide conclusive evidence of non-compliance. It's a catch-22 for both sides."

"And yet the Iraqis assure us they have granted access to every facility we have asked to inspect."

"Not every facility, Sir. Saddam's palaces remain off limits. That's where we believe he's storing weapons."

"But you still have no definitive proof?"

"No, Sir."

"And what reason does Saddam give for refusing access to the palaces? By so doing, surely he is playing into the Americans' hands?"

"Saddam claims the inspection team is a front for the CIA. That the Americans are intent on gathering intelligence for future air strikes."

"He has a point."

The grainy image of a high-ranking officer began to materialise as the image on the screen stabilised, affording Brokenshire his first clear sight of Phillips's office, bookshelves crammed with history books and mementos of a lifetime of military service.

"But if we can't follow the trail of intelligence we've established, then the UNSCOM mission in Iraq is guaranteed to fail."

"Through official channels, yes, that's correct," replied Brokenshire with a pained expression.

"You mentioned the work of this Harris character in your report."

"Yes, Sir, there's another side to the story we're exploring."

"Perhaps you can remind me why we are placing so much faith on the word of one man?"

"Sir, Blake Harris has been our eyes and ears in Baghdad for some time. No one has a better read of what's going on here."

"So what does this Harris say?"

"That Saddam has an active weapons programme. It's highly mobile. Capable of being brought online in a matter of weeks, even days."

"An opinion based on what, exactly?"

"He's been on the security detail for several UNSCOM teams

and on inspections of more than a dozen Iraqi facilities in the last three years, feeding us first-hand intelligence since day one."

"And you mentioned he's one of ours?"

"Yes, Sir. Harris served with Four-two Commando. Royal Marine. Twice decorated. Two tours in Northern Ireland, one in Bosnia."

"But I noticed most of his service record is redacted," challenged Phillips, flicking through the briefing document in front of him.

"Not uncommon for someone with his background in covert operations, Sir."

"I see. Do we know why he left in '94?" asked Phillips, checking the document in front of him.

"Like many of his generation, highly paid consultancy projects lured him away. Oil companies, NGOs, non-governmental overseas agencies and the like. He became something of a go-to resource in the Middle East. Fluent in Arabic. Mother was Egyptian. Spent significant time in Saudi, Libya and the last three years in Iraq."

"And the MOD vouch for him?"

"Absolutely. One hundred per cent, Sir."

"Thank you. Carry on."

"As I was saying," continued Brokenshire, "with its current remit, the UN inspection programme is proving of limited value. Saddam is much too savvy to get caught red-handed."

"And, in your view, is this current crop of inspectors to blame? I note Harris claims there is a question mark over their suitability."

"They are the best of the best."

"Then how do you explain their failure to find anything?"

"Sir, in my view, all the low-hanging fruit has already been plucked."

"Plucked?"

"Yes, after six years of inspections, we estimate that over ninety-five per cent of Iraq's chemical and biological munitions have already been destroyed."

"Then perhaps you blame the quality of our intelligence?"

Brokenshire hesitated, anticipating a trap. "Yes, Sir," he admitted, with some embarrassment. "As you know, the UN team has no dedicated intelligence gathering operation of its own. Our analysts at GCHQ and MI6 have been supplying aerial reconnaissance together with first-hand intelligence from our own sources in Baghdad. The American NSA and CIA have been performing a similar intelligence support role."

"So why the hell aren't we finding anything?"

"Because, Sir, by the time we get access to these sites, the Iraqis have cleaned house. Remote monitoring and satellite images only get us so far."

"What about those no-notice inspections they promised us?"

"They are now happening."

"Then perhaps we simply need to give the inspectors more time."

"I wish it were that simple, Sir. The French are campaigning for an end to all sanctions, citing widespread food shortages, hospitals running short of basic medicines."

"So I hear. The UN Security Council is deeply divided on allowing any extension. Meanwhile, the Americans are pushing hard for military intervention."

"What's the UK government's position, Sir?"

"The PM is standing shoulder to shoulder with the Americans, accusing Saddam of obfuscation and non-compliance."

"And yet we still have no hard evidence to support that view."

"Publicly, the Iraqis have consistently maintained that their weapons programmes were dismantled and their stockpiles destroyed. And they have the photos to prove it. On the face of things, they are complying with the UN mandate."

"But there are discrepancies, certainly," insisted Brokenshire. "Significant quantities of material remain unaccounted for, Sir. The Iraqis have been unable to offer any proof of their destruction."

"When you say 'material'?"

"Several dozen SCUD warheads, potentially armed with biological or chemical agents. Thousands of litres of anthrax, mustard gas and botulinum. Not to mention bombs and other munitions that remain unaccounted for."

"Then where the hell is it all?"

"Buried in the desert somewhere."

"Until we can find and destroy those weapons, the Americans won't risk boots on the ground."

"Why?"

"Sending in troops now could risk a catastrophe."

"In what sense, Sir?"

"I'm reliably informed that simply dropping a bomb on those laboratories is not guaranteed to destroy these types of biological agents. To incinerate anthrax spores, you need intense heat. An accidental release could render half of Iraq uninhabitable for decades."

"I see. Assuming those weapons still exist."

"Quite. Several on the committee doubt whether Saddam would ever consider using anthrax."

"Sir, he's used it before against his own people. We must assume he would."

"Anyway, the Americans are worried a targeted aerosol release of anthrax spores over a forward operating base could create a toxic cloud. We'd be talking about thousands of allied casualties. Even if we could protect our troops, producing that much vaccine would take months."

"How long do we have, Sir?"

"The Americans are proposing targeted airstrikes against selected military targets. I'd assume weeks rather than months."

"Then we need to speed up our plans."

"Brokenshire, tell me again what you know about Al-Rahi's Haboob programme," said Phillips, flicking through the folder in front of him.

"Sir, most of the production sites the UN has inspected so far are what's classed as dual-use. Capable of manufacturing anything from animal feed one month to anthrax the next. They can switch production lines. Harris claims they've relocated their more sensitive research to mobile laboratories."

"Mobile?"

"Yes, Sir. Typically, the size of shipping crates that can be moved to new locations at a moment's notice."

There was a pause as the major general scanned the document in front of him. "Those samples he got for us. From Al Daura."

"Yes, Sir. Are the latest results back from the lab yet?"

"I just got off the phone with Major Farrier. He was highly sceptical. Seemed to think there had been some sort of mix-up."

"How so?"

"Because the samples suggested a level of Iraqi sophistication we had not previously thought possible. His team at Porton is still analysing the data but Farrier's initial assessment is that, at the very least, the Iraqis have developed the capability to modify simple viruses. A feat of technology that surpasses even our own."

"Are you sure this is not just more Saddam propaganda, Sir?"

"The samples prove Iraq has successfully modified a strain of haemorrhagic conjunctivitis. I'm told it causes temporary blindness."

Brokenshire struggled to conceal a snort of derision he

hoped wasn't audible over the feed. "Surely, a nuisance, at worst. Hardly very deadly. Sir, I myself suffer from conjunctivitis every now and again. What of it?"

"Well, Brokenshire." There was a hint of irritation for the first time. "Our experts have reliably informed me that haemorrhagic conjunctivitis is a stepping stone towards manipulating other forms of haemorrhagic viruses. Ebola, Marburg, for example. Another sample suggested they had modified camelpox."

"Why camelpox?"

"Because camelpox and smallpox share many similarities."

A lump formed in Brokenshire's throat. "With all due respect, we all remember the smallpox rumours from last time, swirling around Russia. They were never substantiated. Whatever Farrier believes, our intelligence suggests the Iraqi programme lacks the technology and the experience to genetically modify viruses."

"Until now. The latest samples prove they've made a breakthrough."

"How?"

"You said so yourself. It's unlikely they're working alone. Those Iranian militia groups smuggling resources across the border. The Russian equipment we've identified. There's another school of thought you should be aware of."

"Sir?"

"Farrier believes the Iraqis may have outsourced their R&D to somewhere else. Beyond the reach of the UN."

"You've lost me, Sir."

Major General Phillips sat back in his leather seat, perhaps considering how much he should share. "One of Farrier's colleagues, Doctor Littlejohn, is currently in the Congo, embedded within a World Health Organization expedition operating near Kisangani. He's reporting multiple disease outbreaks in the last few weeks there."

"I don't follow. You're suggesting there's an Iraq connection?"

"Farrier claims Iraq and its partners may be live testing genetically engineered viruses in the wild. Infecting local populations and monitoring their spread. The samples from both locations are a close match."

Brokenshire let out a long sigh, thinking through the implications. "If Farrier is right, the PM will have no choice."

"Without hard evidence, Parliament's never going to support military intervention."

"Then it's time the gloves came off. If the inspections are not giving us what we need, we must consider alternatives."

"What do you have in mind?"

"Give Harris the green light, Sir," implored Brokenshire. "He'll get us the evidence we need."

"Very well. The less detail the committee knows about covert operations, the better. If this goes pear-shaped, there can be no trail back to the committee."

"Understood. All I need is your sign-off," confirmed Brokenshire.

"Very well. Let me bring them up to speed. I'll let you know the committee's decision tomorrow."

Phillips terminated the connection before Brokenshire could thank him. All he could do now was wait.

CHAPTER 24

Kisangani
Democratic Republic of the Congo
9 November 1998

On their way back to the WHO field office, Alice and Professor O'Leary swung by the Embassy and were welcomed with open arms by the French ambassador. A kiss on each cheek, and a third for good measure, much to Koch's amusement as he watched two men kissing. They left Koch flirting with a French aide in the lobby, while the ambassador escorted his two guests upstairs via a grand staircase lined with oil paintings of former French presidents, including an unflattering portrait of the incumbent, Jacques Chirac. He threw open the doors to a palatial reception room complete with marble statues in each corner, where he entertained them with tea and biscuits. O'Leary relayed their conversation with Beaumont, the health minister, being careful not to vent, and explained calmly what help they needed.

"I was just speaking to your boss, Doctor Brundtland, only this morning."

"Oh really? The director general?" replied O'Leary in astonishment.

"Yes, do you know each other?"

"Not personally."

"I met Brundtland in Oslo when I was a junior minister. She'd just secured her second term as Prime Minister. Anyway, I took the liberty of passing on your request for additional resources."

"You did?"

"She said that she was putting her top person on it. Told me to mention they were sending a GS12. She said you'd know what that was."

"What's a GS12?" asked Alice, studying the professor's astonishment.

He shook his head, barely believing the news. "My God. I didn't know they'd actually built one. I advised on the design specifications years ago. It's a containerised level four laboratory. A fully mobile facility that can be disassembled and flown anywhere in the world in forty-eight hours."

"She said to tell you they're mobilising a rapid response team to assist you," added the ambassador.

O'Leary blinked in disbelief. "That's the best news we could hope for in the circumstances. When will they get here?"

The ambassador checked his watch. "Their flight left Geneva at 1100 local time. With any luck, they should be with us by the end of tomorrow."

The professor embraced the ambassador once more. A clear breach of protocol, but one that was warranted in the circumstances.

"You're welcome," said the ambassador, straightening his jacket.

"Right, where to next?" asked Koch when they were back in the vehicle. A digital squawk from the portable radio beside him suggested he was reporting their every movement.

"Back to the animal testing centre, please," replied Alice.

Each day since Alice's almost disastrous first autopsy of the infected marmoset, her team had spent every hour injecting the animals with a barrage of candidate vaccines and treatments. Nothing seemed to be working so far, but, at the end of each day, they took more samples and shipped them back to the support team in Geneva, running computer simulations and advising on how best to limit further loss of life.

The extended WHO team was working at warp speed. In any normal situation, they might study a pathogen like this for months before having any hope of a breakthrough, and yet here in the Congo, Leclerc expected them to work miracles. Somehow, this virus had learned to adapt, to become even more infectious and deadly for humans. That was no mean feat.

In the latest experiment, even the control monkeys had developed symptoms. Three days after the first monkey had been infected, all twelve animals tested positive for the virus. The control monkeys were in two sets of cages, separated from the others by over twenty feet. It was impossible, thought the researchers, for the animals to have contracted the virus through direct contact. The only plausible explanation was that the virus had travelled through the air. The conclusion terrified all involved.

Even by monkey standards, the stench in the holding area was hard to stomach. Alice would later refer to the smell that permeated their supposedly airtight suits as "death and faeces" mixed together. Compared to her last visit, the silence was overwhelming. Gone were the familiar screeching, grunting, hooting sounds. Those animals not suffering advanced symptoms paced from side to side, others appeared listless and lethargic. In the stainless-steel trays under each cage an unholy ooze of blood and bodily fluids collected.

Alice asked Ntumba, the chief veterinarian, for his team's observations.

"Once their internal organs liquify, fluid pours out of every orifice until their lungs, intestines and liver empty," Ntumba explained, watching the colour drain from Alice's face. Her stomach lurched at the description, but she was too proud to admit any squeamishness. Not in front of Ntumba anyway.

Her colleague, Maxine, had volunteered to monitor the animals day and night, recording her observations on a clip-board. Alice noticed her French counterpart stumble in her Racal suit, momentarily bracing herself against the side of one cage.

"Be careful," warned Ntumba, cautioning her back, aware of the danger should one of the monkeys reach through the mesh and claw at her suit.

Alice rushed to Maxine's side, catching her before she collapsed to the concrete floor. Through the fog in her helmet, Alice could see Maxine was red in the face, panting. The French scientist appeared woozy, her movements imprecise. At first, Alice assumed exhaustion was to blame. Perhaps the battery pack powering her suit fan needed changing. God knows, the heat was unbearable at the best of times. Maxine's cheeks were flushed, her forehead noticeably blotchy.

"Why don't you take a break," Alice said. "Go sit down."

"I'm a little faint, that's all. I didn't sleep much last night."

Alice could testify to that. The few hours she had spent back at the hotel were disrupted. Her room-mate had tossed and turned most of the night. Alice sat her down and gently asked her some diagnostic questions. Maxine complained of blurred vision, loss of smell, loss of hearing.

"I've been feeling off all morning."

Alice supported her back to the staging area and helped her through the decontamination process, paying special attention to Maxine's uncharacteristic confusion. Alice decided they should both keep their suits on for the time being.

"Everything just seems off today," admitted Maxine. "It's hard to explain. Like someone washed all the colour from the world."

Alice deposited Maxine in an isolation room where she could rest in peace while she went to fetch the rucksack containing her medical kit. When she returned, her room-mate appeared non-responsive, melancholy, her face visibly drained of colour, pale beyond belief. Perhaps it was the harsh overhead light, but her cheekbones appeared more prominent somehow, her face drawn tight, like a living corpse. Her lips were thin and cracked. Alice finished recording her medical observations and struggled to conceal her worst fears. Maxine saw through Alice's professionalism and recognised a fellow doctor's concern.

"It's the virus. I'm going to die, aren't I?"

"We don't know that. It could be anything," she said, trying to make light of the symptoms she recognised only too well. "We're all working crazy hours. Why don't we run more tests first? It could be a simple fever, even heatstroke," Alice lied unconvincingly.

"I took every precaution." Maxine's shoulders slumped, tears streaming down her cheeks.

"We all did." Alice thought of all the late nights Maxine had spent fraternising with effervescent nurses and doctors, drinking moonshine.

Maxine knew better than anyone that the onset of symptoms

would be rapid, but there was something else. "Alice, I need to tell you something."

"What is it?"

"I'm pregnant," she said, with a shallow sob.

Alice swallowed hard. "How far along?"

"Just a few weeks. I haven't told anyone yet."

Maxine should never have made this trip if she knew she was pregnant. It was against every WHO guideline.

"Who's the father," asked Alice.

"He wouldn't care. He's married."

"But he has a right to know."

"Please. Not now," implored Maxine, pained by the effort of explaining herself. Alice nodded in sympathy. "We both know what this thing does to an unborn foetus."

"Let's not jump to any conclusions. Why don't we get you out of here? Some place you can rest up. You'll feel better once you've slept."

"I wanted to call her Lilly. After her grandmother," she said, a faraway look in her eyes.

"Come on, let's get you out of here."

Koch jumped out of his vehicle, stubbing out a cigarette, as soon as the two doctors reappeared. When he saw they were both still wearing their Racal suits, he hesitated, keeping his distance. He volunteered his driver to take them to the hospital or wherever they needed to go, while he would stay put and check in with the senior veterinarian to wait for the next transport.

As Alice helped Maxine into the back of the waiting vehicle, a troubling realisation dawned on her. If Maxine was infected, there was a strong chance she was too. They'd shared a room, hadn't they? What would the professor say if he found out?

CHAPTER 25

Baghdad, Iraq
9 November, 1998

Since the Joint Intelligence Committee's decision to approve covert reconnaissance of suspected Iraqi weapons storage sites, Harris had been busy, making two more midnight visits to Al Hakam alone. The evidence he had retrieved was now being pored over by experts back in Whitehall.

Brokenshire congratulated Harris on his photography skills. Several now empty animal holding facilities still retained signs above their doorways confirming the cages had once housed monkeys, birds, even pigs. Of more interest were the aerosol chambers, sophisticated air handling systems and a laboratory suite which had been deep cleaned. All the evidence suggested they had used this facility for animal testing. The boffins in London suspected multiple pathogens. Something about the place reminded Harris of pictures he had seen of Nazi death camps. Cages large enough for humans. The whole place still reeked of death and decay.

Eight further locations had been identified and allocated to other teams still scouring Iraq for suspected research and production sites. Harris still had two more targets to scope out over the coming days.

Brokenshire summoned Harris back to the south-east Baghdad safe house for an urgent video call to update Major General Phillips, who was now eager to speak to Harris directly. To Harris's surprise, he recognised the United Kingdom's Defence Minister sat listening at the far end of the conference table in London.

"If the committee plans to advise the PM to support this bombing campaign, then we need to be damn sure that those weapons are there, Harris," insisted Phillips.

"Sir, there's no longer any doubt that Iraq has retained core elements of a weapons programme."

"Whether Saddam is prepared to use it is another matter. Our Whitehall experts maintain the Haboob programme is a deterrent. A bargaining chip. We can't afford to take that risk. We have to act based on what we already know."

"Yes, Sir. Many of the research and production facilities can be brought online in a matter of days. They're hiding in plain sight, Sir. With sufficient time, I'm confident that we'll find more munitions hidden in secure bunkers in the desert."

"The ones immune to air attack."

"Yes, Sir."

"Very well," said Phillips. "Keep up the good work, gentlemen."

"Thank you, Sir."

Brokenshire ended the connection, and the screen went blank. "You did well, Harris."

"I said what you told me to say."

"Exactly. You stuck to the script. For once."

"Now, perhaps you can tell me what's really going on?"

Brokenshire was true to his word. "The Americans are lobbying for punitive action. They've already drawn up a list of targets and they're moving assets into position."

"About time."

"They're calling it Operation *Desert Fox*. There's a carrier force of US Navy fighter bombers from USS *Enterprise*, B52s from Diego Garcia supported by F-16s, RAF Tornados from Italy, plus dozens of cruise missiles."

"Targeting what?"

"Communication infrastructure, command and control, air-defence installations. The final list of research and production sites hasn't been determined."

"They can't stop Saddam. They know that, right?"

"This is as much a show of force as anything. A warning shot."

"So diplomacy has failed?"

"No, there's still hope a 'shock and awe' campaign can drag Saddam back to the negotiating table. The PM is walking a knife-edge between supporting Bush and giving the inspectors sufficient time to complete their work. We're counting on you to give us something definitive we can use."

"How soon can they execute *Desert Fox*?"

"Forty-eight hours. Possibly less."

"That doesn't leave much time."

"It doesn't."

"We'll have to gamble on which of the remaining sites to focus on."

"I've been thinking about that. I had the team in Whitehall pull an all-nighter, reviewing all the intelligence again. They drafted in a new set of analysts. Fresh eyes. They do that from time to time to tell us what we've been missing."

"And?" asked Harris impatiently.

"They've come up with this."

Brokenshire unfolded the blueprints for what looked like an underground complex buried within the foothills of a mountain.

"Al-Mansulijah? Not this again. Last time we decided it was a non-starter."

"I know. Just hear me out." Brokenshire produced a series of aerial photos time stamped from the preceding days showing a railway line disappearing into the mouth of a tunnel. A goods train was pictured with some thirty wagons covered by tarpaulins heading for Al-Mansulijah. Harris used a magnifying glass to inspect each of the wagons. Two armoured trucks attracted his attention. One was mounted with twin heavy machine guns and more than a dozen armed guards. The other appeared to have an anti-aircraft gun and a mobile air-defence missile system.

"There's no question. This was a military operation. While we can't be sure what they were transporting, there's every chance they were weapons. This is the break we've been waiting for."

The satellite imagery was otherwise inconclusive. The outbuildings surrounding the tunnel entrance were nondescript. Time and again, the Iraqis had proven inventive in their attempts to disguise buildings. Before the Gulf War, they painted rooftops to appear fire damaged or derelict. As Harris knew only too well, there really was no substitute for on-the-ground intelligence.

"We've had several reports of suspicious cargo making its way by train under cover of darkness. The analysts think they could be missile components, warheads being moved to secure locations throughout Iraq in anticipation of air attacks."

Harris turned his attention back to the aerial photos and

blueprints. "Has anyone actually been inside these tunnels? Do we know what's there?"

"We've contacted one of the original engineers in Germany who project managed its construction. That's where these blueprints came from."

"What did he say?"

"It's designed to be bombproof, impregnable to air attack. Six storage levels buried more than one hundred and fifty metres deep, extending far beneath the mountain. Capable of housing thousands of tonnes of materiel and strategic supplies. A huge bunker complex hidden within a mountain, impenetrable to attack."

"But there's no way of knowing if there's any link with the Haboob Project."

"No, but the blueprints show hermetically sealed temperature-controlled areas that would suit the storage of sensitive biological material."

"So you want me to get in there, find you more samples?"

"No, we've moved to a search and destroy phase. This is it, Harris. Our last chance. We may not get another."

"What's my point of entry?"

"Here," said Brokenshire, pointing to an anonymous service building high on the hillside. "There's an emergency access shaft that descends over a hundred metres to the complex below. You can get in and out without being seen."

"Great, but if I blow that place up, don't we risk one of those toxic clouds you were so worried about? One that would poison half of the Middle East for decades to come?"

"Don't worry. Our boffins have been sweating the detail. Their risk assessment confirms that a high-energy detonation deep underground would incinerate any anthrax spores or chemical ordinance."

"What about security? There must be a small army guarding that much material."

"Not if no one knows it's there. This could be Saddam's best-kept secret to date."

Harris was nodding, going through the details in his mind. "What about backup?"

"I've requested an armoured support unit to be on standby, just over the border. But your orders are to get in, get out, blow the place."

"But what if your analysts are right and I do find more samples, you're going to want me to bring them back, right?"

"Your primary objective is to destroy."

"But if circumstances permit..."

"I'll have two Sea Kings on standby, just in case. Don't worry. We'll get you out."

Harris grunted his approval. Sea King helicopters meant they were a commando force. Reliable, dependable. "When do I go in?"

"We'll need you to sync up with the air attacks. Timing will be critical. But within forty-eight hours, I'd say. With any luck, the Iraqis will be so distracted they won't know what's hit 'em."

Harris left a message with Sadi's cousin at the café to call him back. The phone rang within five minutes.

"We're on. That job came through."

"If it's surveillance, do me a favour and find someone else. My hip still hurts from last time."

"This is the real deal."

There was a moment of silence.

"Listen, if you don't want the work, I can find someone else," Harris lied.

"Fine. Where to this time?"

"The bunker I told you about."

"That's a long drive. Why do you want to go there anyway?"

"What's the word on the street about what they store there?"

"Supplies, equipment."

"Military?"

"I don't think so. But who knows?"

By the time Harris made it back to his hotel, he discovered the UN inspectors waiting in reception with their bags packed.

"What's going on?" Harris asked Marchand, the French scientist.

"We're shipping out. Tonight."

"No one told me."

"We just heard ourselves." He leaned in, eyebrows raised, his voice barely above a whisper. "Some coded warning. They've postponed the rest of the inspections. Indefinitely."

Harris played along, promising to make some calls, but he already knew the truth.

The last few days had been frustrating, to say the least. The investigations had become deadlocked. The UN Security Council had refused repeated requests from the Americans and British for tougher enforcement action. Progress had come to a standstill. As the Iraqis dug their heels in, attitudes hardened. The time for inspections was over. They had instructed UNSCOM teams to cease operations, with immediate effect. That could mean only one thing. US patience with Iraq's leadership was at an end. Operation *Desert Fox* was imminent. It was no longer safe for the inspectors to stay.

CHAPTER 26

Kisangani Airport
Democratic Republic of the Congo
10 November 1998

The newly arrived GS12 self-contained mobile laboratory was a design marvel to behold. Alice arrived at the airport two hours early, eager to watch in wonder as two ordinary-looking shipping containers were carefully unloaded from a giant military cargo plane borrowed from the French air force. Deposited in a secure hangar, end to end, a team of technicians busied themselves extending the middle concertina section, elevating the entire structure on what looked like stilts. The two containers were then connected via a suspended walkway. Technicians set about assembling the other component parts stored inside. The GS12 had its own built-in generator but on this occasion would be hooked up to the hangar's power supply.

With a satisfying hum, the GS12's internal lights blinked on and, with a hiss, both pods pressurised. The air handlers fitted on the roof powered up with a low whirr. The lead technician, a Swiss engineer with a handlebar moustache, stepped back, hands on hips, to admire his handiwork. He invited Alice and Littlejohn to suit up for a private tour of their new high-tech laboratory.

To Alice, it was like stepping inside *Doctor Who*'s Tardis. Compact on the outside, but dim recessed lighting and clever use of mirrors made the interior space seem cavernous. The first zone was a staging area where two space suits hung from pegs, gloves, masks and respirators at the ready. A bank of monitors and screens displayed the rotating logo of the manufacturer. The GS12 was a workspace large enough for two scientists to operate in relative comfort with modern equipment in a safe, hermetically controlled environment. Through the airlock at the far end, Alice could see the self-contained level four laboratory, connected by a covered walkway. Negative pressure ensured that, in the unlikely event of an accident, nothing would escape. Air would leak in rather than out. Dangling from the ceiling between the two workstations on either side were coiled orange air hoses to which the scientists would connect their suits.

Littlejohn inspected everything, pushing buttons and checking seals until he was satisfied the laboratory would meet their exacting requirements.

"Satisfied?"

"It's not quite up to British standards, but we can make do," he joked with a playful wink, to the obvious annoyance of the Swiss technician. "Certainly a step up from what we're used to in the Congo."

The GS12 technician ignored Littlejohn's petty one-upmanship and explained to Alice how to operate the chemical decontamination spray and the procedure for safely exiting the pod.

"Once you're inside, the main door locks automatically. It's totally secure. The only way someone can get in is if you push this release button and let them in."

A television monitor showed the entry zone where the professor's face was pressed to the glass as he tried to peer inside. Alice yawned loudly, suddenly overcome with tiredness, covering her mouth with embarrassment. "Sorry." What would her mother say? thought Alice.

"When was the last time you took a break?" asked Littlejohn.

"A while. Yesterday morning, I guess."

"Why don't you have a rest now? You're no good to us tired."

Alice knew Littlejohn was right but was too stubborn to admit she had boundaries. She would push herself as long and as hard as her male colleagues. She thanked the technician, joining the professor in the hangar. O'Leary seemed content to appreciate the GS12 from the outside.

"Don't you want to see inside?"

"No need. I saw the prototype back in Geneva."

"So there are more of these?"

"Well, this is the first one off the line. They've made some modifications, I see," said the professor, noting the location of the air vents. "No doubt there are still some bugs to iron out."

Alice nodded with a loud yawn. Exhaustion had finally caught up with her.

"There's a comfy chair in the staffroom you might want to take advantage of. I know, I was just there myself," said Littlejohn. Seeing Alice's reluctance to leave, he added, "Go on. I'll cover for you."

"Thanks, boss," she replied with heavy sarcasm.

"I mean it, you're too close, Alice. Remember, this is a marathon, not a sprint. You need to look after yourself. Stay sharp." He softened his approach, putting an arm around her shoulder, mindful of how stubborn she could be. "Come on. I know what crisis situations like this are like. They can be all-consuming. You can't see the wood for the trees. But, I promise you, you'll see things more clearly when you've had some rest. Now go on before someone else grabs your spot."

Grudgingly, Alice sloped off towards the hangar staffroom, where she found an unoccupied faded leather armchair still warm from its previous occupant. She sank into its threadbare cushions, massaging the stiffness in her neck and shoulders, resting her eyes for what felt like a few seconds. When she opened them again, her watch said thirty minutes had passed. The professor was right. She had been running on empty for too long.

Once she was awake, Alice found it impossible to get back to sleep again, her brain churning on all the different conflicting inputs. When she tried closing her eyes, all she saw were images of sick patients. A pregnant Maxine screaming in childbirth. And to think, Alice had waited her whole life for an opportunity like this. Now she was face to face with the true scale of an outbreak she was more terrified than she would have imagined. The stakes could not be higher. The consequences all too clear. If they could not contain its spread, they risked a catastrophe of unimaginable proportions.

She closed her eyes again, trying to organise her thoughts, to focus on her breathing, to remember her training. Clues were so easily missed in these early days of an outbreak. Attention focused on the wrong areas, mistakes made, data misrepresented. Intelligence can often become fragmented. To those on the ground, the scope and scale of a humanitarian disaster is not always clear. She craved perspective. The professor was right; she had allowed herself to get too close. Perhaps worse still, she had become emotionally invested. Her problem had always been that she cared too much about people like Maxine, about all the innocent victims she had formed an attachment to. Young people with their whole lives ahead of them. She envied the professional detachment exhibited by her male peers. Did women simply care more than men? She wasn't sure.

Alice checked her watch. It would be dawn in two hours. She splashed water on her face in the handbasin, reapplying some lipstick to make herself look less washed out, less like someone who hadn't slept properly for nearly forty-eight hours. In the deserted staff canteen, she found JP nursing a cup of black coffee.

"I thought you'd already gone home."

"Where you go, I go." He smiled with a resigned shrug. He looked exhausted, too.

She returned the smile, grateful for his support and protection. "I need someone to drive me to the warehouse on the far side of the airport."

"Right now?"

"I wouldn't ask if it wasn't important." She had an itch that needed scratching.

The ever-expanding WHO logistics team had relocated their base of operations from an empty hangar to their current location next to the main building. However, they were yet to bring across all of their stores.

"We'll need to find someone to let us in. I don't have keys."

It was still dark outside. Dawn was an hour or more away. The night sky was beginning to brighten on the horizon. There was no danger of air traffic at this time of day, so they drove straight across the runway to the far side of the airport enclosure. Alice couldn't help but look left and right, scanning the skies for any approaching aircraft. She did the same thing at railway crossings.

JP parked the Land Rover outside a darkened storage unit, beeping the horn to attract the attention of the night guard who stumbled out of an office, rubbing his eyes, flustered by their unexpected arrival.

JP followed a few steps behind, no doubt curious as to the nature of Alice's pre-dawn excursion. She hurried towards an orderly line of pallets, checking the numbers against a printed packing list she held in her hand. She stopped at one of the crates, which, according to the manifest at least, contained a library of medical textbooks. JP whistled to get the security guard over, who used a crowbar to lever open the splintered wooden container, stepping back for Alice to inspect its contents. It took her several minutes to find the correct volume.

Printed the previous year, but still the de facto "bible" for infectious diseases doctors, the index of the multi-volume medical reference compendium contained just a double-page spread that matched her search. In matter-of-fact language, reminiscent of *The Hitchhiker's Guide to the Galaxy*'s quirky view of Planet Earth as "mostly harmless", the book's research team referenced the now infamous historical outbreak of infectious disease at a Behring Works in northern Germany in 1967 within a single page. She had heard the professor refer to this outbreak on more than one occasion, and was curious to learn more. The name of the town was Marburg, on the picturesque Lahn River.

She read the entry several times, angling the page towards the overhead strip light. It provided a brief history only, with multiple footnotes and references to other studies. Back in the day, Behring Works had produced vaccines made from the kidney cells of green monkeys. Out of several hundred monkeys imported mainly from Uganda in that year, they had found a handful to be infected with a mystery virus which spread quickly from cage to cage, eventually killing several animals. Not only had the Marburg virus, as it later became known, succeeded in jumping between different species, a feat managed by only an elite few pathogens, Marburg had infected the Behring employee responsible for cleaning out the cages. The parallels with Maxine's unfortunate predicament were obvious.

She had been in direct contact with the animals, assisting in multiple autopsies.

The patient autopsy results were cited in a footnote for further reading. "Organs liquified", "bleeding from the eyes, nose, rectum". A single black-and-white photo accompanied the entry. It didn't take a genius to see the connection with the Congo variant they were dealing with, so why had the professor been so reticent to admit the link when she asked him about it? She continued reading. The health authorities in Germany had contained the outbreak, but not before it had killed six workers and infected dozens more. As a precaution, all the monkeys were destroyed. The prompt action of those involved had avoided disaster. The textbook noted in plain language that the virus was unlike any other encountered previously. The drawing that accompanied the entry was immediately familiar to Alice. A thread virus, shaped like a ring. Part of the family of filoviruses she'd studied during her doctorate. When viewed together, thread viruses looked like a bucket of snakes, intertwined, a writhing mass of deadly spaghetti. There were differences to the Congo variant, of course, but the likeness was unmistakable.

Staring at the image of the thread virus, an idea began to form. A sixth sense had been screaming at her. A nagging suspicion she was missing something. She slammed the textbook shut, placed it under her arm and marched back towards the Land Rover. JP followed a few steps behind.

"Can you drive me to the field office, please?" There was something she needed to check. Right away.

"Your wish is my command," he replied with a theatrical bow.

CHAPTER 27

Alice changed into her lab coat at the WHO field office in Kisangani where they had stored the monkey autopsy samples. Wriggling her hands into protective latex gloves, donning eye protection and a mask, she strode into the biosafety level three laboratory, too excited to speak to the professor or share her hunch with colleagues.

The laboratory stank of disinfectant and bleach, the floors still slick from their daily scrubbing. She powered up her monitor, the familiar whir of her computer's CD-ROM drive spinning up. She took a bite of a bread roll, stale and rock-hard, but it would give her grumbling stomach something to think about.

She prepared a fresh cell culture collected earlier from one of the infected marmoset monkeys, identical to the samples express shipped to the WHO team in Geneva for further analysis. In her state of exhaustion, she struggled to focus as she peered down the microscope, waiting for the image to come into focus. What she saw sent a chill down her spine.

This most recent strain had a distinctive ring shape to it, not dissimilar to Marburg. What made the Congo variant so beguiling was its rare talent for misdirection, to fool and potentially disable the body's natural defences. The result was an overreaction, filling the lungs with liquid as organs became starved of oxygen.

"Clever little bastard," whispered Alice through gritted teeth. She zoomed in further. At least now she knew what she was looking at. To her trained eye, it was like staring into the eyes of a natural born killer. This latest variant was a pandemic waiting to happen. A virus capable of changing the course of history.

The professor's cough at the doorway interrupted her train of thought. It took a moment to break through her reverie.

"Geneva just called. They've completed their analysis of those first samples we sent them. You were right, it was a novel strain of H5N1."

"Bird flu?"

"They're calling it Epsilon5. They've promised to fax over the data within the hour. I've booked a call for 1130 to discuss next steps."

Alice barely reacted, her thoughts still elsewhere.

"I thought you'd be pleased. Discovering a new variant is a big deal."

"Sorry, Stephen. That's great news. Really. I'm a bit preoccupied, that's all."

"Preoccupied with what, exactly? The monkey pox samples?"

Something made her hesitate. She wanted to be sure before she told the professor about her discovery.

"I thought I told you to prioritise the bird flu?"

"I will. I mean, I am."

"Good." He checked his watch. "Let's talk through what you're going to say to Geneva."

"Me?"

"Of course. You identified the variant. You should get the credit."

She nodded. She'd nearly finished her report on H5N1, but that seemed irrelevant now.

As soon as the professor left the room, Alice put in a call to one of her contacts in Geneva to find out what else they had on file about Marburg and Ebola. These diseases were so rare, very little was known about them. Other than the professor, most experts only knew what they read in books. The professor's experience, along with a handful of others, was somewhat unique.

"Jean, it's Alice. Thank God you're up early too."

Geneva was one hour behind Kisangani.

"We're all working double shifts supporting you lot," Jean replied, an edge to her voice. Everyone was stretched to the limit right now.

"We're all grateful. Really."

"So, what can I do for you?" Businesslike as ever.

Alice lowered her voice. "I need a favour."

"Sure. Anything." They had been friends and colleagues for years, but Jean, a veteran of multiple WHO expeditions to central and West Africa, played by the book.

"What can you tell me about Marburg?"

Jean hesitated, as if taken by surprise by the question. "A little. Why?"

"Because I think we're dealing with at least two separate outbreaks. Not just one."

"What makes you say that?"

"The range of symptoms is too broad. Besides, the mortality rate is far too high for H5N1."

"How many cases are we talking about?"

"At the last count, seven hundred confirmed cases. Give or take." She was met with a stunned silence. "And that's likely only ten per cent of the total cases out there."

"I had no idea it was that many. And how many fatalities?"

Alice checked her notes. "As of midnight last night, out of the seven hundred admitted to Kisangani Hospital and other health centres, nearly six hundred have already died. And that's in five days. That number's only going one way."

"That's unbelievably high, even considering what we know about Marburg."

"Exactly."

"How is this thing spreading so fast?"

"Littlejohn has several theories. But I'm not convinced by any of them."

"Go on."

"All the previous evidence for haemorrhagic fever points to monkeys being the carrier, hence my question about Marburg. I was rereading the reference book again, looking for clues. Back in 1967, WHO investigators established a clear link between historical Marburg cases in Germany and the shipment of monkeys from Uganda."

"Correct, but, as I remember, no witnesses were prepared to go on record."

"Even Professor O'Leary seems reticent to consider Marburg."

"Why?"

"I'm not sure. He's been AWOL for large parts of this trip."

"The last time I was in Uganda and Zaire, we spun our wheels investigating links with monkey shipments," explained Jean. "Animal trappers were quick to deflect blame. They're a powerful lobby group with local government. Most of the trappers refused to go on record. But one spoke on condition of anonymity. He claimed the infected animals came from much further east. As far away as Lake Victoria. Other trappers told juju stories about a mythical plague island."

"The same mystery island they tried to blame for AIDS in the '80s?"

Jean laughed. "They love their folklore and superstition in Africa. Look, whenever animals are captured, put in cages and shipped long distances in unsanitary conditions, you create the perfect conditions for disease."

"Tell me about it. Did you see my photos of the living conditions we witnessed in the affected villages?"

"Another hot mess. Pigs, chickens and humans living together, exchanging genetic material." Jean paused, as if struck by a thought. "Have you considered that maybe you're not looking at two pathogens but one combined virus? With patients exhibiting different symptoms?"

"Littlejohn convinced me it was a red herring, but now I'm not so sure."

"Hmm. Ben Littlejohn? The military scientist? What's he doing there? You're sure he's not trying to misdirect?"

"Ben? No, he's a good guy when you get to know him. I've got no reason to distrust what he's saying." Jean's silence spoke volumes. "Why is there virtually nothing written about Marburg or Ebola?" continued Alice. "They're not exactly new viruses."

"Try asking at the local hospital. Logic suggests both viruses have been circulating for decades, possibly centuries. I'm sure if you look hard enough, you'll find what you're looking for. "

"Nobody's talking, Jean, and I want to know why. Without those historical patient records, we have no way of knowing if this type of outbreak has happened before."

"I did read somewhere a while back that one of the professor's predecessors, Doctor Schmitt, I think it was, wrote about a mystery haemorrhagic fever in Orientale Province back in the '60s. I'd need to check, but I'm fairly sure Schmitt documented cases of cross-species infection."

"Can you find that source and send it to me?"

"I can try. Anyway, even if this is Marburg, everything we know about past outbreaks should reassure you that filoviruses are really hard to catch other than direct contact with a carrier or bodily fluids. It'll run out of people to infect soon enough."

"This variant may have unique characteristics. More resilience. More longevity. This thing spreads so easily."

"I'm telling you, viruses just don't evolve this fast, Alice. Unless..." Jean paused again.

She was silent for so long, Alice thought the phone line may have gone down. "Unless what?" she repeated.

"I was just thinking. Remember what we saw in Hong Kong? Influenza and swine flu merrily exchanging genetic material. What if Mother Nature got lucky? A chance meeting between two viruses?"

"A mythical chimera virus?" Alice laughed. "Deadly as a filovirus, but with the transmissibility of avian flu?"

"I wish I was joking."

"Did my autopsy samples arrive yet?"

"Yes, about that. I'm so sorry, Alice, but they were unusable."

"Oh no. Did I do something wrong?" said Alice, worried she had packaged them incorrectly.

"No, no. I'm told the FedEx refrigeration unit on the plane was defective. Everything was too badly decomposed. All the internal organs were liquified."

"I'm so sorry."

"I can't work with goo, Alice."

"What about the cell cultures?"

"Yes, they survived the journey. I'll call you back as soon as we get the results."

"How long will that take?"

"Tomorrow morning. Maybe sooner."

"What if we don't have that long?"

"I can chase them up. Why? How are your monkeys doing?"

Alice cleared her throat. "I'm expecting an update. But as of 1900 last night, Ntumba, the vet, said the control subjects were hanging in there but every other monkey we injected with live virus has developed symptoms."

"Within forty-eight hours? Wow! That's fast."

"Two dead so far."

"But both controls are now symptom-free. Which confirms what?" Jean asked in a school-teacher voice.

"That our variant is not airborne."

"Because?"

"They're in cages on the far side of the room. That's the only way for them to be infected."

"Exactly. You wanna hear my theory?"

"I'm all ears."

"Remember your Master's thesis postulating that the emergence of new viruses was caused, in part, by a decline in biodiversity?"

"You mean the same thesis that nearly got me laughed out of Cambridge?"

"Don't be so hard on yourself."

"Jean, half the faculty ridiculed that paper as an 'overreach based on inconclusive data'." Alice still smarted at the unwillingness of the scientific community to consider alternative explanations, rigid in their long-held views.

"But what if you were right, but had everything back to front?"

"Jean, you think everything ties back to deforestation?"

"Because it's so obvious, Alice. Deforestation contributes to the retreat of animal species everywhere. Why would it be any different in the Congo? The ongoing destruction of natural habitats for intensive farming in Central Africa is definitely responsible."

"You're talking about the decline of bird populations, specifically?"

"Exactly. We all know that birds act as a natural barrier to cross-species infection. A rapid decline in species diversity could easily lead to a spike in infections like the one you're seeing in Kisangani."

"For bird flu, maybe, but I don't see how that affects monkey or bat populations." Alice slammed her fist on the counter in frustration. "Why do I still feel like I'm not seeing the full picture?"

"A word to the wise, Alice. You won't find the answers in that lab. Go talk to the local doctors. Go to the source."

Alice nodded. The answer seemed tantalisingly close. "You want to hear another theory?"

"Sure."

"Remember how, in Hong Kong, we proved pigs were the natural reservoir for the DNA of multiple viruses? Pigs sit between birds and humans in a typical chain of infection."

"Yes. Excuse my ignorance, but are there that many pigs in Kisangani?"

"You're kidding. They're everywhere, Jean. Over a million of them. Living in tiny mud huts with chickens and humans, sharing the same enclosed spaces. We know cross-species contamination is common. What if nature just found a way? And the perfect genetic combination emerged, ready to infect humans in large numbers."

"But tell me this, genius. How is it possible that a strain of avian flu, only previously recorded in Hong Kong, suddenly appears ten thousand kilometres away, on a separate continent?"

"Migrating bird populations?"

"You're seriously suggesting that an infected bird could fly halfway around the world?"

"It's possible. Especially if the birds are carriers and exhibit no symptoms whatsoever."

"There has to be another explanation."

Alice thought back to what the Congolese vet had told her. All it takes is one sick transported animal to bypass quarantine.

"Remember that Marburg outbreak in '67? They blamed illegally imported animals back then," said Alice. "Once they release animals back into the wild, there's nothing to stop them interacting with local species. Once that happens, anything is possible. And we know Kisangani is a distribution hub for the whole north-east of the country."

"Has O'Leary bored you with his theory about bats?"

"What about them?"

"I've read a few studies suggesting fruit bats could act as the natural reservoir for several haemorrhagic fevers."

"Maybe in Uganda, but no one's talking about fruit bats here." Alice checked her watch. "Shoot. Look, sorry, I have to go. I'm meant to be presenting my preliminary report to this committee in forty minutes."

"I know. I'm on the same call. Along with just about everyone in the department."

Alice swallowed hard. She was so under-prepared. "Listen, I really appreciate this, Jean."

"Seriously, any time. Good luck."

CHAPTER 28

The next morning Alice begged JP to drive her and Littlejohn out to the remote villages north-east of Babudjala, where they had documented the first confirmed cases of this new strain of haemorrhagic fever. Babudjala was much further than their previous field expeditions and would require an overnight stay.

JP summoned four of his most trusted security personnel, all former Foreign Legion soldiers, together with Philippe, their local guide, and two Congolese porters. They persuaded Leclerc to spare two long wheelbase Land Rovers, together with food and supplies, including four lightweight tents suitable for jungle expeditions. To reach their final destination in the north-east corner of the territory they had to cross the Uele River. Philippe pointed out a crossing point on the map equipped with a floating platform and nylon lines stretched from one side to the other, where one could pull across foot-passengers and equipment by hand. Beyond the Uele River, they would be on foot for the remaining five-kilometre hike to their destination.

Alice worried that, by the time they got there, the threat of conflict would have driven any remaining inhabitants from their villages. Reports of soldiers streaming over the border, joining forces with the Congolese militia groups operating in the area, had set in motion a huge exodus of indigenous people heading west towards Kisangani, Bangui in the north, or Kinshasa to the south-west, spreading disease to new areas. Many migrants had already arrived exhausted and hungry in the UN camps on the outskirts of Kisangani, renamed "death camps" by the locals.

Alice had seen one such camp with her own eyes. Watchtowers at each corner, armed checkpoints to get in and out, chain-link fences topped with barbed wire. The site was poorly equipped to handle a worsening humanitarian crisis. Unsanitary conditions were unavoidable. Local government officials now blamed the United Nations and other overstretched aid agencies for failing to offer more support.

The roads heading east out of Kisangani were hard-topped and easily navigable, unlike the last time they had travelled this way. Once they had left the main road and entered more forested areas beyond Babudjala, for Alice it was like entering a wild, unforgiving world, untouched by human hand. Dappled sunlight pierced the tree canopy, cattle wandered untended across dirt roads scavenging for food. JP directed Alice's attention to one poor beast caught on the barbed wire. Another was trapped in a ditch, one of its back legs badly broken. There was nothing they could do for them, other than put the beasts out of their misery. JP despatched them both with a single shot to the head before calmly walking back to the vehicle, eyes lowered. They all agreed it was the humane thing to do.

Further along the cratered, rutted track they found the rotting corpse of a cow lying by the side of the road alive with a swarm of flies. In the first human settlement they reached, rabid dogs prowled deserted streets searching for scraps, howling at their passing. Not a living soul to be seen. Crops lay withering in the fields. Everyone had left this ghost town while they still could.

Two miles further north-east, where the track narrowed, meandering through dense forest, the driver screeched to a halt, narrowly avoiding a collision with a fallen tree blocking their path. A shirtless man advanced towards their vehicles, brandishing an AK-47 held aloft, shouting something in Lingala or Swahili, ordering them out of their vehicle. Alice noticed two other men hiding behind trees, watching them. A tribal elder in floor-length dark red robes, face painted in vibrant colours, emerged from the trees, warning them to keep their distance. Philippe, their guide, held up a hand in welcome, half-recognising the village elder.

"Why have you come here?" the elder shouted, signalling for the shirtless youth to lower his weapon.

JP moved slowly to the rear of the vehicle, his arms raised, and slowly reached in to the cardboard boxes stacked in the back, producing a medical bag with a red cross emblazoned on its side.

"We bring medicine for your sick."

Philippe translated, prompting the elder to relay the message to those waiting out of sight.

"What are they saying?" asked Alice, wiping her brow with the back of her sleeve, suddenly deprived of airflow through the open windows in the stifling heat. The humidity was oppressive, even in the shade. Monkeys chattered in the surrounding trees. The forest was alive with the hum of insects and birdsong.

"They're scared," explained Philippe. "They're not sure whether they can trust us."

"Fear is what's kept them alive," admitted Littlejohn. "Complacency kills."

The villagers continued to discuss the arrival of the strangers and whether to allow them through the blockade.

"This is learned behaviour, Alice," continued Littlejohn, pushing his wire-framed glasses back up his nose. "It's what communities around here have always done in times of disease. It's an evolutionary response to danger."

"Barricades won't protect these people," countered Philippe. He had shared many stories of the widespread looting, rape and murder of villagers by marauding gangs, raiding parties crossing the border.

They were both right, thought Alice. The villagers had learned from bitter experience that sealing off their community from the outside world was their best chance of survival. It was a crude but effective defence against the threat of disease.

The village elder finally relented, enlisting the help of the young men present to lift the improvised barrier to one side and allow the WHO party through to the settlements beyond. Round the next bend the vista opened out to reveal a clearing where a whitewashed church stood proudly in the middle of a dozen single-storey wooden structures topped with thatched roofs. To her surprise, Alice noticed a school, a village hall, a temporary hospital, iron-framed beds without mattresses and a football pitch, dry and dusty, the surface baked in the midday sun. The village was much larger than they had led her to believe. To their right, two shirtless youths levered a heavily stained mattress onto the crackling flames of an enormous bonfire, smoke rising high above the treetops.

They parked up next to the dilapidated church and donned their suits and helmets. An officious-looking tribal elder met them, bare-chested, his body decorated with beads, paint and feathers. The shrunken skull of a monkey hung around his neck. Two local women in colourful robes and headdresses flanked the elder. The other villagers fell silent, crowding round, staring at the scientists in their suits, pointing in wonder at Alice, her fair skin and blonde hair, angling their heads to listen to their conversation.

"Why have you come?" challenged the tribal leader in passable English, cautioning the villagers to stay back.

"We're doctors with the World Health Organization." Alice gestured towards the crates stacked in the back. "We bring medicine to treat your sick."

"We don't need your help. We have our own medicine."

Alice recognised the juju sack hanging from the elder's neck, and the familiar stench of rotting fish, trusted by locals to ward off disease.

"The spirits have protected us." The Swahili translation rippled through the crowd as they repeated the incantation in hushed tones.

"How many cases do you have here?" asked Alice.

"Two. Both in isolation," the elder announced with noticeable pride, pointing towards crudely constructed wooden enclosures on the far side of the football pitch, where hands and feet were visible beneath a padlocked door. One of the buildings was badly scorched, its wooden frame half-burned.

"What are their symptoms?" asked Alice. "Fever, headache, bleeding?"

"Yes, but we quarantined them straight away."

"Good. Do you know how they became infected?" asked Alice, recording the responses in the notebook she carried everywhere.

"They went to visit friends in the next village. Disobeyed our rules. We locked them up when they returned."

"Good. Are there no other cases?" asked Alice, encouraged by the elder's prompt action.

"None for three days."

"That's the best news we've had in days," admitted Alice, turning to Littlejohn with a smile.

The tribal leader appeared confused at their excitement.

"Most of the other villages near here are not doing so well. The hospital in Kisangani has closed to new patients," she explained.

A murmur of concern spread through the assembled crowd.

"City people are weak," claimed the tribal leader. "Our faith protects us," he said.

"Quarantine will protect you," countered Alice.

The irony of their visit was not lost on Alice and the WHO team. Despite their good intentions, their expedition actually risked spreading disease. "With your permission, we'd like to take some blood from as many healthy volunteers as possible."

"Why?"

"We believe your people will have developed antibodies. Low-level exposure to the virus has given you immunity to infection. We can learn a lot from your people and why they didn't get sick."

"My people are strong."

"Yes, your blood is strong," said Alice, directing her words to the crowd by way of encouragement. "You can help us develop a medicine to save more lives," she explained, not sure they understood her meaning.

"How long will this medicine take?"

"Weeks, maybe longer. Quarantine is your best option until we return."

"The village is well prepared."

"Providing the rebels stay away and your animals remain healthy," said Littlejohn under his breath.

"The spirits will protect us," insisted the tribal leader. His words were repeated once more through whispered oaths.

"Quarantine will protect you," repeated Alice under her breath. She couldn't help but admire their stoicism, the unshakeable faith of those who lived in remote rural areas like these. Why worry unnecessarily about some invisible evil spreading in the city? Here in the rainforest, danger was all around them. It was a way of life. Grinding out a living came first. Tending to crops, feeding their cows and chickens. Sealing themselves off from the world outside. That was their best chance.

Littlejohn and Alice invited a dozen volunteers to come forward to give blood. Children pressed closer to watch Alice as she worked, each sample carefully labelled and packed securely in Styrofoam cases.

When they had finished, the scientists took it in turns to disinfect the suits and scrub down their equipment, before packing the crates back onto the Land Rovers' roof racks. Philippe wished the villagers good fortune, and they continued on their journey north. Children ran alongside their vehicles, cheering and laughing until they passed beyond the settlement, enveloped once more by the forest.

"They don't need scientists like us to tell them how to survive," admitted Alice, sharing a smile with Littlejohn.

"Theirs is a fatalism borne of acceptance. What will be, will be. If the spirits will it," added Littlejohn.

"Who are we to question their beliefs?"

It was a philosophy that resonated at a fundamental level. Alice laughed inwardly at what her mother might say of such stoicism. Had the villagers visited the hospitals and clinics in Kisangani, she was sure they might have been more concerned about the genuine danger lurking in the surrounding forest.

CHAPTER 29

Uele River
Democratic Republic of the Congo
21 November 1998

A stone's throw from the banks of the Uele River the expeditionary group set up camp near a dilapidated brick building reclaimed by the forest. They pitched their tents beneath a giant Afrormosia tree, covered in liana creepers that caressed the ground in the breeze. Ripening seed pods littered the fertile soil which burst when disturbed. The nearby river was a languid reddish brown, coloured by iron oxide, which drained into the Congo River further downstream.

JP's men set to work hammering stakes into the ground as they erected four tents large enough for their party of nine. As the only woman, they allocated Alice her own tent, despite her insistence that she be treated like everyone else. Privately, she would admit she was terrified of being alone in a tent.

As the sun set behind the treeline, the Congolese porters

collected firewood strewn across the forest floor. JP hacked at low-hanging branches with his machete, stripping them of their foliage before dragging the limbs back to camp. They piled the wood several feet high within a stone circle. The ensuing flames sent shadows dancing in the gathering darkness.

When the fire had sufficiently died down, they set a giant pot of beef and vegetable stew to heat through. Alice marvelled at the night sky. She had never seen so many stars. The smoke from their fire rose uninterrupted into a cloudless sky. As darkness fell, the absorbing sounds of the rainforest came alive around them, hooting monkeys, calling birds, the steady rhythmic hum of insects. Alice was mesmerised by the glowing embers, enjoying every crackle and spark whenever someone threw on another log. JP and the other men smoked cigars, sharing stories from their travels.

Alice startled at the sound of a branch snapping in the darkness behind her. The men's conversation paused. JP reached for the rifle propped beside him, but the forest noise levels resumed a few moments later. Alice remained permanently on edge, imagining shapes and shadows in the darkness, hoping someone would come and sit with her. JP collected bowls and wandered over, joining Alice on the log the men had dragged closer to the fire.

"You look cold?" said JP, noticing Alice shiver, snaking an arm around her waist, pulling her in tight. "I can get you a rug if you like. There's one in my tent."

Initially, she resisted, but soon relented, realising how much she had missed the warmth of human contact these last few long weeks. Now she remembered, she had barely spared a thought for her fiancé, Richard, back at home in Oxford. He would have hated camping in the rainforest.

"I'm fine," she lied, resting her head against his broad shoulder, fascinated by the wall of insect noise coming from all around them, overwhelming the senses. "It's so beautiful here. So noisy."

"You get used to it after a while. Is this your first night in the forest?"

She nodded. "First time camping in years. Life back home will seem so boring after this."

"Oh, you can never go back," said JP.

The rustle of leaves from a foraging creature made Alice flinch once more, prompting JP to hug her tighter.

"Is there anything I should be afraid of?" she said.

"You mean apart from the snakes and spiders?" he joked. "Not to mention the hippos and crocs this close to the river."

She laughed, nudging him playfully in the ribs. She felt completely relaxed in his company. Her own personal bodyguard watching over her wherever she went. She could get used to this. JP couldn't have been more different to her bookish fiancé. Camping was Richard's idea of hell. The more time she spent here, the more she was falling in love with the Congo. For the first time in years, she felt so connected to the natural world. Like a child again.

As she nuzzled into JP's chest, she became aware of Littlejohn's disapproving stare from across the crackling fire. With a shake of the head, he got to his feet, stretching his arms high in a yawn, before retiring to his shared tent for the night. Alice didn't care. Why shouldn't she be happy? She had every right.

The pair of them sat together in a silent embrace, gazing at the stars, listening to the other men's stories, laughing into the night, oblivious to their quiet intimacy.

JP leaned in and kissed Alice full on the lips. She closed her eyes and kissed him back. When she opened her eyes again, the fire lit up his face, his pupils reflected the glowing embers as he studied her reaction. She pulled away, and the moment was gone.

"I'm sorry. I can't." She held up her hand, her engagement ring glinting in the flames.

"I just wanted to kiss you, that's all."

Alice freed herself from his clutches, stretched and bid the group goodnight. She crawled into her tent, carrying the lantern, zipping the entrance tightly closed behind her, meticulously checking the interior for any creepy crawlies. Lying in her sleeping bag, she listened to the symphony of sound from the rainforest, too excited to relax until, finally overcome by exhaustion, she slipped into a dreamless sleep.

The following morning, they left the Land Rovers parked in the shade of the Afrormosia tree. They loaded their equipment on to the rickety floating wooden platform, tethered together with vines. A thick nylon rope stretched almost one hundred feet from one side of the Uele River to the other. The men heaved their way across the fast-flowing waters swollen from all the recent rain. Alice wondered whether there were any hippos or crocodiles lurking in the shallow water, nervous at every ripple, eyes drawn to any movement or shapes breaking the surface.

On the northern side, the rainforest became denser. Nothing had quite prepared her for the sheer immensity of the cavernous space beneath the tree canopy, like some Gothic cathedral filled with earthy smells, sights and sounds. Their Congolese porters strode ahead, hacking at low-hanging branches and creepers, clearing a path, as their small group became enveloped by nature. Alice stared in wonder at trees fifty feet in diameter, two hundred feet tall, soaring in search of light, a vibrant habitat for hundreds of birds, insects and exotic animals. Every shade of green: teal; emerald; neon; lime; laurel; fern; but little else by way of fauna. A duotone of vibrant greens and browns. When she tried to take a photo, the light was so poor, she could barely distinguish what she was looking at through her viewfinder. Their guides moved swiftly along a well-trodden path, barely pausing to acknowledge the presence of a giant snake curled around a low-hanging branch. Alice hurried past, with one eye closed.

The air was close, humid and hot. Everything here seemed wet to the touch, drenching her clothes. Alice had grown accustomed to the swampy stench from all the water pooling around the base of trees. This was an environment every bit as hostile to humans as the laboratories she worked in. She dared not touch anything, staying tight behind JP, his machete in hand, surrounded by imagined dangers. It was understandable how the rainforest here had served as a continuous crucible for life since time began. Everywhere she looked was another wonder to behold.

They emerged into a clearing to discover a settlement of some thirty huts. Stakes driven into the ground creating pens, now empty, fit for cows and pigs. Smoke from a still smouldering fire clung to the tree tops, undisturbed by any breeze. Alice had half-expected a crowd to welcome them. The scientists assumed the village's remote location might have protected its people from exposure to all the disruption caused by the combined threat of civil war and disease rampaging through other communities.

They suited up before venturing further, their decision immediately justified by the victims they found, lying where they fell, unburied. Congealed blood had haemorrhaged from their noses and mouths, soaked into the earth around their bodies. In one case, lack of oxygen had mottled one victim's lips a dark blue, his chest and stomach sagging like some spent vessel. A scavenging bird had pecked out his eyes. As Alice inched closer to take a sample, a rat hidden within the victim's clothing scurried away.

Finally, just when Alice had given up hope of finding anyone alive, a dishevelled African male wearing Western clothing, jeans and a T-shirt, stumbled from between buildings, surprised at the sight of the doctors in their Racal suits. JP drew his weapon, cautioning the shell-shocked stranger to stay back.

Alice noticed dried blood crusted around his nose and mouth, a handgun tucked into his belt. He stood blinking into the sun, too stunned to speak, barely believing his eyes. He half-stumbled, lurching towards them, his legs stiff and awkward.

"Stay back," ordered Philippe in Swahili.

JP cautioned his team to hold their fire as they trained their guns on the approaching threat. The stranger pointed to his throat. JP threw him a plastic bottle of water from his rucksack, which the stranger drained in one, allowing the empty container to fall at his feet.

"Everyone's dead," croaked the sick man in accented English, interrupted by a coughing fit, spitting blood into the dirt. "They're all dead."

"Who are you?" said Littlejohn.

"Guthrie. I'm a doctor with Médecins Sans Frontières," he rasped, shaking his head.

"What happened here?"

Guthrie ignored the question. "We were too slow, too slow to isolate the sick." He shook his head, burdened by the guilt of survival. "Why did no one listen?" Guthrie pointed to an animal shelter with a padlock on the stable doors. "We locked them in there, but it made no difference. It was too late. By then, trust had collapsed. That's when things got really bad."

"Where are the others in your party?"

"There's just me. I'm all that's left." Giving voice to his grief seemed to catch up with him, eyes half closing in anguish. He looked around him at the bodies of fallen friends and villagers strewn on the ground. He threw his hands in the air, as if pleading to the heavens for mercy. "This is no way for Christians to die."

He crouched next to the body of what Alice took to be a fallen colleague, resting a comforting hand on his shoulder, closing the victim's eyes in peace. "Why did you come back?" he asked in a childlike voice.

Alice exchanged a confused glance with Littlejohn.

"Back? No, we just got here. We're with the WHO out of Kisangani," she repeated.

"Then I met your colleagues last week."

Alice was unaware any other team had made it this far north.

"They were wearing the same Racal suits. Two of them spoke Russian."

Alice assumed Guthrie was delirious. Talking nonsense.

"What other team? You're saying another team was here?" asked Littlejohn.

"I didn't imagine it. They said they were trialling some new vaccine. We all knew it was a lie. Some prototype vitamin injection or other. By the time villagers started dying, your colleagues were long gone. I don't blame them. There was nothing more they could do."

Alice had been studying Littlejohn's reaction. He didn't seem totally surprised.

"We should start back," warned JP, mindful of the fading light.

Alice insisted on completing their search of the rest of the village to make sure she hadn't missed anything, taking tissue samples from several of the recently deceased. Someone, perhaps Guthrie, had propped up the victims' bodies in the shade against walls and in huts wherever she went. Everyone was dead, like Guthrie had said.

Littlejohn grabbed Alice's arm, bringing her back to the here and now. "We got what we needed. It's time to leave."

Did we? thought Alice. She had hoped for survivors. Anyone with developed immunity. All they found was more victims of this terrible disease.

They offered to take Guthrie back to civilisation, but he declined. He knew what was coming. He chose to face his fate here in the forest, among his tribe, the fallen villagers he had cared for. On the long walk back to the river and their vehicles, tears streamed down Alice's cheeks. She vowed never again to boast about scientific progress made in the West, to admit humbly her impotence in the face of Mother Nature's fury.

CHAPTER 30

Al Mansulijah, Iraq
16 December, 1998
2200 hours

The Mitsubishi truck driven by Harris's trusty sidekick, Sadi, bumped along a steep mountain track better suited to goats than cars as Harris braced himself in the passenger seat. Headlights off, Sadi was enjoying the novelty of Harris's night vision goggles, navigating the many boulders and debris that had fallen from the steep hillside above. It was slow-going, the engine permanently in first gear, whining in protest. After almost an hour's relentless climb, they reached a relief, providing access to a vantage point with sweeping views over the valley below.

From here, Harris was on his own. A two-kilometre hike across the next hilltop followed by a steep descent towards his objective: a nondescript service building high above what appeared to the untrained eye to be a cavernous railway tunnel entrance that led deep into the mountain and the bunkers beneath.

The schematics for the Al-Mansulijah complex showed a disused emergency access ladder that descended hundreds of feet into the storage facility below. The steel door to the anonymous building crudely constructed from breeze blocks was padlocked, but there was no other visible security. No CCTV cameras, no alarm. It took Harris less than ten seconds to cut through the toughened steel loop with bolt croppers to secure access.

Inside the darkened building he found rusting machinery, a bulldozer and tipper truck for removing dirt. Both had flat tyres. It took Harris a couple of minutes to find the access hatch hidden behind dozens of heavy crates and half-empty oil drums. The hatch was circular, painted shut by successive layers of what looked like creosote. He spent five arduous minutes attacking the paint with his Leatherman multi-tool, chipping away at the seal until, with a grunt, he levered open the hatch.

The escape of dank, fetid air sounded to Harris like the groan of some mountain demon released from the underworld. He sat on the rim, dangling his legs through the narrow gap. Flicking on his head torch, he panned the beam around the shaft's narrow entrance before it disappeared into the chasm below. The ladder and tube-shaped shaft stretched down as far as he could see. He reorganised his webbing and equipment, dangling a pouch containing the explosive charges from an ankle strap and secured his matt black Heckler & Koch MP5 behind his back. Once inside, he pulled the hatch cover closed behind him; it squeaked shut on rusted hinges, plunging the escape shaft back into darkness.

The schematics had not showed the exact height of the

ladder, but he estimated it was at least two hundred feet, meaning a long, slow descent, hand over hand, to the bottom. Light danced off the smooth walls of the shaft as it plummeted into the abyss, picking out specks of dust disturbed by his movement.

After what felt like an age, his brow beading with sweat, his head torch picked out the first of the hatches providing access to the uppermost sub-level. A hollowed-out point in the shaft large enough for a person to crawl through into whatever lay beyond. On the heavy metal door with a rusted handle was stencilled SL-5. Sub-level five.

He stopped for a moment to catch his breath. He could no longer see the hatch above him, nor could he see anything below. It reminded him of some of his more unpleasant night dives. Excursions from a submarine. Zero visibility. Feeling his way by hand down the length of a line through tunnels or cave systems to an objective, trusting the team around him. These days he worked better alone.

After another five minutes of slow descent, he arrived at his destination, SL-2, and removed a tiny can of lubricant from his webbing which he squirted around the handle and hinges, waiting for the oil to penetrate the mechanism. He swapped his head torch for night vision goggles secured to his helmet before gingerly levering up the handle. With only minor resistance, the latch released, and the door swung inwards as quietly as he had dared hope. He peered inside the darkened chamber, listening for any footsteps, before clambering through.

Inside there was a low-level electrical hum from a distant generator. Other than a few blinking lights from inactive machinery and the pale glow from an emergency exit sign directing personnel to the nearest stairwell, it was as silent as a tomb. The temperature was already much cooler down here compared to the arid desert hundreds of feet above. After the long descent, it was like stepping into a refrigerator.

He took a moment to acclimatise to the new surroundings, adjusting his equipment and bringing the semi-automatic weapon to bear. After the claustrophobia of the tunnel, it felt good to be back on level ground with the use of both hands. The chamber was solidly constructed, concreted-lined, walls carved out of solid rock. Electrical cables ran along the ceiling, and from the gurgle he guessed the larger of the pipes carried water. Air handlers somewhere were pumping fresh air around the facility. All signs were encouraging so far that this was an active site, not another mothballed relic of a pre-Gulf War era of Saddam rule. The question remained: what were they storing here?

Planting his feet carefully in the darkness to avoid disturbing the thick layer of dust, he advanced down the passageway between empty metal racks, weapon at the ready. Every fifty feet he found open double doors to storage chambers that appeared recently emptied. Tyre tracks from a forklift truck were imprinted in the dirt. He froze at the sound of distant voices, listening to the guards' conversation in Arabic as it faded once more down the tunnel. Once silence resumed, he moved off again.

Ahead was an intersection. A service tunnel large enough for two trucks to pass abreast. According to the blueprints, the lateral tunnel connected to dozens of other storage areas just like the one he was in. A vast underground complex hidden beneath the mountain, hundreds of chambers that could feasibly store enough material to support a prolonged war effort. It puzzled him that so many of the chambers appeared empty.

His search of the next section was more fruitful. Stacked one on top of the other were crate upon crate of weaponry.

Hundreds, possibly thousands, of wooden storage containers, each stencilled with an alphanumeric number sequence. After checking he would not be disturbed, he crowbarred open several of the nearest crates. Inside, he found an assortment of LD-250 and R-400 aerial bombs, neatly packed in foam. What intrigued him were the different markings on each; some had yellow circles, others had red crosses or green diamonds. He assumed the markings related to the contents of their warheads. He took photos of a sample selection with a pocket camera from his webbing, risking a flash to capture their detail. In another room, he found what looked like aircraft drop tanks and some sort of aerosol dispersal device that reminded him of crop-dusting tanks slung under the wings of light aircraft back home. Room after room, packed floor to ceiling with munitions and military equipment.

From his rucksack he unpacked the first of the explosive charges, which he hid behind a stack of crates. He could rely on secondary explosions to destroy everything in these chambers. He had seen no evidence of a fire suppression system. The resulting inferno would damage or destroy everything on this level, before, with any luck, spreading to other storage areas. It was even possible entire tunnels might collapse, burying some bunkers for years to come.

In the next cavernous chamber that stretched as far as the eye could see were hundreds of sealed metal oil drums. Another section housed rack upon rack of protective equipment, hazmat suits, respirators, masks and gloves.

He continued onwards towards his objective: a temperature-controlled storage area shown on the blueprints he had committed to memory as SG-17.

He stayed close to the side of the tunnel, pausing at every sound, dropping to his knees as the headlights from a turning vehicle silhouetted a figure smoking a cigarette standing not fifty metres from his position. His senses were heightened. He could hear every drip from the overhead pipe, the rumble of an idling engine, the electrical hum from a distant generator. He moved deeper and deeper into the complex, his exit route now far behind him.

Large black letters stencilled on the spray-concrete wall announced his arrival at the entry to SG-17, a suite of four pressure-sealed sub-chambers. From his rucksack he produced a hazmat hood and respirator, together with thick rubber gloves. The entry keypad was a model he had encountered several times before. He released the retaining screws and set to work reconnecting wires to a code-generating device he carried with him, which defeated most types of security within thirty seconds. With immense relief, the door lock released with a hiss and Harris stepped inside.

Motion-activated lights powered up on his arrival as he closed the door behind him and removed his night vision goggles. As expected, this section was temperature controlled, zero humidity, hermetically sealed, capable of storing biological and chemical weapons in secure environmental conditions. The briefing documents had explained how normal temperatures might affect the integrity of the materials stored. The desert was arid in normal circumstances, but down here the air tasted almost metallic, like compressed air from a cylinder, as if filters had extracted all the moisture.

To his consternation, he noticed a CCTV camera high on the wall covering the entry door, although there was no red light to signify it was working. He wondered whether this was a dummy like some others he had seen or whether it was connected to a central command centre. It was too late to back out now. He took careful aim with his silenced pistol and fired a single shot, destroying the camera lens and housing. He had to hope there was no one watching at this time of night. It was just after 2330. With any luck, the guards would be undertaking their half-hourly patrols. They couldn't be in all places at all times. It was a calculated risk, but one he had little choice but to take.

The first two chambers were deserted, their industrial refrigeration units standing unplugged like passive sentinels. Dozens of racks and shelving units were capable of storing hundreds of litres of whatever they normally produced here.

The next chamber had a pressure door that reminded Harris of a submarine hatch. With some effort, he spun the wheel in the centre and the rubber seal released and the door swung inwards. A crude set of plastic curtains hung from the ceiling, providing a second protective screen from whatever lay within. He held the plastic aside and passed through the gap. Inside were a dozen metal freezer units he recognised from the photos in the shipping documents suitable for storing viruses or vaccines at very low temperatures. He released the centre lock and reached inside with a gloved hand, removing a selection of half a dozen sealed test tubes, each with a different coloured lid, bar code and liquid inside.

From a pouch in his webbing, he produced a storage case with foam cut-outs and placed the test tubes securely within. He repeated the process in the next freezer unit until all twenty-four slots in the case were filled and tucked safely back in the pouches on his webbing.

His oxygen supply started to beep, warning him he had only twenty-five per cent supply remaining. He removed the bottle and gave it a shake. It should have been full. He would have to cut short his time here. He checked his watch and allowed himself five more minutes to explore the remaining rooms. When he had documented everything, taking photos, he planted another explosive charge, setting the timer for 0100. It was imperative that any biological material was completely incinerated. In this confined space, the temperature would reach over a thousand degrees; sufficient, he had been assured by Brokenshire's experts back in Whitehall, for his purpose.

He was on his way back out when he spotted a doorway to a manager's office he had almost missed, tucked behind a row of filing cabinets. Inside were three workstations for the chief scientist who worked here and his two assistants. He crowbarred open the desk drawers and found dozens of folders related to the projects they had undertaken here. He scanned the handwritten notes in Arabic, flicking from page to page, folder to folder, barely believing his eyes. File upon file detailing Iraqi experiments. It was likely a treasure trove of intelligence, one Brokenshire would give his right arm for.

There was one significant problem. There was no way Harris could take this much documentation back up the ladder. The marathon climb required both hands. He took stock, considering his options. If he ditched much of his equipment, he might make space for a handful of files, tucked inside his jacket and webbing. He rifled through the folders once again, shaking his head at the level of detail provided. Measurements, calculations, quantities, data reports. Far too valuable to leave behind.

The only option was for him to improvise. To abandon his planned exit route and find another way. There was only one other exit route, and that was the heavily guarded main entrance. He rifled through the next set of documents, still debating whether there was any alternative. Brokenshire's words loomed large. They might not get a better chance to prove the scale of Iraqi deception. What if he held in his trembling hands the evidence the inspectors had craved since day one? Proof beyond any reasonable doubt. His watch alarm started beeping. His time was up. Two minutes of oxygen remaining and just twenty-eight minutes until the first charge would detonate, setting off a chain reaction. He had to make a choice.

From his rucksack, he removed two heavy-duty bin liners and grabbed as many files and folders as he could carry. It would be a dead weight if he had to fight his way out, but it was worth it, wasn't it? He dumped the non-essential equipment from his webbing and got ready to move out.

CHAPTER 31

Kisangani WHO Field Office
Democratic Republic of the Congo
16 December 1998

Back at the laboratory, Alice was unable to focus. She remained troubled by the professor's continued absence and lack of transparency, whether imagined or not. Why had he been so preoccupied since the expedition's arrival in Kisangani, leaving Alice and Littlejohn to handle the lion's share of the work? Was this a sign of the growing trust he placed in her or something else entirely?

Come to think of it, had the professor always been this removed, so indifferent to her concerns? She was beginning to wonder whether he had lured her to the Congo on false pretences. Whether the professor's intention had always been to pursue his own interests and simply piggyback on the WHO expedition? At least Littlejohn had been clear about his motives for being here. In short, she doubted everything. She felt like an imposter playing a game she barely understood.

The discovery that a rival Russian team was sneaking around the same villages, collecting their own samples, administering their own treatments, all seemed so cloak-and-dagger. Alice never had much time for secrets. It reminded her of her mother's attempts to disguise her alcoholism, hiding empty bottles in neighbours' bins. That deception had almost destroyed what little trust remained between them.

She resolved to confront Littlejohn, to ask him point-blank why the military scientists were really so interested in a remote corner of Central Africa. She interrupted his silent study, as he sat hunched over a microscope, surrounded by computer monitors displaying analyses of the latest samples.

"Those photos you showed me back in Oxford, the modified Ebola and West Nile samples. Where did you really get them?" she said.

Littlejohn blinked back at her, the hint of a smile on his lips, as if amused by her naivety.

"Alice, I was straight with you from the start. They came from the laboratory in Iraq I told you about."

"Stop playing games, Ben. You used me. You used all of us."

He shook his head. "Come on. You knew the rules. I thought you were smarter than this."

Alice nodded. So did she. She had been a fool from the very beginning, doing Porton Down's dirty work, blind to the emerging truth. "You knew the Russians were here all along, didn't you?"

"I suspected. I didn't know for sure."

"How? How did you know?"

"Because they've been coming here for a long time. Two expeditions to the Congo in the last four years. One to Uganda. And those are just the three we know about."

"But why here? Why now?"

"You said so yourself, this is where the action is. Like us, they want to study viruses endemic to the region in their natural habitat. To pilot anti-viral treatments. You have to admit it makes for a mouth-watering list. Marburg, Ebola, West Nile, Rift Valley, Lassa fever."

"But why haemorrhagic fevers in particular? It doesn't make sense."

"I could ask you the same question." He paused, as if making a point. "I assumed that was why the professor campaigned to have you come on this expedition in the first place." Alice had often wondered the same thing. "He always boasted of your ability to see patterns, to make connections, to join the dots. Perhaps he was mistaken."

No one was more disappointed in her own performance than Alice. She had always been her own fiercest critic.

"I came here to learn, Ben. I was naive enough to think I could make a difference to these people."

"You still haven't figured it out. You still can't see the complete picture, can you?"

During the many sleepless nights and long journeys from one village to the next, she had often wondered what might be eluding her. Some commonality linking the outbreaks, in different regions, in different countries. No doubt, Littlejohn blamed the Russians somehow, but she didn't want to encourage his conspiracy theories.

"Something tells me you already know the answer, Ben."

"If I knew the answer, don't you think I'd tell you?"

Alice remained unconvinced by his reassurances.

"The professor put his faith in you, Alice," he said. "He believed you might hold the key."

The key to what? thought Alice.

Even though they were alone in the laboratory, Littlejohn

lowered his voice to barely above a whisper. "Look, a few years ago now, we obtained copies of several studies undertaken in Russia attempting to modify bat-borne viruses retrieved from this area. The latest samples seemed to suggest unprecedented breakthroughs with genetic engineering. Advances we didn't think were possible."

"What were Russian samples of Congolese viruses doing in that lab in Iraq? I'm confused," replied Alice with barely disguised scorn.

"You're not the only one," admitted Littlejohn. "Look, the Russians spent millions trying to weaponise smallpox in the '80s. They knew the West had run down their stocks of vaccine as we eliminated cases. They saw an opportunity."

His voice trailed off, as if thinking through the permutations of what he was suggesting. The concept of biological weapons had always seemed nonsensical to Alice. Why start an outbreak of infectious disease? An outbreak over which you could have almost no control. It was the equivalent of an arsonist starting a fire on his own doorstep. The consequences would be devastating for everyone.

"An opportunity for what?"

"Do I really need to spell it out?"

"Actually, I think you do."

"The more military science knows about these pathogens, the better we can prepare the world for any future outbreak."

"Don't pretend you care what happens to these people, Ben."

"Alice, I've always been straight with you. My priority is UK national security, but I'm not blind. I can't ignore what's happening here."

"You expect me to believe that Porton Down doesn't share the Russians' interest in using these viruses as weapons?"

"It doesn't matter whether or not you believe me. Right now, we both want the same thing."

Alice's eyes narrowed. "No, Ben. I came here to learn. To help stop an outbreak. Whereas, you? I don't know what you want any more."

Littlejohn blinked rapidly, but didn't dignify the accusation with an answer. "We both know the Official Secrets Act prevents me from discussing certain matters with you. I've told you as much as I can."

"After everything we've been through?"

"I can't, Alice. If you really want answers, why don't you ask the professor?"

Alice remained puzzled by the professor's level of involvement. "He tells me nothing. How much does he really know?" asked Alice.

"He's been advising the government for nearly a decade. I thought you already knew that. "

Advising on what? thought Alice.

From the corridor outside came the sound of footsteps and raised voices. Alice's first thought was an emergency or a fire in the building. JP was shouting Alice's name, looking in each of the laboratories. She met him at the doorway.

"Thank God," said JP with noticeable relief, embracing her, before realising she was not alone.

"What's going on?" demanded Littlejohn.

"We're evacuating everyone to the airport. The rebels are on the outskirts of town. They could be here within the hour."

"Wait, what about all our research? We can't just leave everything."

"Take whatever you can carry. We're leaving in ten minutes."

"Where's the professor?"

"He's already at the Embassy. We'll meet him there."

CHAPTER 32

Less than ten minutes later, the entire lab team, carrying various folders and storage containers, loaded into the convoy of waiting vehicles, ready for departure. A further two armoured vehicles carrying two squads of UN soldiers would meet them at the French Embassy to escort them the remaining sixteen kilometres along a contested roadway to the international airport terminal where a passenger jet was being readied to fly them to Kinshasa.

The French ambassador and Professor O'Leary jumped in either side of Alice in the back row of the people carrier. JP rounded up the last of the passengers before climbing in, weapon at the ready, talking rapidly on his walkie-talkie in French to the rest of his security team, each allocated to one of the WHO vehicles. Littlejohn had joined another group, perhaps eager to avoid answering any more of Alice's questions.

"I was so worried about you," admitted Alice, gripping the professor's arm. "Where have you been?"

"It's a long story. I'll tell you later."

"That's everyone. We should get moving," interrupted JP, waiting for the ambassador's nod. The normally jovial Frenchman's cheeks were puce, clearly flustered by the rapid evacuation. "We could hear the fighting last night. From the Embassy rooftop you could see buildings on fire to the east. Rebels are looting shops and houses, burning everything."

"Bastards," muttered the professor. "They're marching on Kinshasa to overthrow Kabila, aren't they?"

"They won't admit it but government forces are on the back foot. The security situation has been getting worse all week," explained JP.

"Has there been any news from the villages east of here?" asked Alice, remembering her promise to Sister Francine and those in the direct path of the rebel advance.

"Most of the settlements were already deserted. They knew what was coming. The rebels won't take prisoners. They'll burn those villages to the ground."

On the radio, a burst of static was followed by a strangled, high-pitched voice shouting in French over the sound of gunfire.

"We're running out of time," said JP. "The rebels are advancing two miles east of the airport road."

An explosion in a street to their left made everyone sink lower in their seats, but it was far enough away not to concern JP, encouraging their driver to stay tight behind the truck in front. Another massive explosion less than half a mile away to their right quickly dispelled any sense of security. A plume of smoke rose over the buildings and homes of Kisangani.

"Incoming mortar fire," shouted a voice over the radio, as the rebels zeroed in on the roadway and the convoy's route.

"I thought you said this area was safe," shouted the ambassador, as their vehicle swerved to avoid debris in the road.

"This could only be a raiding party. The main rebel force is still forty miles from here. Once we're beyond the city limits, we should have a straight run. We'll be safe once we get there."

"How can you be so sure?" asked the ambassador.

"The UN peacekeepers have established a perimeter. More than two hundred soldiers massing there from all over the region."

Almost as soon as JP finished speaking, a rocket-propelled grenade streaked towards the armoured vehicle at the head of the convoy.

"RPG," screamed a voice on the radio, too late for the lead driver to take evasive action. The explosion sent the Humvee careering left and right before flipping onto its side, sliding down the tarmac until it came to a halt at the side of the road, smoke and flames pouring from the engine compartment and cabin. None of the occupants emerged from the wreckage.

The Mitsubishi Land Cruiser immediately behind was now exposed to incoming fire. It accelerated past the crash site only to come to a screeching halt, skidding sideways as three rebel vehicles raced into view, blocking the road at the next intersection. From the back of a flatbed truck, a mounted machine gun spat fire at the convoy, sending the column of vehicles veering left and right as they tried to take cover on either side of the road.

JP and the other security personnel dismounted, grabbing their weapons. They took up defensive positions behind parked cars. Quick bursts of suppressing fire, followed by rapid movement, leap-frogging closer to the rebel position. Alice and the others were suddenly alone, keeping their heads down, as instructed by the ambassador. Several rounds ricocheted off the bonnet of their MPV, shattering the windshield, prompting screams from the passengers.

Alice could hear JP shouting instructions in French, encouraging his team to keep advancing. The heavy machine gun on the flatbed truck abruptly stopped firing for a few seconds until another rebel took the fallen gunner's place.

Gunfire from the turret of the second UN armoured vehicle

switched its attention to their left flank. A voice on the radio warned of a renewed threat. Further up the road, Alice could see JP's security team suddenly falling back, retreating under heavy fire, alert to the new danger. Something had spooked them, but Alice was too shell-shocked by all the noise to understand what.

A uniformed soldier in a beret threw back the sliding door of the people carrier and thrust a machine gun into the ambassador's face. He was shouting in a language Alice didn't understand, ordering them all out of the vehicle with their arms raised. She glanced over her shoulder, searching out her protector, but JP was pinned down, unable to reach them. The rebel soldier grabbed Alice by the arm and dragged her clear.

"JP," screamed Alice.

The passengers were force-marched through the backyard of a school at gunpoint to a waiting vehicle, engine revving in the next street. Alice wrenched her arm free and was rewarded with a stinging slap across her face from the back of the soldier's hand. There was no room for all six hostages so they forced Alice and the ambassador down on to their knees, hands behind their heads to wait. The car sped away, leaving the two of them shaking with fear. Every time Alice looked up, the two remaining rebel soldiers shouted at her to keep her eyes down.

With a soft pop, the rebel closest to Alice collapsed, legs folding beneath him. The second soldier suffered a similar fate, his weapon firing as he fell, nearly deafening Alice. JP rounded the corner and hurried to her side, checking she was uninjured, while his teammate ran to help the ambassador to his feet.

The rotund Frenchman appeared in some discomfort, breathing unevenly, grimacing with pain. JP lifted the ambassador's corduroy jacket and discovered a red stain spreading across the fabric of his shirt. JP clamped a hand to the wound, maintaining pressure as he shouted for a medic.

Alice sat back on her haunches, barely taking in what had

just happened, tears streaming down her cheeks. JP hauled Alice to her feet, dragging her to safety, too shell-shocked to speak, back to the waiting people carrier. JP unceremoniously manhandled Alice into the backseat and slammed the sliding door shut. They accelerated towards the roadblock now controlled by UN soldiers.

"Where's the professor?" asked JP, counting heads.

Alice couldn't answer; her voice had deserted her. She simply shook her head.

The driver barely slowed as the vehicle negotiated the narrow gap between the two abandoned rebel vehicles, picking up speed, following the car in front now racing towards the airport.

CHAPTER 33

Al Mansulijah bunker complex, Iraq
17 December, 1998
0000 hours

Harris half-carried, half-dragged the heavy-duty refuse sacks containing a treasure trove of intelligence from the Iraq lab back towards the tunnel entrance. He took his time, ducking low as each service vehicle trundled past, depositing even more supplies in the hundreds of chambers that made up the vast underground storage facility at Al-Mansulijah, buried deep within the mountain complex.

At ten minutes to midnight, Harris felt the ground shake as the distant impact of heavy ordnance exploding at ground level sent dust raining down from the ceiling above. He imagined the night sky lit up by explosions as cruise missiles zeroed in on strategic targets throughout Iraq. B52s flying high overhead would target the railway and tunnel entrance. Timing was critical. At 0030, the first wave of bombing would pause, allowing him a window to make good his exit. For now, he would remain hidden, edging closer to the tunnel entrance. Whatever happened, come 0100, when the first explosive charges planted at strategic points throughout the bunker detonated, he would need to be far away if he wanted to survive the resulting firestorm.

Hidden in the shadow of a truck, Harris listened to the successive surface blasts, secure in the knowledge that even ground-penetrating ordinance couldn't reach this deep within the hillside. Harris's primary concern was that a direct hit could jam the blast doors and destroy the tunnel entrance, trapping him underground.

The sound of surface explosions ceased at 0025. Harris booted up his satellite phone, wondering if he was close enough to the entrance to acquire a signal. The phone normally locked onto an orbiting satellite within a few seconds, but this far underground the signal bar remained empty. He fished out his backup radio from a pouch in his webbing but the white noise in his earpiece told him there was no reception within the tunnels. Somewhere high overhead, Harris knew a circling AWACS aircraft would be orchestrating the combined air attack. An airborne battlefield command centre monitored by a team tracking dozens of aircraft, warships and ground forces would relay updates and instructions to those involved. Harris was just one asset in a complex operation that required meticulous coordination.

He edged closer to the cavernous chamber within the blast doors and was rewarded by two bars of signal. He keyed in a coded alphanumeric sequence that would be relayed to the command centre, requiring priority level one extraction from his alternate rendezvous point. Harris could expect an immediate response from a helicopter rescue team based just over the border in Jordan. If the sat-phone didn't receive acknowledgement for any reason, he would need to broadcast on an open radio channel and risk pinpointing his location to any surface guard force tasked with defending Al-Mansulijah.

As quietly as he dared, he climbed onto the sill of the nearest truck and levered open the door. The driver's paperwork sat ready on the passenger seat, neatly secured in a clipboard next to a flask of coffee and a snack wrapped in brown greaseproof paper. Perhaps the driver had just stepped out for a moment to use the restroom. He reached under the dashboard to locate the ignition wires, only to realise the keys were on the dashboard.

At 0055 precisely, Harris checked his mirrors and turned the key. Inside the now silent tunnel, the throaty roar of the diesel engine was deafening. Harris half-expected guards to come running from every direction, but the tunnel remained deserted. He put the heavy goods vehicle into gear and rumbled forward, bumping over the railway track that ran along the centre of the tunnel. Turning the corner, he found the blast doors firmly shut, unbreached by the impact of the allied bombs. The guards were nowhere to be seen. Perhaps they had taken shelter during the bombing raid.

Harris left the engine running and jumped down on to the dirt floor. To the right of the heavy blast doors, inside a guard hut, would be a hydraulic mechanism. He engaged the gun-metal lever and ran back outside to watch the doors squeak back on their rollers, revealing the nightmarish scenes of destruction outside. Two outbuildings had been destroyed, an inferno burning out of control. The railway track leading to the tunnel complex tangled by the explosions. But the blast doors had done their job, blackened and burned. They had stood firm, protecting the bunker and its contents.

The noise of the blast doors opening finally attracted the attention of the guard force stirring from their hiding places. Raised voices had Harris sprinting back, climbing up into the cab of the truck, crunching into gear as bullets ricocheted off the side of the vehicle. The heavy doors inched opened, the gap still too narrow, but it was now or never. If he stayed here, he would be surrounded. He revved the engine and accelerated towards the widening gap, ducking down as bullets shattered the passenger side window and fractured the windshield. He removed his sidearm and directed three shots towards his pursuers, without pausing to aim.

Harris corrected course, unconsciously breathing in, hoping to squeeze through by the skin of his teeth. One of the wing mirrors paid the price. The canvas tore back, exposing crates stacked inside. He swerved past an enormous crater, still smouldering from the impact of heavy ordinance, sending dirt scattering into the darkness. Behind him, the guards emerged from the tunnel, shouting instructions. Two jeeps set off in pursuit. One appeared to be mounted with a machine gun, which spat inaccurate fire in his general direction. He spun the wheel, sending a cloud of dust billowing behind him.

He grabbed the sat-phone again. Three bars on the display. Signal acquired. He keyed the pre-programmed number. It was answered without delay.

"Angel 7, this is Warthog."

"Warthog, Angel 7, go ahead," replied an American voice.

"Jackpot, jackpot, jackpot. Proceeding to RV Bravo. Repeat, Bravo."

"Copy. Rescue team en route to RV Bravo. ETA 15 minutes."

"Copy that. Warthog out."

Great, thought Harris. Fifteen minutes to drive the five kilometres to the extraction point. Fifteen minutes to survive.

CHAPTER 34

Al Mansulijah, Iraq
17 December, 1998
0100 hours

Harris checked his one surviving wing mirror once more, keeping a close eye on the chasing jeeps. They seemed content to keep their distance. Perhaps they had been ordered to stay back. He wondered what was in the back of the truck. He hadn't thought to check. If the crates contained LD-250 and R-400 aerial bombs like the ones he had photographed, there was a risk of explosion. Alternatively, they might be driving him towards a patrol lying in wait on the service road, ready to ambush him in a hail of bullets.

He pushed the truck to its limits, foot to the floor, engine screaming in high gear up the slope. Even with his headlights on full beam, he found it hard to judge the contours of the roadway, dodging rocks and debris from the hillside perhaps dislodged by the explosions. Suddenly he hit a dip, suspension crunching, wheels screeching in protest. Up ahead was a bend in the road, hugging the contours of the steep slope. He spun the wheel into a tight corner, leaving a cloud of dust behind him before veering left, careering on to a dirt road, hidden within a wadi, extinguishing the truck's lights and flipping down the night vision goggles secured to his helmet. He turned off the engine and rolled down the uneven road in neutral. To his immense relief, the Iraqi jeeps continued along the service road, seemingly oblivious to his detour. The ruse would only buy him a few seconds before they doubled back.

He took a chance. As the truck's momentum slowed, trundling down the shallow slope, he carefully lowered the bags out of the cab on to the roadway below and threw his rucksack after them. Leaving the engine in neutral, he jumped down after his equipment. With any luck, the truck would continue for several hundred metres before losing its battle with gravity but, by then, he would be long gone.

He shouldered his rucksack and took one of the heavy refuse sacks in each hand, staggering under their load. There was a good kilometre and a half to the rendezvous point and he had less than ten minutes to make it. The extraction team would wait as long as they could, but no longer.

He left the dirt road and headed across uneven ground, strewn with rocks and scrub, picked out in dark shapes and shadows by the night vision goggles that bathed everything in green. Across the wadi, dry at this time of year, and up a shallow slope. He counted down the seconds in his head. Five minutes remaining.

Behind him, the jeeps had doubled back, searching out their quarry on the service road. He was already several hundred metres beyond the truck, growing in confidence in the darkness. The patrol would waste time searching the surrounding area for the vehicle, assuming the driver was wounded. If they had night vision equipment, they would find him, but they were unlikely to cover the open ground, unsuitable even for all-terrain vehicles, with its gullies and rocky contours, in time before his extraction.

Further to his right, about two kilometres away, he noticed torchlights dancing in the darkness, hoping to trap him in the closing trap. Harris redoubled his effort, half-running, half-walking. He was less than five hundred metres from the rendezvous point when the reassuring sight of two Sea King Mark IVs roared into view over the hilltop, swooping low, circling the landing area. Good, thought Harris. Sea Kings meant they would be Royal Navy. Dependable.

The lead helicopter came into a hover, dropping vertically until its wheels touched down and a squad of what he assumed were commandos exited the aircraft. He counted six soldiers, now taking up defensive positions in the darkness. Harris was less than three hundred metres away now, breathing heavily, his lungs bursting.

A single shot rang out, pinging off a rock beside Harris, who ducked down, hoping to make himself a smaller target. He couldn't stop. There was no time to take cover. The nearest commando returned fire towards the muzzle flash in the distance. The circling Sea King banked hard towards the approaching patrol, its heavy machine gun firing, raking the Iraqi position, sending the guard force scurrying for cover.

Harris's leg buckled under him as a second shot tore through the muscle in his thigh. He writhed in agony, screaming at the shooting pain, dragging himself behind a nearby rock. A friendly voice was by his side a moment later, helping him upright again, imploring him to get to his feet.

"The bags," shouted Harris, refusing to move without the intelligence haul he had risked his life to recover. The soldier hesitated and grabbed both sacks, one in each hand, dragging them the remaining distance towards the waiting helicopter.

One bag tore, spilling its contents. Files, folders, documents and computer disks scattered in the dirt. Harris tried to kneel to scoop them up, but his leg screamed in protest. A steady trickle of blood soaked his trouser leg. Sheets of paper began blowing across the ground in the helicopter down-draught.

"Come on. Time to go," shouted the soldier, half-supporting Harris's weight, dragging him onwards.

They staggered the remaining distance to the landing zone, where a crewman helped get Harris into the helicopter. To his surprise, the arm that reached down to pull him aboard was Brokenshire's. They lowered Harris on to the cabin floor and a medic set to work on securing a tourniquet to his thigh, bandaging the wound and staunching the blood flow. Harris felt the warm fug of morphine as the medic made him comfortable for the return journey.

Harris was dimly aware of the returning soldiers crowding in to the cabin as the helicopter took off once more, gaining altitude, rotors whining. The aircraft banked sharply as one soldier shouted a warning. A shoulder-launched rocket-propelled grenade passed dangerously close to the open cabin door, disappearing into the darkness before exploding against the hillside.

Below them, Harris could make out the headlights of three Iraqi vehicles moving to encircle the landing position, firing up into the night sky, more in frustration than hope of bringing down the helicopter. A couple of rounds pinged harmlessly against the helicopter's armoured underbelly.

The two Sea Kings flew in formation, low over the desert, skimming hilltops in the low light.

Brokenshire kneeled beside Harris. "You did good, Harris. You did good."

"They knew we were coming."

"Relax. No one knew you were coming. It's the morphine," reassured Brokenshire, patting Harris's shoulder.

"Have you heard from Sadi?" whispered Harris, struggling to focus, his vision blurring. "Did he get out safely?"

Brokenshire seemed to hesitate. "We don't know. He missed the check-in call."

"Then we have to go back," said Harris through gritted teeth, trying to sit upright.

"No one's going back."

"I can't just leave him."

"If the Iraqis have him, we must assume they'll make him talk."

"No, Sadi will tell them nothing." His thoughts had become clouded, but his loyalty to his friend burned through.

"Everyone talks in the end, Harris. You know that as well as I do."

"Not Sadi."

"He'll buy us as much time as he can. But no one can withstand interrogation forever."

"I'm telling you, someone talked."

Brokenshire shook his head. "Face facts, man. There's no going back."

"You know I can't rest until I know..."

"Listen to me. Your work here is done."

Harris slumped back against the rucksack he was using as a pillow, giving in to the waves of morphine-induced numbness spreading throughout his body. He just hoped his friend had made it out.

"Once tonight is over, Iraq will be in chaos. It's not safe for any of us here any more. They'll round up any Westerners suspected of helping the Americans. I'm getting you on the next flight out of here."

CHAPTER 35

Kisangani
Democratic Republic of the Congo
17 December 1998

The convoy deposited Alice and what remained of the shell-shocked WHO group outside a two-storey utilitarian airport passenger terminal made of weathered concrete and glass. Raised letters welcomed them to the "Aéroport International de Kisangani". Fluttering proudly outside the entrance was the recently adopted flag of the Democratic Republic of the Congo, sky blue background, yellow stars, which Alice initially mistook as the European Union flag.

They led the wounded members of the team inside the building's spartan interior with exposed steel beams, its dusty floor strewn with rubbish. The Congolese minister and his entourage were waiting to receive them, sheltering from the heat. Inside it was noticeably cooler. As Leclerc and Alice entered, the minister shuffled forward, brow furrowed, hands clenched together in supplication, in a thinly veiled charade of solidarity. Alice well remembered the minister's earlier refusal to help when he had the chance.

He shook hands with each of the WHO team, making loud promises about conducting a "thorough investigation" to get to the bottom of this "wicked act". On learning the news that the professor was not among them, he seemed to backtrack in his rhetoric, playing down the incident.

"When they discover who he is, the rebels will release him. A case of mistaken identity, I'm sure."

"And what if they don't?" asked Leclerc.

"Then my government will negotiate his return. That's how these things normally work."

"How long will that take?"

"Monsieur Leclerc, whatever you may think, the rebels are not savages."

"Didn't they kidnap a senior NGO official only last week?" asked Leclerc.

"It's true. Kidnapping is on the rise again. Sometimes a ransom must be paid," he conceded with regret, "but attacks against the United Nations are, thankfully, extremely rare. Last week's was a simple misunderstanding. Nothing more. The individual in question has already been released."

"A misunderstanding?" protested Leclerc, in an uncharacteristic display of frustration.

"Yes. A rebel patrol stopped him at a checkpoint. Searched his vehicle. As soon as the other NGO representatives identified themselves, they were allowed to continue on their journey."

Alice glanced at JP, whose expression suggested otherwise. There was more to this story than the Congolese politician was prepared to divulge.

"Minister, what news from the villages cut off by the rebel advance?" asked Alice.

"Until the security situation stabilises, we have no way of reaching them. But if the rebels have any sense, they will avoid the entire area."

"Sir, with respect, if medical supplies don't reach them soon, many more will die," implored Alice. She felt so guilty, powerless to keep her promise to Sister Francine. Those villages had been abandoned to their fate.

"The situation would have been much worse had it not been for your brave efforts, Doctor," congratulated Leclerc, trying to put a positive spin on the WHO's interventions. "Many more Congolese lives would have been lost."

"Disaster seems to follow you wherever you go, Doctor Bishop," countered the Congolese minister with a wry smile. A thinly veiled reference to her time in Hong Kong, she presumed. "Perhaps this is no coincidence."

"I beg your pardon?" challenged Leclerc, indignant at the dangerous accusation.

"Allow me to speak plainly. My sources inform me that members of the British team are, in fact, military."

"Excuse me?"

"Doctor Littlejohn over there is a spy."

"A spy?" repeated Leclerc. "Doctor Littlejohn is one of the UK's leading experts on infectious disease!"

"He's also a military scientist, is he not? From the now infamous Porton Down. We are all aware of the research undertaken there. Military research."

Leclerc seemed unsure how to respond, leaving Alice to defend Littlejohn, despite her own long-held suspicions.

"Minister, with respect, we have the Porton team to thank for one of the anti-viral treatments we've been using. Littlejohn is renowned for his pioneering work on haemorrhagic fevers.

They developed one of the candidate vaccines being used by the WHO at Porton."

"A vaccine, I'm told, that works no better than a placebo."

"On the contrary, it's proven highly effective."

"Then you also deny Littlejohn was a late addition to your team?"

"Following a last-minute health issue, yes."

The minister scoffed at the claim. "Do you also deny that bribes were paid?"

"Bribes?"

"Very well. A generous donation made to the professor's institute shortly after Littlejohn's inclusion. Perhaps the timing was a coincidence too?" the minister mocked.

Alice was beginning to wonder where the politician was getting his information. Could the professor have boasted about their source of funding? How else would anyone know?

"Your team has shown a blatant disregard for the welfare of my people from the start."

"I assure you, Minister, our only priority is saving lives."

"This entire expedition has been an unmitigated disaster. My people are not lab rats, Sir."

"With respect..." Leclerc tried to intercede, to make their host see reason.

"The behaviour of your so-called peacekeepers has been nothing short of reprehensible. Drunken behaviour, fornication, looting. The United Nations is no better than the last lot of colonialists who came here," he claimed, referring to Leclerc's Belgian heritage. "They stole our riches, claimed our land."

"You go too far, Minister."

"No, Sir. Hundreds of my people are already dead. Hundreds more are dying. Your superiors have not heard the last of this, believe you me."

With a dismissive wave, the minister turned on his heels and strode towards a waiting limousine.

Koch couldn't resist having the last word. "I hope you got what you came here for," he snarled as he brushed between Alice and Leclerc.

Alice considered responding, but thought better of it.

CHAPTER 36

JP escorted the remaining members of the WHO team out onto the tarmac to board the waiting aircraft, whose engines were already powering up as the captain and first officer prepped for take-off.

Halfway down the cabin's interior, Littlejohn craned his head above the seat backs, motioning for Alice and JP to join him. He had been watching the exchanges with the minister from a distance, ears burning. Alice relayed the main thrust of the long list of rumours and claims to the Porton man's growing annoyance.

"Talk about biting the hand that feeds you," added Littlejohn.

"I wonder if the Russian team got a similar send-off," said Alice mischievously.

"I doubt it," said Littlejohn.

"What makes you say that?"

"Oh, those cigars you mentioned. The gift box signed Leo, the one you told me about on the minister's desk."

"What about it?"

"I spoke to Farrier. He explained. Leo is short for Lev."

"Lev who?"

"Lev Nikolayevich Alexeyev. The Head of Research at the Vector Institute in Siberia."

Alice had never heard of Alexeyev or his institute.

"The State Research Centre of Virology and Biotechnology is where the Russians conduct most of their military research into infectious diseases, vaccine development, that sort of thing," answered Littlejohn.

"Bit like Porton Down?"

"Similar. Not the same."

"And you think the cigar box was a gift from the Russians?"

"Farrier was sure of it, and he's met Alexeyev. But the Head of Vector wouldn't get his hands dirty. He'd only send his underlings to do that."

Alice spun round to face Littlejohn. "Why didn't you tell me all this before now?"

"Look, I'm sorry. Like I said, I didn't know for sure."

"Doctor Bishop," came a voice from the front of the plane. Leclerc was counting heads and checking off names from the roster. He needed Alice for something. He began with an apology. "I'm sorry about just now. The minister had no right to blame you for what happened. Don't take it personally. Politicians can get a little passionate at times."

"I won't, but thank you."

His furrowed brow suggested there was something else he wanted to discuss. "I just spoke to Thierry at the hospital. He was sorry he didn't get a chance to say goodbye in person."

"Did he say how Maxine was doing?"

Leclerc's hesitation frightened her beyond words.

"I'm so sorry." He scrunched up his eyes. "The nurses found her a few hours ago."

"What happened?"

"I'm told her condition deteriorated overnight." He paused,

as if still coming to terms with the news. "Thierry said she became monosyllabic, disorientated, barely able to speak or confirm her name. This morning she slipped into a catatonic state, totally unresponsive to treatment. Alice, I'm so sorry. She overdosed on morphine."

"How?" Alice shook her head. "Where did she get the morphine?"

"Thierry assumed it was her own supply. No one thought to check her belongings."

Alice covered her mouth in horror, unable to find the words to make sense of what had happened. Maxine had sworn Alice to secrecy about the pregnancy. She was just a few weeks along, but she would have known only too well what this disease would do to her unborn child. No mother could live with that burden.

"She took her own life rather than face the horror of a progressive illness," confirmed Leclerc. "I'm so, so sorry." He rested a hand on Alice's shoulder before turning away to complete the boarding of the remaining WHO staff.

Alice returned to her row in silence, hoping the faded leather seat would swallow her up whole. Tears streamed down her face as she watched the remaining luggage and equipment being loaded into the hold through the grimy window.

Perhaps this was what it felt like for doctors working in crisis zones. Totally helpless. Unable to stop an invisible force tearing through once vibrant communities. All the WHO could do now was scuttle home, back to their laboratories, to return when the outbreak had run its course. To pick up the pieces. To learn the lessons for next time.

Alice knew better than most that there would always be a next time. Novel viruses were coming thick and fast. It was only a matter of months, maybe years, before the next variant emerged. When it did, the WHO would descend en masse once more to shut down the affected area, establish quarantine. No one in, no one out. Those trapped inside would be left to face their fate. As the professor had explained, if this is what it took to protect the wider world, then so be it. Humanity would cut its losses. Live to fight another day. No one liked it but it was just what needed to happen. Go back to the lab and start again.

Alice was dimly aware of the aircraft doors closing and the bumps and jolts as they taxied for take-off. She noticed the wing nearest her, paintwork peeling, bouncing up and down more than she might expect on the potholed asphalt surface. This was a workhorse that had been kept flying through love and money.

Littlejohn in the row behind Alice was talking loudly about the "true test to come". She wondered what he was referring to.

"Didn't you see the newspaper? Tutsi militia shot down that passenger jet," said another voice.

"Really?" exclaimed an excitable Belgian scientist. Alice didn't want to turn round to engage with their idle conversation, consumed by her own private grief at the news of Maxine. The pitch of the engines rose to a shrieking roar as the aircraft accelerated down the runway. The shaking became all-consuming. Alice braced herself, gripping the armrests.

With a final lurch, the plane left the runway, soaring into the late morning sky, gaining altitude as it roared west over the outskirts of Kisangani. They were only a couple of thousand feet off the ground when the plane banked hard right, shaking violently. The cabin pitched at an impossible angle, Alice's face forced against the grimy glass. Trees, houses, dirt roads flashed past the window, terrifyingly close.

Just as suddenly, the plane banked left to renewed screams from the passengers. Her seatbelt dug into her abdomen, her entire body weight held in place by the flimsy buckle. She braced herself against the armrest. She imagined panic in the cockpit as the pilot wrestled with the aircraft controls, rolling dangerously close to the hillside to their right, screaming back over the runway before climbing again.

Alice noticed a small puff of smoke on the ground below, fire and flames, and then it was gone. To her horror, she noticed what looked like a projectile streaking towards them, zeroing in on their heat signature. She pressed her face to the glass, dumbstruck, barely believing what she was seeing, unable to speak, to shout out, to warn someone. They were a sitting duck at this altitude.

A tremendous explosion shook the aircraft, close enough to send a shock wave through the airframe. A stunned silence replaced the ensuing screams as the passengers realised they were still alive.

JP hurried down the aisle, making for the cockpit, checking everyone was okay.

"What happened?"

"Shoulder-launched missile," replied JP over his shoulder. "Russian-made. Never the most reliable," he added, as if he was talking about the weather. "It was the rebels."

"What happened? Did they miss?" asked Leclerc in disbelief.

"I don't believe so. I'd say they shot it down. We were lucky."

"Who? How?"

"The airport has an anti-missile system. After the rebels shot down that Boeing 727, the government ordered one for Kisangani."

"Thank God," said a voice behind her to a chorus of relief.

The entire WHO team cheered, applauding the pilots for their tremendous skill.

Alice picked up her belongings from the floor around her and settled back into her seat, heart racing, adrenaline still coursing through her veins. She concentrated on the ground below as they continued their climb over dense forest, far beyond rebel-held territory.

Patches of mist and fog still clung to the valleys below, shrouding the hillside from their passing. The shadow of their aircraft raced over the contours of an unbroken canopy of trees extending as far as the eye could see. Hidden from view, beneath the treetops, was a wild, primeval ecosystem teeming with untold species. Somewhere beneath that dense tree canopy, was a vast natural world that fascinated Alice. Her newly adopted wonderland. Alice's wonderland. Novel forms of life, lurking unseen, evolving at a dizzying rate, totally indifferent to mankind's attempts at mastery. Oblivious to the scientists' departure.

Alice knew now that her work as an infectious diseases specialist would never be done. All she could hope for was to stay in the game. To track the emergence of novel pathogens as early as possible. To buy the West more time. Science consigned to play a waiting game, forever a few steps behind Mother Nature's invention. Now, at least, Alice knew the rules and how the game must be played. Control had been an illusion. A dangerous one. But the scales had fallen from her eyes and her curiosity burned brighter still.

EPILOGUE

London, United Kingdom
7 January, 1999

Blake Harris stepped out of a black London taxi outside the Foreign Office building on King Charles Street in White-hall, dressed in a tailored suit and sober tie. On Brokenshire's suggestion, he had trimmed his beard to look "less like a jihadist". After all, he didn't want to scare his paymasters.

It was Harris's first time back in London since he officially left the UK Armed Forces. He had always hated stuffy government buildings. Too claustrophobic. He intended to get the formalities over and done with as quickly as possible. His ticket home to Poole was booked for late afternoon, two hours away by train from London Waterloo station, just over the bridge from the Houses of Parliament and Big Ben.

He let the crutches take the strain, levering himself through the double doors. He half-expected a welcoming committee for a returning war hero, but the entry lobby was a hive of activity. Civil servants and special advisors coming and going, oblivious to his presence. He stared wide-eyed in wonder at the soaring painted ceilings, gilded domes, marble statues, walls lavishly decorated to impress foreign visitors. The whole place was steeped in history he knew dated from the time of Queen Victoria at the height of her power. A far cry from the dusty warren of back-alleys where he lived in Baghdad.

The receptionist directed Harris to a stateroom on the first floor where he found a host of others similarly attired, waiting for their names to be called. From the ceiling hung two vast crystal chandeliers, an intricate web of crystals, polished so brightly they glowed like a thousand stars on a clear desert night in Iraq. The whole place reeked of Empire, the musty smell of old carpets, leather and furniture polish. The heavy curtains, portraits and paintings appeared to muffle the familiar sounds of London traffic outside.

After a brief delay, a junior staffer in a suit invited Harris to receive his medal in a private ceremony. The Victoria Cross would join a growing collection stored in a shoebox under a bed, marking tours of duty in Northern Ireland and Bosnia. Another honour never to be officially recognised in his lifetime. That was the job.

Major General Phillips, wearing full military regalia, got to his feet and extended a hand in welcome. “Congratulations, Harris.”

“Thank you, Sir,” said Harris, resisting the urge to salute.

“How’s the leg?”

“Getting there. The doctor said it’ll be a few weeks before I’m fit for active duty again.”

“I was sorry to hear about your batman, Sadi, was it?”

“Yes, Sir,” said Harris, staring at his shoes. “I’m grateful for what you did for his wife and family.”

"Please pass on my condolences," Phillips continued. "He was a good man."

Harris nodded. He still missed his friend and collaborator.

When they had recovered Sadi's body, dumped in a back street of Baghdad, they found his hands still bound behind his back, face and torso blackened and blue. Scorch marks to his armpits and groin suggested a prolonged exposure to electrocution at the hands of military police. Harris only hoped Sadi had not suffered too long before confessing his part in the attack on the underground facility at Al-Mansulijah. No one deserved to die like that.

"I hope it was all worth it, Sir," commented Harris through gritted teeth, fighting back his emotions, still raw at the memory.

The intelligence haul Harris recovered from the bunker complex had included a detailed inventory of Iraqi research programmes together with audio and video recordings made by the scientists involved. Their first-hand accounts confirmed what the Iraqis had claimed all along: that the vast majority of Saddam's weapons programmes had been mothballed several years before. What remained was a shadow of its former self. Ninety-nine per cent of the chemical munitions had been declared and destroyed. They had turned biological research and production facilities over to civilian industry. However, military munitions experts had determined the photos of shell casings with strange markings were capable of carrying a biological or chemical payload, albeit stored empty. The better news was that the shells, warheads and any biological material stored at Al-Mansulijah had been completely destroyed by the intense heat from the explosive charges Harris had planted prior to his escape.

"What about the samples I recovered, Sir?"

"Still being analysed by the team at Porton." Phillips added with a shrug, "I fear they'll match the others you recovered from Al Hakam."

Harris struggled to hide his disappointment, risking life and limb, the torture and murder of Sadi, and for what? Confirmation of what they already knew. The smoking gun had eluded them once more. Phillips noticed Harris's frustration.

"We all hoped for better news," said Phillips, placing a comforting hand on Harris's shoulder. "Brokenshire tells me he still has some promising leads to follow up. The search for those damned weapons of mass destruction continues."

"Yes, Sir."

"Before you head home to Poole, Harris, there are some people I'd like you to meet."

Harris straightened, uncomfortable in these overly formalised surroundings, wondering who it could be. On the mantelpiece, the bust of Winston Churchill caught Harris's eye. Harris took a deep breath. He smelled a trap. Brokenshire had not mentioned anything about this. Harris recovered his composure before Phillips became aware of his discomfort. The officer nodded towards his aide-de-camp, who went in search of the other waiting guests before returning a few moments later.

"Blake Harris, I'd like you to meet Doctors Alice Bishop and Ben Littlejohn, recently returned from their World Health Organization expedition to the Congo."

Harris shook hands with the two scientists, his curiosity piqued. Littlejohn barely merited a second glance, thinning hair, piercing blue eyes, a grey pallor that suggested too much time spent in a laboratory, barely able to look Harris in the eye. As for Alice, there was an air of challenge, even defiance. Confident, attractive, privileged, definitely the kind of woman Harris avoided if humanly possible.

"I take it you're the one we have to thank for recovering the samples from Iraq?" said Littlejohn.

Harris nodded by way of a response. "And how do you fit in?"

"I'm one of the geeks trying to figure out what Saddam is up to." There was a kind of goofy humour to Littlejohn that Harris instantly warmed to. "Please, call me Ben. How much do you know of XC-4328?"

"The so-called 'Congo Variant'?" replied Harris rather melodramatically, as if he were talking about the Loch Ness Monster. "Only what I've been told."

Littlejohn deferred to Alice to explain. "It's a strain of haemorrhagic fever responsible for more than a thousand deaths in Central Africa this last month. Not dissimilar to Marburg or Ebola," she added.

"We've been waiting for another variant to emerge," said Littlejohn. "We just didn't know when. But the real question is what XC-4328 was doing in a lab in Iraq in the first place?"

"I'm sorry," said Harris, struggling to hide his incredulity. "Perhaps no one explained what I've been doing these last few months. The Iraqis are obsessed with anything they can weaponise."

Harris's blunt response seemed to surprise everyone. Littlejohn waited for a nod of approval from Phillips before responding. "Opinions differ on that point. We prefer to think that the Iraqis' interest mirrors our own."

"Which is?"

"That the more the world can learn about these viruses and how they spread, the better we can protect the West."

"You don't honestly believe Saddam cares about advancing the health of his citizens?" mocked Harris. "Have you not heard of the Haboob Project?" All except Alice nodded. "Then there should be no doubt about his intent to develop weapons of mass destruction."

"Whether they intend to use those weapons remains the

subject of much debate in intelligence circles," replied Phillips, with renewed authority. "Nevertheless, we now know that UN inspections have left few places to hide. It's possible that those programmes have moved underground or even been re-shored."

"Re-shored?" asked Harris.

"Yes, you see, our enemies are not stupid. Saddam couldn't risk being caught red-handed by the inspectors. We think he moved most of his R&D elsewhere, perhaps to the front line."

"You're talking about the Congo?" said Alice.

"Yes."

"But surely the Congolese authorities would know that?" she challenged.

"How do you think they paid for all those new roads and rail links, Alice?" said Littlejohn.

"In return for what, turning a blind eye while military scientists experiment on the good people of the Congo?"

"They would argue they're partners, providing essential aid to some of the world's poorest people," explained Phillips. "It's a shame you weren't able to secure a sample of this vaccine you say the Russians were administering to locals."

To Harris, the common-sense explanation was staring them all in the face. In his experience, scientists were often blind to the truth. "You really think the Iraqis synthesised a vaccine in such a short time?"

"Only if you believe the outbreak was zoonotic and didn't originate in a lab," said Phillips provocatively. "The timeline remains a little murky."

"Until I see evidence to the contrary, the only sound scientific explanation is zoonotic," insisted Alice.

"Right now, we're giving the Iraqis the benefit of the doubt," added Littlejohn. "At least now we know what XC-4328 is capable of in the wild."

"And it's worse than Ebola and Marburg combined," admitted Alice.

"I was under the impression your team contained the outbreak?" said Harris.

"Officially, yes, but honestly, the outbreak was already dying out," explained Littlejohn. "A victim of its own success. It literally ran out of victims to infect. You see, XC-4328 kills people too quickly to spread far and wide."

"It still infected thousands," countered Alice.

"Let's assume for one moment that the Iraqis really did engineer XC-4328, managed to inject a few dumb villagers who didn't know better. So? What have they really learned?"

Alice bridled at Harris's use of the word "dumb".

"Imagine a bio-engineered virus like this in the hands of Islamic fundamentalists. It doesn't bear thinking about," insisted Phillips. "Saddam could already have supplied biological material to several terror groups. We've had reports suggesting Osama bin Laden is training a small army of sleeper agents embedded within Western countries. State-sponsored terrorism is already rising to the top of the American threat list. A clear and present danger. Eliminating the threat at its source remains the top priority. Which brings us back to Iraq."

"The inspections are done. There's no going back now. Anyway, those factories and research facilities I saw were just pawns," admitted Harris. "Saddam was happy to sacrifice them. His most prized assets remain hidden away in royal palaces and underground complexes like the one we destroyed at Al-Mansulijah, beyond the prying eyes of the inspectors."

"And our precision-guided bombs."

"No, Saddam is playing a longer game. He's still bragging to other leaders in the Middle East about his weapons of mass destruction. Standing up to the US plays well in the Arab world.

As long as we allow them to, the Iraqis will continue to deny anything we can't directly prove."

"Whether or not those weapons exist doesn't really matter," countered Phillips. "The threat of that deterrent sufficed to galvanise the allies into taking action. Saddam could never hope to win in a conventional war. Sowing the seeds of fear was likely the real prize."

Terrorists mounting an attack on foreign soil with a bioweapon? Harris had to admit that was clever.

"The Iraqis have been busy recruiting Russian scientists to accelerate their programmes. We're working on the assumption that Professor O'Leary may have been kidnapped to order. Plugging a gap in their knowledge." Phillips quickly explained to Harris who O'Leary was and how he fitted into this scenario. "With the professor on board, there's no knowing what they'd be capable of."

"Have there been any updates from Kinshasa?" asked Alice, anxious for news of her former mentor.

"The rebels claim they don't have him. Our sources suggest O'Leary is no longer in the country." Alice struggled to hide her distress. "Don't worry, Alice, we're going to find him. That's actually the reason I wanted you three to meet."

They all turned to face Phillips, curious to understand what he had in mind.

"The Defence Secretary has asked me to put together a new joint nuclear, biological, chemical expeditionary unit, ready for operational deployment in the spring of next year. Doctor Bishop, I thought you might be interested in joining the team."

Littlejohn gave Alice an encouraging wink.

"I'm flattered. Thank you, Sir. I'd need to think about it."

"Excellent. Well, don't take too long. You'll be working with Mr Harris here as soon as he's fit and able to go back in."

Phillips's aide-de-camp appeared in the doorway and beckoned over the major general. "I'm sorry. I have some other people I need to see. Why don't I leave the three of you to get acquainted?"

Alice, Littlejohn and Harris waited until the door was closed before expressing their collective relief and surprise. Harris wasn't sure he was ready to go back to Iraq. Not yet anyway. He wondered why Brokenshire had mentioned none of this earlier. Things were moving quickly. Too quickly.

"So you think the Iraqis really have the professor?" asked Alice.

"It's possible," admitted Harris. "They've brought in several overseas experts. If he's as important as you say he is, then why not?"

"No one knows more about Marburg or Ebola than he does."

"Except you, Alice," said Littlejohn. "It's no longer that hard to imagine a virus that spreads like the common cold but kills like Ebola."

"And if we've learned anything about Saddam, that would be the real prize. A weapon that could bring the West to its knees. Factories closed, shops shuttered, planes grounded. An outbreak in a developing African nation is one thing, but one in the West would be devastating."

Alice took up the baton from Harris. "The West has been complacent about the risk of a major outbreak for years. The UK government still thinks pandemics are some distant threat, like climate change or rising sea levels. We're not talking about some random event, like a meteor strike. It's a question of when, not if. And the time to prepare is now, not when those first cases are identified in emergency rooms."

"There's no budget for that and you know it," countered Littlejohn. "We're talking billions."

"Only because we're failing to make the case, Ben. Most politicians simply shrug their shoulders when we experts talk about the risk. There's a sense of fatalism. Why prepare for something that may never happen?"

"Then perhaps the best that can be hoped for is some short, sharp shock to the system," conceded Alice. "An outbreak that makes people sit up and listen. Recognise the danger we live under." Both Harris and Littlejohn stared at Alice as if she had lost her marbles. "We all know nothing will change until countries pool their resources and start working together. Pandemics don't respect borders. We saw that in the Congo," she added.

"Countries will cooperate when the time comes," insisted Littlejohn.

"No,' countered Alice. "There's too much self-interest for that to happen. Look at how the authorities responded in Hong Kong and the Congo. The truth was suppressed."

"If the Iraqis really do have your professor, then there's no knowing what they could achieve," said Harris.

"Our analysis predicts that Iraq's ability to master genetic engineering is only a few years away," admitted Littlejohn. "What was cutting-edge science a decade ago is commonplace today."

"With all the risks that accelerated development implies?" challenged Alice.

"This is no longer science fiction but science fact, Alice. To create new strains of viruses, whole genomes even."

"In other words, to play God," countered Alice.

"Then we need to find your professor. Before it's too late."

"It seems the dark ages really are back," joked Littlejohn. "Back on the gleaming wings of science."

A look of confusion passed between Harris and Alice. Harris assumed the doctor was quoting from some obscure religious text.

"The Bible?"

"No, Churchill."

The penny finally dropped, remembering the unflattering bust of Churchill on the mantlepiece. "Then, victory, however long and hard the road may be," countered Harris, fixing Littlejohn with an unblinking stare, reciting the lines he knew by heart. "For without victory there is no survival." He was something of a Churchill fan himself.

Littlejohn nodded his approval. "For all we have to give is our blood, toil, tears and sweat."

A little obvious, thought Harris, but fitting.

Alice rolled her eyes at the men's verbal jousting. "Heavens preserve us," she added, reluctantly playing along, with a resigned shake of the head. "And may we never surrender."

It was at that precise moment, Harris realised he would be catching the later train home. Phillips was right. The three of them had so much to learn from each other.

ABOUT THE AUTHOR

Robin Crumby is the British author of *The Hurst Chronicles*, a post-apocalyptic series set on the south coast of England in the aftermath of a deadly flu pandemic. Since reading John Wyndham's *Day of the Triffids* as a child, Robin became fascinated by end of the world dystopian literature and was inspired to start writing by Cormac McCarthy's *The Road* and Emily St. John Mandel's *Station Eleven*. Why? Because post-apocalyptic fiction fires the imagination like nothing else. Pondering what comes next, who would survive, what life would look like. His Eureka moment came when wandering the shingle beach at Milford-on-Sea, inspired by the beauty and rich history of the Solent. Where better to survive the end of the world than a medieval castle surrounded by water? Robin spent much of his childhood messing about in boats, exploring the many waterways, harbours and military forts of the Isle of Wight, where *The Hurst Chronicles* series is set.

ALSO BY ROBIN CRUMBY

Hurst

Sentinel

Wildfire

Harbinger

Congo Variant

The Hurst Chronicles Reader Newsletter

Sign up for the Hurst Chronicles newsletter and be the first to hear about new books in the series as well as reader offers and exclusive content.

Sign up now at Hurstchronicles.com

Reviews

If you enjoyed the series, please take a moment to write a review.

Reviews help other readers discover new books. Your feedback also helps authors become better writers

and storytellers.

Printed in Great Britain
by Amazon